VERTŪ PUBLISHING
A Component of Vertū Marketing LLC
Ordering Information:
Quantity sales. Special discounts are available on quantity
purchases by corporations, associations, and others. For details,
contact the publisher. Orders by U.S. trade bookstores and
wholesalers please contact: Tel: (866) 779-0795.
publishing@vertu-marketing.com
Printed in the United States of America
The Body Auction:
ISBN: 979-8-9870674-4-4

Redemption

By: Lisa Mathis

Redemption: The action of saving or being saved from sin, error, or evil.

Prologue

Some dreams are incredibly vivid, blurring the line between blissful slumber and reality, leaving you in a state of confusion upon waking. Your heart may pound fiercely within your chest, the remnants of sleep assaulted by the harsh light of consciousness. As you struggle to discern the truth, your breath shallows and your tense muscles slowly melt into relaxed masses beneath your skin. Yet, even in the darkness, the fear lingers—a fear of the lurking monsters in the inky black corners of your bedroom, their shadowy figures haunting your thoughts. A whisper creeps into your psyche, questioning the authenticity of your experiences: "What if it wasn't a dream?"

People often dismiss their most harrowing experiences, claiming, "It didn't feel real. It felt like a dream." Sadly, for some, horror transcends the realm of imagination; nightmares bleed into reality.

Kayleigh found herself trapped in a waking nightmare, a ghastly tale playing on an endless loop in her mind. The events of the past few months, surreal and horrifying, seemed fit for a macabre movie, yet they were tragically real. She recalled the moment headquarters had called, informing her about a woman nearly buried alive. An investigation had unraveled a group of physicians who perfected a method to render women seemingly lifeless, selling them in a Body Auction. Families mourned these women, believing them dead, while they were sold for organ harvesting or sexual slavery. It was a sinister trade, orchestrated by a web of officials, politicians, and influential figures. The love of Kayleigh's life, someone she had failed to recognize as the mastermind, was part of this dark conspiracy. The pain of her broken heart was a raw wound, causing her to question her own judgment and instincts.

Her attempts to protect those she befriended became a relentless assault on her own soul. Each mistake felt like a sharp ax striking her chest, leaving her filled with self-reproach. The once-burning fire within her had been extinguished, replaced by a hollow darkness. Deprivation gnawed at her, driving her to consume anything, even insects, in a desperate bid for survival. The agony of hunger and the breakdown of her body tormented her, the pain intensifying with every passing moment. She longed for death, seeking solace in the prospect of eternal rest, yet it remained elusive.

The sound of occasional noises and the false hope of rescue left Kayleigh shattered, a mere shell of her former self. Mental anguish tortured her, and she lay curled in the fetal position, enveloped by pitch darkness. Her only wish was for someone to acknowledge her absence, to recognize the Bureau's failure. As her grip on sanity slipped, she imagined a distant future where her remains would be discovered, a grim testament to her suffering.

And then, in her weakest moment, as she teetered on the precipice of surrender, she heard footsteps. A glimmer of hope flickered within her, but skepticism lingered. Was this another trick of her mind, a final illusion, before succumbing to the sweet embrace of death? Yet, the footsteps persisted, and the door creaked open, flooding her dark prison with blinding light. Her feeble attempts to rise were thwarted by weakness and dizziness, and for a moment, she dared to believe that death had finally claimed her. But reality crashed in, dispelling the fleeting hope. A silhouette stood before her, an unexpected presence in her desolate world. Struggling to focus, she glimpsed the figure, dressed as if it were an ordinary day at the office, and realized this was no hallucination. But before she could comprehend the situation, darkness engulfed her once more, the door remaining ajar. This was no rescue; her fight had only just begun.

Chapter 1

Time seemed to creep slowly after I returned home. The adjustment to our new lives had been hard. I didn't immediately return to my position as a Nurse Practitioner. After being trapped inside my own coffin, almost buried alive and sold in a Body Auction, and caught up in the most intense and depraved series of criminal events imaginable, my mental status had become unstable. I was terrified of leaving home. I jumped at every sound. I went into counseling along with Aubrey, but the process of mental freedom was slow, for me at least. Nonetheless, I remained determined to overcome my fears, and I steadfastly refused to let the depravity of mankind and my victimization by that self-same wickedness ruin my life.

Aubrey had taken the aftermath of those events extremely hard, especially the loss of Kayleigh. She needed extensive trauma counseling and therapy, but finally began to recover. In fact, she had gone beyond recovering to thriving. She found strength she didn't know she had. So much so that through an intense time of self-reflection and a striking shift of life events, they gave her the opportunity to apply for consideration as a member of the FBI. Her hope when she applied was just to get in and maybe eventually work as an agent in a special unit devoted to human trafficking. I would like to say that her acceptance surprised me, but it didn't. I could see it lighting her up inside. I witnessed the spark in her eyes; a mother's intuition never falters. Before we knew it, she embarked on her training journey at Quantico. I felt a mixture of nerves and pride for her. She had confronted the monster head-on. It was clear to me that this path was her calling, a means to keep the darkness at bay. In the end, she was my inspiration. Her drive and resilience ignited the fire in me, too. I doubled down on my healing efforts. Instead of hiding from my fears, I began facing them, using them as fuel to ignite something new. That fire inside me started small but soon roared as I absorbed as much information as I could about human trafficking and how so few people were truly trying to make a difference. I became obsessed. Tripp hated it. I was consumed by research and data. I scoured the internet for information on how trafficking works and how it was possible for so many people to disappear without a trace. I was a woman consumed. All I could think about was Kayleigh, and how she'd sacrificed so much for us, only to be sucked into the bowels of something sinister.

After a lot of soul-searching, my admiration for Aubrey's

newfound purpose, and of course, my obsession with fighting back, along with some encouragement from the many contacts in law enforcement we had never wanted but now had, I decided to join the FBI Special Advisor Program. It gave my life a newfound purpose, a sense of meaning that surpassed my experiences in medicine. The prospect of making a unique difference appealed to me the most.

Meanwhile, Tripp resumed his normal travels, but his demeanor remained fractured. The trauma had strained our relationship to the point it could no longer be ignored, and he intensely struggled with the fact that both Aubrey and I refused to let go and move on, choosing instead to join the fight. I understood his worry, but I also knew he could never fully grasp our resolve. We faced hardships on all fronts, especially after attempting to return to our "normal" lives, but we remained committed to each other and persisted in our efforts to salvage our marriage.

Being a Special Advisor was nothing like being an agent. Thank goodness for my sake, but some training was required. I went to Quantico, met with agents, and learned what my new role would look like. All the while, I still had one thing on my mind: Kayleigh. Where was my friend? Was she alive? Was she being tortured like Rhonda had been? The uncertainty of that reality was the hardest part for me. She had disappeared trying to save us, to save me. She had vanished before they dismantled the auction. Worse still was the realization that she did not know we had gone to Dubai and rescued Rhonda. She didn't even know that we had survived and ended a huge, evil ring that profited from the worldwide trade of women. She also didn't know we had killed the love of her life.

Agent Johnson touched base with me often, but there were never any updates. They had no idea where Kayleigh was. He was also very disturbed by her disappearance since he had played an intricate part in the initial investigation. The US government had been called in to assist with the raid in Dubai, and the whole situation had caused significant tension between the two governments. No one wanted the true details of the Body Auction to leak out. The ramifications of something of such magnitude would cause a worldwide panic. Physicians who made women appear dead, their families mourning them, but instead of death, they were actually fodder in a sick moneymaking scheme. Can you imagine if the press got hold of the information? The chaos of families who'd unexpectedly lost loved ones would be demanding bodies to be exhumed to prove they weren't trafficked instead. People would search worldwide for loved ones, making wild assumptions. Hysteria would ensue everywhere, and all the government officials involved knew it. While some expressed embarrassment that it had happened on their soil, others were suspiciously quiet. Everyone suspected that there were people in the upper levels of the government who had their hands in the profit, but no evidence of that had ever surfaced.

Ishmael was practicing medicine again, and Krissy had gone to work for him. I was happy for her. She needed it. It was good for her to be busy too. Ishmael was overjoyed that his daughter, who had been a long-grieved victim, was rescued and safe, no longer in the hands of the psychopath in Dubai who had purchased her. He had such a good heart, and he felt so badly for Krissy who, being a young physician's assistant, had lost her very best friend in the auction. In her efforts to find her friend, she had collaborated closely with the FBI but was devastated to learn that her friend had been one of the victims harvested by the psychopath in Dubai who had bought her. It devastated Krissy. She tried to be happy, but she couldn't. All she could do was mourn the loss of her friend.

Whitley had been Krissy's best friend since childhood. They even attended PA school together. When Krissy learned Whitley had been harvested in the Body Auction, harvested alive, it had almost destroyed her. She was in constant contact with the FBI to help with leads, no matter how slim they seemed. It seemed like dead ends were all they wound up with. They had arrested multiple men in Dubai, but we learned that lots of them had either bribed the government to be released or simply refused to talk. Records were heavily encrypted, and even though Ahmed was a cyber-genius who worked tirelessly, he couldn't get enough information to fully track the sales. Since he was involved in finding his sister Rhonda and clearly had a penchant for cyber investigations, he continued consultant work with the FBI alongside their technical team.

We all knew that hundreds, maybe thousands, of women had been auctioned. The thought of being sold for sexual slavery and living a life of torture haunted me and was in my dreams almost nightly. When faced with the alternative, part of me thought that being harvested would be merciful. Rhonda had closed herself off to everyone but her brother. Her method of self-preservation was self-isolation. We all knew she would never recover from the trauma. Knowing what had happened to her, her own torture, and the suffering of those women still out there seemed to make her worse. She had survivor's guilt, and therapy was not breaking down the immense wall she had built around herself.

I lived a new life, plagued by nightmares and sleepless nights that I could never escape. I consciously avoided dwelling on it and only mentioned it when absolutely necessary. I still couldn't trust anyone, except for those closest to me. Losing my friend left me overwhelmed with guilt and worry. I was determined to find her, even if it killed me!

Chapter 2

Being in the FBI special advisory program meant I gathered information and reported back to my assigned leadership. They typically used the program in a management capacity, but my situation was unique. The FBI also used informants, and they used consultants. So, my role was designed as a combination of special advisor and consultant. I was assigned to go into a hospital or medical setting where leadership suspected an investigation might be needed. Obviously, there weren't many FBI agents who also had medical degrees, so leadership believed I could go into any hospital or clinic setting undetected and report my findings so the shot callers could decide if there was even a need for FBI intervention. It was supposed to be a simple information gathering role. I wasn't qualified to do anything in depth. If I uncovered the information they needed, then "real" agents would come in. I was scared, but also ready to do something, anything, that might make a difference. My first assignment was in a small town in the foothills of Tennessee, working at a rural hospital.

Tripp remained a good husband, as he had always been, but I felt as though we had grown further and further apart. I understood, of course. The auction had rocked his entire world, too. But on top of everything else, I had actually accused him of being part of it. I had broken his heart because I doubted him. I couldn't blame him. I would have been crushed if the tables were turned. But the truth is, during those dark days, I didn't trust anyone. It wasn't intentional, and I didn't intend it to be personal. My counselor said it was a self-preservation mechanism, but that didn't stop Tripp from taking it hard. Looking back, I wonder how I could dare think such a thing about a man like my husband, but I couldn't change the past. After everything that had happened, he was one hundred percent against me consulting for the FBI. He desired normalcy. He longed for life prior to the auction. It was hard for him to accept that he was no longer married to the same woman. Time, and everything about me, would forever be marked by befores and afters.

"You're being selfish! Why would you do this to our family? First, you actually accuse me of being involved in probably the worst thing I've ever heard of in real life, then you just up and leave to save the world? I don't want this life. I want my wife back! I want our life, our home! I don't want any of us to be constantly looking over our shoulders. It's bad enough our daughter has chosen this life, with your blessing I might add, but now you, too?" Tears welled in his eyes as we argued, a sight rarely seen that ripped at my heart. But no matter what was said or how many times he said it, I knew I would leave anyway. I had no way to explain myself, except that I simply had to do it. He dealt with my alternative path by traveling more and more for work. During that time, we hardly spoke. Aubrey was still in training, but we communicated as much as we could. And so, with my home life hanging in a perilous limbo, I set out to start my new role as an FBI consultant/Nurse Practitioner.

A rented SUV was waiting for me when I landed at the small airport. My cover? A temporary stand-in for an absent physician. The quiet facility, nestled in the town's embrace, had been plagued by a series of baffling and unexplained deaths. Patients spanning a wide spectrum of age, race, and gender would be in stable condition, some even ready for discharge, but would code and pass in the night. No one could prove foul play, but they were certain something was happening in the hospital. It could all be completely innocent, perhaps natural causes that needed uncovering, and the FBI did not want to waste resources. But at the same time, the local authorities truly believed there was something deeper at play. So, they assigned me to look into the situation and report my findings.

The roads were narrow and winding, like a snake around and around the mountain. It was almost sickening how curvy the roads were. I drove from the airport into a very rural area. The homes were quite tiny, some yards manicured, but some overgrown with weeds and large briars. Despite their worn and rotting state, the porches sometimes hosted a small, random flowerpot. I found that amusing; in all the ugliness, a hint of beauty. Every few miles, a large skeleton would arise on the horizon of a factory that had long ago become extinct. It probably had been a large area of industry at one point and had fueled the economy many years ago. But like the factory, only the shell of the town remained. There were political flags in more than a few yards, clearly a very conservative area, with signs supporting the freedom of religion and the Second Amendment on nearly every corner. I even saw that some people had the Ten Commandments posted on yard signs. I couldn't believe a killer could be hiding in this town somewhere. They sent me to find out if that was possible, and my heart was racing with excitement for my first job.

My small apartment was a room over a garage, and the home belonged to a retired police officer, J. Reavis. He was sitting in a rocking chair on his front porch when I pulled in. They had informed me he had worked undercover for the

FBI when he was younger and had been a Navy Seal. His son was now the Chief of Police. They had briefed me and assured me that I could trust him with my life. He knew I was a consultant and was on an information-gathering mission. The town's sentinel, Mr. Reavis alone would bear the knowledge of my true purpose in town. The warm breeze against my skin as I walked up the rock driveway carried whispers of stories untold, mingling with the scent of Old Spice, a nostalgic aroma that danced with memories of my grandfather. Although his face was round and friendly, stress lines were evident. His white fluffy beard had a neat manicure. His appearance and demeanor made me feel comfortable and safe right away.

"Good afternoon Mrs. Matthews, welcome to my home." His voice was deep and seemed serious, but his smile was a contradiction, as it was warm and welcoming.

"Nice to meet you. Please, call me Layla. Thank you so much for your hospitality." I reciprocated with a cheerful smile.

After the brief introductions, I excused myself to the apartment. Walking up the old white steps that needed a fresh coat of paint, I was worried about what my sleeping quarters might look like.

The garage was quite run down, and I had a fear of staying in a nasty, bug-infested room. As I opened the door, I was beyond shocked. From the outside, the place looked like a hot mess, but on the inside, it was lovely. Exposed beams lined the ceiling, fresh paint made the room bright and cheery. In the corner, a fully furnished modern kitchen and, on the other side, a huge entertainment center. I could see that they had installed the latest technology with a gigantic computer and multiple screens. The FBI had really done a great job setting this up. It impressed me. As I stood, mouth gaping, I heard Mr. Reavis behind me. "I cannot believe this." I'm here solely to consult and verify whether the FBI plans to open a case. I could not hide my surprise or excitement.

A deep chuckle came from his chest. "Well, this isn't just for you, sweetheart. The FBI has discrete hubs set up in multiple areas. Nashville isn't far from here, and Lord knows a lot of things happened there. Are you happy with your apartment? I also have a large command center in my basement that you will have access to." His voice was breathy from the flight of stairs.

"Oh my! It is very impressive. Thank you again!" The sound of my voice made me cringe as I sounded almost giddy.

"Please make yourself at home and also join us for some supper tonight. My wife is quite the cook. My son will also join us, and he can update you and answer any questions you may have." His southern accent made me smile.

"I would love a good home-cooked meal and would be

happy to join you." I expressed my gratitude, and he left me to unpack.

Mrs. Reavis was an adorable, sweet southern lady. She had fixed the typical southern supper with fried chicken and all the fixings. It was delicious! We discussed no business during dinner, just small talk and introductions. They caught me up on the small-town gossip and the typical way of life here. After the best strawberry cobbler, you could imagine, Mr. Reavis and his son led me to the basement.

It shocked me to learn that the Chief of police knew who I was and why I was there. But that quickly subsided with complete awe as I descended the stairs. The room held a quite impressive computer system. The wall had been lined with the latest technology. I could not help but chuckle at the thought of this hiding under the white farmhouse. It made me wonder what was hiding above garages and under farmhouses in my little hometown.

It only took a few moments of conversation to know that Mr. Reavis was not the typical country farmer. Mr. Reavis had a very impressive vocabulary and was extremely well educated, but he was also southern to the bone. I could not help but think of the cliche, "Never judge a book by its cover."

Across from the wall of screens was a working board. Photos of all the victims were hanging with names, ages, etc.

There were young faces, old faces, smiles, frowns. No common denominators that I could see at first glance. As I was staring at the vast information, Mr. Reavis gave me the details.

"The hospital is a 150-bed facility, so it is relatively small. They transfer anything very serious, like the need for bypass surgery, out to a larger healthcare facility. The first few deaths were not too much of a concern, but as the numbers climbed, we knew we needed the FBI's help."

"I am sad to say we have no leads at all. No similar family members, all patients had different diagnoses, we could not find any true similarities. I suspect either a nurse or a physician. The patients all died in their sleep, peacefully of sudden cardiac arrest."

Adrenaline surged in my veins. But should I feel guilty? I was almost giddy with excitement knowing I would get to be undercover, but people were dying. A red flush of shame crossed my face. I hoped they didn't notice.

"I have made copies of the information that we have obtained and you can use my resources anytime."

"Thank you so much. This is very helpful and a great start!" I knew the excitement in my voice was on the obnoxious side, but there was nothing I could do to hide it.

He had great access to the FBI system. It puzzled me that a retired FBI contractor had high-level government clearance. I, as a consultant, had only what he provided me. I felt like there was more to this kind southern gentleman than I knew, but I would worry about that later. I graciously thanked them for the help and retired to my apartment. My shift started at 7am. But always in the back of my mind was Kayleigh, and what I might be able to find with his access. Could I sweet talk this old man into helping me?

Chapter 3

I had been a nurse for many years before becoming a Nurse Practitioner, so I was aware of how dynamics varied at different hospitals. As I pulled into the parking lot, it wasn't that different from my own hometown, just smaller and with fewer businesses. Only a spattering of locally owned restaurants and a Hardee's. Food Lion was the only grocery store for miles. There were no malls or fancy hotels. This was a quaint little town, tucked away in the serene foothills of Tennessee, exuding an aura of quiet isolation.

The head of the hospitalist program, Dr. Harris, briefly met with me and I liked him immediately. He escorted me to the doctors' lounge where I would find out which in-patients I was to see on my shift. He had no idea of my true identity. He was an older man, but I wouldn't have known if he hadn't told me how long he had practiced medicine, as he looked incredibly young. His smile was pleasant, and I could see why he was well-respected in the area. I made a mental note to look further into his background. After all, the seemingly "nice" ones, as I knew from experience, could harbor the deadliest secrets.

I would have a certain number of patients to see during the day and some admissions from the ER, nothing I couldn't handle. There would be one more provider with me during my shift. Sometimes a physician, other times another physician's assistant or nurse practitioner. But what I needed was the night shift, and it was clear that I needed to be patient. This might take time.

Next up on my introduction tour was Alisondra, the Physician Assistant I'd be partnering with on most shifts. She was a tall, leggy blonde, her hair adorned with highlights that probably cost a small fortune. There was an air of late-blooming confidence about her, and her innocence added an extra layer of charm to her demeanor. Dr. Harris, who clearly found her irresistible, practically drooled over her during the introductions. Instantly, I felt a connection with her. Her infectious personality and sharp sense of humor had me laughing so hard that tears rolled down my cheeks within the first fifteen minutes of our conversation. We embarked on our rounds together and shared a delightful lunch.

Alisondra quickly became my go-to source for hospital gossip, filling me in on all the juicy details: who was romantically involved with whom, who had recently untied the knot, and who was on the brink of getting fired. She even handed me a carefully curated list of top-notch physicians to consult and a few to steer clear of. Her information was a goldmine, flowing so rapidly that I had to activate my ear recorder, one of my favorite pieces of FBI tech, to catch every detail. Wearing the ear recorder made me feel like I was living in a spy movie. It felt like power, a secret strength only I had. Interestingly, Alisondra mentioned that they often needed assistance on the night shift, a revelation that instantly brightened my day.

My first day was good overall, and I felt like once I had a chance to compile my data, I had a good start. By the time I got home, I crashed, but not before I downloaded the recording. After a long, hot shower, I inserted my earbuds to listen once again to Alisondra's rant that I recorded during lunch. I thought I could start putting the names in the database the following day. Just as I drifted off to sleep, I heard something that made me sit up in bed, and that was all it took to give me my first sleepless night in my new "home."

I replayed and replayed the sentence, and I was correct. She said, "Dr. DeWhite." I remembered the name from researching the victims. He had, at some point, seen them all. He was not working the night they died or the day prior, but in the data collected when they looked for similarities, he had seen them all. The police had ruled him out as suspicious. But, Alisondra's description had piqued my interest in him.

"He is an older cardiologist. He is brilliant and very charismatic. The younger physicians look up to him and seek him out for advice. Being a veteran gives him structure and discipline. I am not a fan. I feel like he needs to be more aggressive with newer treatments, but he is stuck in his old ways." Alisondra's voice through my earbuds was high-pitched and squeaky in my ear. By that point, I had listened for what seemed like hours. I saw an Excedrin Migraine in my near future. "He does not like to use Physicians' Assistants and won't even speak to me." She disliked him because of this, but I felt like he probably didn't flirt and give her the attention she was used to getting from the other male physicians.

I wrote down the facts I knew about him and would get more details as soon as I could. I finally rolled out of bed at 5am to get ready for my day. I was hopeful about finding out more details. I would be with my new friend the rest of the week, and I was excited to get started!

Darkness

Kayleigh slowly blinked her eyes open, her senses clouded by the aftermath of sedation. The world came back to her in fragments, like shards of glass forming a blurry mosaic. The stiffness in her limbs, the pounding in her head, all screamed of a fierce hangover. As she lay in the back seat of the car, she focused her senses, trying to piece together her surroundings.

In the front seat, two distinct figures came into view. The driver, Lam, was compact but strong, his arms sculpted, bearing the mark of an old tattoo on his forearm, its contents indecipherable, but she could tell the markings were Asian. Beside him sat Jody, an overweight man with a penchant for indulgence, evident from his protuberant belly and the stench of stale cigarette smoke that clung to him. The car carried the unmistakable aura of Marlboro Reds, marking one, or possibly both, of the men as long-time smokers.

Kayleigh remained still, feigning unconsciousness, her mind sharp, observing the subtle nuances of their conversation. Her memory was shrouded in a fog of uncertainty, punctuated by a sudden jolt of realization. The face, the shock, the raw ache in her heart—she had previously given in to despair, embracing death. But with the image of that face in her mind, a fiery determination now blazed within her.

For the first time in what felt like an eternity, sunlight streamed through the car window, its warmth a soothing balm against her skin. The hope she thought had deserted her began to flicker back to life. She was no longer confined to the dark abyss of her captivity. The task at hand was clear: escape, find her friends, and uncover the truth about the twisted world that had ensnared her.

Despite the discomfort of lying still, Kayleigh forced herself to endure. Every itch, every urge to move, was suppressed as she absorbed the invaluable information flowing from the men in the front seat. Jody's occasional touches, her thigh, her arm, though unsettling, as they were layered with a malice that made her skin crawl, did nothing to betray her facade.

The revelation that they were in the United States shocked her. The sedative had kept her unconscious for three days, blurring the boundaries between reality and nightmare. Their destination, a house "off the radar" according to Lam, meant they were deep in the countryside. The car bounced along gravel roads, each jolt sending waves of pain through her fragile body. Yet Kayleigh's training kicked in. She meticulously noted their surroundings, her survival instincts sharpening her focus.

Lam, the apparent leader, spoke with a thick accent,

occasionally challenging comprehension. Beside him, Jody's drawl was casual, disguising the sinister undercurrent beneath his words.

"We've got to meet the others and get the boss's latest plans," Lam's voice crackled with authority, his intentions shrouded by something in his tone that Kayleigh couldn't pinpoint.

Jody's tone, on the other hand, reeked of malevolence. "Think we can have some fun with her before we hand her over? No one would know, right?" His laughter was a grotesque symphony of cruelty, filling the car like a noxious perfume.

Panic threatened to consume Kayleigh, but a glimmer of hope emerged. If they planned to profit from her, they would have to nourish her, make her stronger for whatever grim fate awaited her. The realization sparked a surge of determination within her. This would not be her end. With fear supplanted by resolve, she began to devise her plan, her mind racing as she plotted her hope of escape.

Chapter 4

The following weeks unfolded surprisingly well. I swiftly adapted to the job, finding comfort in the routine. The patients were endearing, their warmth filling the hospital halls with a sense of belonging. Having grown up in a small town myself, I relished the camaraderie that small-town life offered; it felt like family, a genuine connection that ran deep. Shadowing Alisondra, her infectious personality made each day enjoyable. As days turned into weeks, I found myself developing those unmistakable "work bestie" feelings for her. Loneliness had crept in; I missed the closeness I shared with my friends, particularly Krissy, who had become like a sister to me. Tripp's visits, though promised, were sporadic, his absence leaving an ache in my heart. And then there was Aubrey, my baby girl turned FBI agent—sometimes it felt like I was living in a surreal dream, my mind struggling to grasp the reality of it all.

My first assignment had begun with naive expectations. I anticipated discovering something ominous immediately, a clear clue leading me back home. But reality had a different plan for me.

As the days passed, I became accustomed to my new role, gradually blending in with the hospital staff. The nurses, typical southerners, welcomed me warmly, their hospitality easing my transition.

I had also befriended a nurse who worked on the weekends. Angel, she was a hairstylist on the side and worked at a salon near the hospital. She offered to fit me in when I needed a touchup, and since it was just a short walk, I took her up on the offer. I am from a small town, but this place was beyond small. I had an idea of what the salon would be like, expecting a "beauty shop" vibe like one you might find on an old TV show. But the salon, despite my expectations, exuded a modern ambiance. The scent of perms and hairspray stung my nose the moment I walked in, the air thick with a medley of scents. Angel introduced me to Sheree, the salon's owner, a woman my age, who had carved out a successful business for herself. The other stylists, older and experienced, greeted me with smiles. Among them, I recognized one face—her husband had been one of the deaths under investigation. My excitement surged; this was an opportunity to gather more information.

My mindset shifted instantly, my focus on gathering intelligence sharpening. As I settled into Angel's chair, I sensed an opportunity beyond a simple haircut. Angel skillfully wielded both scissors and questions.

"What brought you here? Are you married?" Her inquiry flowed effortlessly, matching her expertise with my hair.

"It's a travel assignment, just filling in. And yes, I'm married. Tripp is his name," I replied, my eyes catching glimpses of Angel's tattoos in the mirror. "He travels a lot for his job, so he can't join me on this assignment. What about you? I love that you are a cosmetologist and also a registered nurse. That is awesome."

"I never married, not my thing," she confessed, her eyes veiled with mystery, clearly keeping her personal life close to the vest. "Hair was my passion, but Mom pushed nursing on me. So, I do both now."

With Angel engrossed in my hair, I turned my attention to Sheree, the salon owner, who approached with curiosity.

"Hey, I'm Sheree, the owner here. Welcome to town. How do you like it so far?" Her words tumbled out with a naturally energetic rapidity.

As I engaged in conversation, I studied Sheree, observing her warm demeanor and genuine hospitality. She shared details about Shirley, the oldest stylist, recently widowed, her husband passing away unexpectedly while admitted for pneumonia. The emotion in Sheree's voice resonated, her eyes clouded with sorrow. Meanwhile, Angel continued her work, her concentration unyielding.

Amidst the buzz of salon chatter, my excitement bubbled. I had found a way to gather information outside the hospital walls. The salon visits, disguised as hair appointments, would serve as my gateway to unraveling the town's mysteries. And with my newfound friends, who seemed all too eager to spill the latest gossip to the new stranger in town, the secrets were bound to surface.

Chapter 5

After my appointment, I went straight back to my apartment and started taking notes. The older beautician had been married to one of the first victims. He was 72 and a pillar of the community. The picture in the obituary showed an elderly-looking man, but with strong features; he did not look weak or ill. Little round glasses perched on a cute button nose. He reminded me of some of my old patients I cared for when I was in pulmonary medicine. I adored them, truly, and they held a special place in my heart. Thoughts of them often crept into my mind, and the void their absence left was palpable. The love we shared was pure and mutual. Every time they stepped into my office; warm embraces ensued. As they left, our parting words were always the same: "I love you. See ya next time." When one of them left this world, I felt the weight of the loss keenly. As I read about his passing, tears welled up in my eyes. The newspaper had crafted a poignant tribute, highlighting his dedicated service to the town and his illustrious military career.

He had been robust for his age, but a bout of flu coupled

with the complications of pneumonia proved to be his undoing. It was heartbreaking to learn that he had been on the road to recovery, set to be discharged in a matter of days if fate hadn't intervened. I delved into the hospital notes from the day he breathed his last, seeking answers in the minutiae of his final moments.

Physician progress note:

The patient looks good this morning. He is making progress on current antibiotics and nebulizers.

Chest x-ray reveals fewer infiltrates, and he has remained fever-free for 24 hours. He reports his cough has decreased and denies chest pain. Plan.

DC in the a.m. if no changes overnight.

The next entry in the chart revealed the CODE BLUE sheet.

Code Blue called 2400:

Pt found in cardiac arrest. ACLS protocol initiated.

After 42 min of CPR and multiple code drugs, pt had no return of pulse.

Please review CODE BLUE sheet for detailed record and medications given.

Time of death 2442

Wife notified of pt death.

The nurse assistant discovered him during her midnight

vital sign rounds. I imagined the scene, because it was one I had lived many times before. In my mind, I could see the events unfolding... The urgency of the situation would have struck hard. The Code would have echoed through the corridors, and the code team would have hurriedly assembled, but despite best efforts, too much time would have slipped away, robbing the man of life. The whole team would have felt the loss. Not necessarily out of emotion or connection, but in some cases, because they would have felt as though they'd failed.

According to the last recorded note, he was perfectly fine at 10 pm, but something had transpired within those two hours, leading to his sudden demise. At 72, he was vulnerable to a myriad of health issues–heart attack, emboli, or stroke, to name a few. However, his recent heart checks had come back clear, making a heart attack improbable. The presence of blood thinners made a clot less likely. Thus, a stroke loomed as a potential cause. Yet, in the midst of unexplained deaths, the sheriff demanded an autopsy, diving into the mysterious speculations. Oddly, the results yielded nothing–no cause of death, no defensive wounds, no answers.

In my quest for truth, I scrutinized the other deaths, searching for patterns. But nothing emerged. I couldn't shake the suspicion that the medical examiner in this small hospital might not be up to the task. There had to be a reason for these sudden deaths. There were no signs of struggle, no defensive wounds–just an inexplicable void.

Turning my attention to the deceased's elderly wife, a woman of elegance and grace, I delved into her history. Born and raised in the town, she had shared a 35-year-long marriage with her late husband. Yet, her past was shrouded in secrecy, harboring extramarital affairs that the town whispered about. A web of tangled relationships, her affairs had painted her life with a colorful, albeit scandalous, brush. I couldn't help but chuckle at the irony of their open marriage, an unusual arrangement for an elderly couple. This intriguing detail might provide a motive, yet, the final judgment was not mine to make; I was merely the bearer of information.

The weekend loomed ahead, and my plans to see Tripp were dashed. I had planned on going home over the weekend to visit, but he had once again gone out of town for work. Since I was off work, I planned on relaxing a little, going to the town social and to church. A small, gnawing hole was developing in my heart. Not sure if it was a dark hole of anger, resentment, or sadness, but it ate away at me nonetheless. Sometimes emotions are hard to differentiate as they overlap one another. I missed Tripp, but did he miss me? What was so important that he could not give me some time, especially when he had made me feel so guilty for taking the job? Resentment—yes, I was feeling resentment, and like any wound, it can get bigger and fester over time.

I decided I might as well get some good food while I gathered more information so, the following day, I would have a little fun. I attempted to call Tripp before bed, but his phone showed "out of range." I couldn't help but wonder if he had found someone else. The small black hole within me seemed to deepen. He remained distant, showing no signs of missing me or attempts to bridge the widening gap between us. A solitary tear landed on my cell phone screen as I texted Krissy and drifted off to sleep. The night was restless, haunted by dreams of the Auction and images of Tripp's face.

My restless night gave way to a sense of impending dread, gnawing at my stomach. An ominous feeling gripped me, urging me to action. Determination propelled me out of bed and into the day, where the sleepy town concealed the possibility of a murderer in its midst and I was going to find out who.

Invited to Sunday morning breakfast with the Reavis family, I dressed in my usual church attire and headed downstairs. I was surprised to find the Chief and his father in the basement. Mrs. Reavis was taking biscuits out of the oven and gestured for me to join them. The atmosphere buzzed with both excitement and anxiety. There had been another death overnight, the first since I'd arrived. A 69-year-old man, initially admitted for a UTI, was scheduled for discharge after IV antibiotics, but he was stable and showed no signs of distress. However, he was found dead during the night. Immediately, I requested a list of all staff who'd worked the prior night and the providers who had seen him since admission. I printed his picture and pinned it to the working board, eager to assist. As I looked on, I imagined what my life might had been if I'd pursued an actual FBI career when I was younger, but this was as close as I would get.

I kicked off my heels and observed the men in action. They worked seamlessly, compiling information while I tried to stay out of their way. As the computer generated the list of nurses and providers, I recognized familiar names. Alisondra had admitted him and consulted urology and cardiology due to his history of irregular heart rate. Dr. DeWhite appeared frequently in his visits. The nurse practitioner had also attended to him and was arranging his discharge. Angel had been one of his nurses too. I could speak to those I knew, gathering their perspectives on what they'd witnessed and heard. Understanding more about visitors was crucial; assuming it was an "inside job" might not be the best approach. We needed to explore all possibilities.

I looked up from the stack I was collecting and stopped to

see the picture taken immediately after the police had been notified. As I stood, staring at the board, I tried to focus on what I was seeing. There were only a few of the deaths with pictures taken, but the ones we had were not helpful. Same type of room, pale yellow walls, small TV, nightstand, small flowers, and a dead body. Some rooms were trashed with post-CODE blue paraphernalia, but nothing really stood out. I made copies of them and would examine them in more detail later. We never made it to church but had a productive morning of getting information on the latest victim.

He was married to a much younger lady, no children, and they seemed to be happy on paper. Very active in church and the community, also a veteran. But once again, no common threads with the other deaths. I printed his records and the sign-in sheets to see who was caring for him overnight. It was Angel, and as I recall, she had also been working some of the other nights. I am certain she can tell me if there was anything strange going on that she could remember. By the end of the afternoon, we had a few different ideas, but I wanted to see the body.

With the evidence mounting that there was, indeed, something malevolent happening in the small town, and feeling almost certain of foul play, I persuaded the chief to let me see the body. A skeptical gaze met my request, but my insistence won him over.

The chief tilted his head, his brow furrowing in confusion. "That's a bit of an unusual request, Layla," he said, lifting his ball cap and absently scratching his receding hairline. "I mean, I don't intend any disrespect, but you're just a consultant, not an agent. You're doing a great job, but let's keep things in perspective. Gather the information you can, share it with us, and then we'll decide, along with the FBI, if we need to open an investigation."

I nodded, my eyes pleading. "I totally understand, believe me," I replied. "But I've been in healthcare for years. I've seen my fair share of dead bodies. What harm could one more pair of eyes do? I might notice something you miss, and besides, I've got nothing else to do. Please, just let me help." I flashed my warmest smile, hoping to sway him. "You know how I've always wanted to live vicariously through you guys." Reluctantly, he nodded his approval.

"Alright," he conceded, his tone firm. "But please, don't touch anything and stay out of the way. If you notice anything useful, please let me know."

"Absolutely, sir!" I beamed, a broad smile spreading across my face. I quickly changed into scrubs, excitement bubbling within me. Together, we made our way to the morgue, where the body awaited autopsy. I was eager to be there, ready to unravel the mystery. Accompanied by the chief, we ventured to the morgue, where the body lay, waiting for answers.

Chapter 6

Morgues are horrible places. Imagine what it would be like if your occupation was working inside a Frigidaire of death. The contents of which was corpses, and that grocery list would never change. The scent of formaldehyde constantly infiltrates your nose along with the stench of flesh, bowels, and the insides of the dead. This was a medical examiner's lot in life. The romance of a medical examiner and fancy morgue on TV could be nothing further from the truth. In real life, the hot detective never strolls in with a one-liner that solves a crime.

The morgue is always deep in the bowels of the hospital, underneath the shiny little florist and gift shops. The aroma of Starbucks coffee couldn't drift that many levels down. The visitors coming and going to see their loved ones don't want to think about what lay beneath their feet. The families coming in to rejoice over the birth of a new baby never let the tomb of death cross their minds. No one wants to think that little granny up in room 203 might end up in the morgue. They would load her up like an old sack of produce after placing her gray, cold, wrinkled body in a black body bag and sliding it in the drawer. No one wanted to explain to little Johnny, "That's where they will cram your granny's cold dead body when she's gone, in the drawer of a fridge." The shame-like location of the place made me hate it even more.

The imposing metal tables loomed before me, their sterile surfaces marred by the memory of countless autopsies. The odors, a macabre blend of disinfectant and decay, assaulted my senses. Despite the eerie atmosphere, I couldn't help but find a strange fascination in the scene. I had promised to remain inconspicuous, yet the lure of the autopsy room was irresistible. My companions, however, shared none of my enthusiasm. Their discomfort was palpable, their unease echoing in the stifling air.

His body laid bare on a tray of gleaming stainless steel, the deceased man was devoid of the dignity a body bag might offer. His skin, once warm and vibrant, now bore the pallor of death, tinged with undertones of gray. His severely unkempt eyebrows, resembling dark woolly worms, arched above sunken eyes. A trivial detail, perhaps, but it grated on my nerves in a way I can't explain. I had always detested bushy brows and unibrows. Why it affected me so profoundly in that moment, I can't say. But, for some reason, it pulled my attention.

I had witnessed numerous deaths over the years and

become desensitized to the lifeless forms before me. Compassion flowed effortlessly for the living, but my emotions seemed to shut off in the presence of the dead. It puzzled me, a peculiar quirk of my psyche that probably begged for therapy. I brushed off the doubts about my own nature and focused on the task at hand.

Under other circumstances, he would have been a nice-looking man, salt and pepper gray hair, nicely trimmed beard and mustache. Why was I so irritated that he had let his brows go? For way too long by the looks of them. He clearly exercised, as he had good muscle tone, especially for his age. Forearms were muscular, but the skin did sag. As a person ages, there is a loss of subcutaneous tissue, and the skin becomes thin and fragile, almost translucent in areas. The dark vessels can look like road maps, but his road maps were gone. When he was moved, his blood pooling to his back and buttock gave him a purple tone. I saw no large scars or wounds. He did not look 69 at all, much younger if I had to guess. I noted that his eyes were open. His pupils were fixed, appearing as large black holes, but no longer rounded. I have noticed that when you die, the moment your heart stops, you turn this specific color of gray, your tongue isn't pink anymore, your eyes go dim. Like turning a light out, they can be bright and shiny, then within a few seconds, they are gone, just blank balls without meaning or purpose.

A solitary tattoo adorned his forearm–a tribute to his military service, most likely a Marine insignia. Déjà vu tugged at my consciousness as I leaned closer to examine it. Just then, the metal door slammed open with a resounding bang, and the medical examiner finally made his grand entrance. I had been waiting impatiently for this moment, eager to witness the autopsy. Mr. Reavis, one of my companions, recoiled, his face drained of color.

Pretending to be a mere observer eager to learn, I approached the medical examiner, a grizzled veteran of his trade. He seemed to warm to my presence, guiding me through the procedure with kindness and confidence. "Okay, let's begin, sweetheart. If you feel light-headed or nauseous, don't hesitate to speak up."

"Thank you, I'll manage," I replied, my true discomfort masked beneath a veneer of composure. In truth, my main source of distress were those unruly masses of black hair crawling across the man's forehead, taunting me. I fought the urge to grab the surgical scissors and rectify the situation. I shook myself out of my own weirdness and back into the present. With a deep breath, he commenced the autopsy.

Hours stretched on as he meticulously dissected the body, dismantling it like a macabre puzzle. Yet, even after the thorough examination, the cause of death eluded him. Layers of skin and muscle were peeled back, organs removed, and bones sawed through with a scream that resonated with horror. The examiner painstakingly documented every detail, his voice muffled by the mask, recounting the weight and intricacies of the man's inner workings.

Finally, the ordeal ended, the body reassembled and sealed with staples, the skull cap replaced. The examiner removed his bloodstained gloves, seemingly nonchalant. "Well, that's it. I'll have to await toxicology, of course, but I see no cause of death. I think he was just old and died." An odd chuckle emerged from his mask. He walked over, pulled his mask down, took a huge drink of coffee, and then ate a chip that was sitting on the table without even washing his hands. Gross... He was bizarre, but whoever does this job would have to be, wouldn't they?

My eyes met with the Chief's. He spoke to the man still chewing his chip, "Well, thank you for your time and hard work." He didn't reach out to shake hands. I giggled with understanding, and we walked outside.

"I hope you don't mind my input, Chief, but wouldn't a more advanced autopsy at a larger facility be better? Something doesn't feel right," I ventured, my voice hesitant.

"I agree, Layla. There's something off about this. I'll make the necessary arrangements. Thank you for coming along. You handled it remarkably well. I can't get used to that," he said, the color returning to his cheeks. I smiled, my true thoughts hidden beneath a mask of professionalism, even as the memory of that poor man's horrible eyebrows flashed across my mind.

Checking the time, I realized it was 4pm. I texted Angel, my hairdresser and fellow nurse, inviting her for dinner. She accepted, and after a quick shower and change of clothes, we met at the local diner. Amidst casual small talk, I probed, trying to glean information about her night.

"So, how was your shift last night?" I inquired, feigning casual interest.

Without looking up from her greasy, oversized cheeseburger, Angel replied, "Same old, same old. Short-staffed, and I had to tolerate that lazy Betsy. You know how it is." She chuckled, bits of food escaping her mouth. As she spoke, I had a hard time staying focused.

Angel forced her words around half masticated fries. I hoped that my face did not give away my disgust. I put my fry back down on my plate and tried to focus.

Her demeanor suggested a typical night, devoid of any significant events. I prodded further; my curiosity piqued. "I'm scheduled for tomorrow. Looks like I'll have a few discharges. Always makes for a busy morning."

"Well, you can scratch one of them off your list, Layla. Smith died suddenly last night. I didn't think they'd even admit him. Just had a UTI, and then bam, they called the code. His wife was devastated, naturally. Sad, but not as sad as the enema I had to give in room 302! She had an explosion down south and I thought I was going to code myself–Code Brown! Code Brown!" Angel chortled at her own dark humor, oblivious to my growing unease. Nurses, I mused, possessed a unique ability to find humor in the most morbid and disgusting situations.

Attempting to steer the conversation back to the topic at hand, I probed further. "That's awful. Any idea what happened to Smith?"

"Who knows? People die," she shrugged dismissively.

A disconcerting feeling settled over me. Something felt off about Angel's nonchalance. I said my goodbyes to her, my mind already consumed with the urge to delve into the enigmatic nature of my friend and colleague. My research took an unexpected turn, focusing now on Angel, my hairdresser, and RN. What was I missing?

The Woods

The car jerked to a stop after what felt like an eternity of suffocating odors and unbearable conversation. Kayleigh kept up her act, feigning sedation while her mind raced with fear and determination. The two lackeys yanked her out of the car, and Jody hoisted her over his shoulder, carrying her inside. She strained her senses, trying to get a glimpse of her surroundings. It was a metal building nestled in the heart of nowhere, surrounded by dense woods. Perhaps a storage unit, she thought, but definitely off the grid. Despite her dire situation, the scent of fresh air and the touch of sunlight stirred a flicker of hope deep within her. Every fiber of her being screamed to run, to fight back, but she knew she had to bide her time. They would catch her if she made a move. So, she forced herself to stay calm, to be strategic.

They dumped her onto a couch in a small room and left her there. Uncertain of who might be watching through hidden cameras, Kayleigh tried to feign restlessness, though she was painfully alert. The door burst open with a deafening bang, causing her body to jerk involuntarily. She continued to appear groggy, opening her eyes just enough to see the entrance. The sound *of approaching high heels reverberated off the metal walls, and the couch shifted under the weight of another person.*

The newcomer was tall, with impossibly long legs, and exuded an odd mix of confidence and warmth. In her hand, she held a glass of water, offering it to Kayleigh with a comforting smile. "You're safe now. Let's get you cleaned up and fed. You'll feel much better in the morning, I promise," she said, her tone strangely perky given the circumstances. Her smile, though, seemed forced and almost eerie. She vanished as quickly as she had appeared, leaving Kayleigh bewildered.

The encounter left Kayleigh feeling torn between reassurance and impending danger. The stranger's kindness was oddly juxtaposed with the alarming situation. There was something about her that stirred a sense of nostalgia, a feeling of déjà vu. Those long legs, the confident posture, the high-pitched giggle—they all felt oddly familiar, though Kayleigh couldn't pinpoint why.

Shortly after, the door creaked open, and a group of older women entered, bearing trays of food. Kayleigh savored the meal, then allowed herself to be led to a bathroom. There, a large tub of hot water and an array of soaps and shampoos awaited her. She immersed herself in the warm water, desperately trying to wash away the horrors that clung to her skin. Hours passed as she completed the ritual, emerging clean and clad in fresh clothes.

Guided to a brightly lit room with absurdly lavish furnishings,

Kayleigh settled onto a plush velvet chaise, her mind sharp and senses alert. She absorbed every detail of her surroundings, determined to memorize every nuance for a potential escape. This was her chance to break free from the nightmare that had ensnared her. The building, though plain from the outside, displayed intricate rooms. Narrow hallways led to closed doors, and various noises filled the air–voices, laughter, and the faint hum of music or a television. She was not alone.

After a while, two men in suits, accompanied by her previous captors, entered the room. They continued their conversation, seemingly oblivious to her presence. Was she invisible? The blonde lady followed suit, her entry marking a crucial moment. Sitting up on the chaise, Kayleigh studied the woman intently, her eyes widening in recognition and shock. Then, her gaze shifted to the lady standing beside her–a petite, dark-haired woman. They were clearly a couple, deeply connected. The conversation flowed, and names resurfaced–names that stirred memories within Kayleigh. The realization hit her like a tidal wave–she wasn't meant to survive this ordeal. They didn't care about her overhearing their conversation, or seeing their faces, because they intended to erase her from existence.

"Layla is our top priority now. She's become too much of a threat. This place, hidden in the mountains, is perfect until it's time for our grand plan," the blonde woman asserted, her voice

laced with authority.

Kayleigh became an unwilling witness to their sinister plot. She realized she had just seen the key players behind the Body Auction on the United States side of operations. Dr. Pierce may have been neutralized, rendered useless, but there were still nefarious elements at play within the United States, and Kayleigh knew first hand just how depraved those elements could be.

"The FBI thought Pierce and Ricardo were in control—how stupid. Pierce's demise was a blessing in disguise, helping us clear our path, and of course they assumed the men were in charge," the woman laughed and continued, her confidence unwavering. The conversation betrayed their intentions—to end anyone who posed a threat, to silence the truth.

Listening intently, Kayleigh knew she had to escape. Her friends were in danger and had no idea just how close they were to death, and the very people they had trusted with their lives were orchestrating the nightmare. It was a race against time, a battle for survival, and Kayleigh was determined not to be a pawn in their malicious game.

Chapter 7

By the time I arrived back at my apartment, it was dark. The only sounds were of the night creatures and the occasional passing car. The lights were on at the Reavis's house, but no one acknowledged my arrival. Mr. Reavis had informed me that they would examine the body the following morning, and a full forensic team would be doing a repeat autopsy.

I thought back to how elusive Angel had seemed when I first had my hair appointment. She asked me all sorts of questions, but didn't actually answer mine. I scolded myself for not looking at her more closely in the beginning. Something just wasn't right with how she reacted to the death. I pulled out my laptop and went to work. I thought maybe I could become a real agent someday. That is, if I wasn't so old, slow, and out of shape.

Angel was a native of the area, born into a military family. Her father, a high-ranking general, had passed away a few years prior, shattering her world. Reflecting on her social media posts, it was clear she battled severe depression after his death. I always find it astonishing what people share on platforms like Facebook and Instagram. Following her father's footsteps, she had joined the Marines, but his swift decline due to terminal cancer left her heart and soul shattered. The enormity of the loss overwhelmed her, leading to a profound mental and physical breakdown. Consequently, the military had to grant her an honorable medical discharge due to her mental health struggles.

After a period of healing, Angel managed to piece her life back together and pursued a career in nursing and, interestingly, cosmetology. She juggled two jobs for years, showcasing remarkable strength. Remarkably, she rarely mentioned her mother, who resided in North Carolina. Judging from the pictures from the past year, she did make holiday visits. Angel had no siblings, no criminal record, and her background appeared flawless. With the help of my neighbor and a few extra phone calls, we managed to access her military records and the physicians' notes that led to her discharge.

For some reason, delving into her files felt like a betrayal of our newfound friendship, as I perused pictures of her father and her. He had been a towering, imposing figure—a man of strength and honor. His impressive record in special ops, adorned with many medals and commendations, made it clear he was her hero. As a daughter who deeply loved and admired my own dad, I couldn't help but feel an overwhelming sadness for her. Angel had left her mark during her brief stint in the military; her records spoke of her exceptional marksmanship skills, showcasing her hard work, determination, and discipline.

Her father's abrupt illness was devastating. He transformed from a robust, muscular man, weighing over 250 pounds, to a mere 125-pound shell of his former self. In a cruel twist, metastatic cancer consumed him rapidly, like a malevolent demon devouring his very soul. It was as though he was being eaten alive from the inside out. He endured a miserable, undignified death, engulfed in agonizing pain and suffering, unable to care for himself in his final moments.

There were pictures in her file and, I admit, I got emotional looking at the sad records. One of the last pictures of her father alive was in the hospital. She was by his side, arm to arm. He was trying to smile, his face gaunt and his skin pulled tight over his teeth, resembling a sad skeleton. The hospital room was normal, flowers everywhere, flags adorned the walls, but then something caught my eye. I jumped up and ran to my stack of photos.

I saw it again, so I threw on a coat and ran to my neighbor's. The bite of the cold air shocked me. The weather had taken a turn; a cold front was coming through. In the Tennessee mountains, it could be 70 degrees one day and snow the next.

Adjusting my jacket, I approached the front door. I had not even looked at the time and wondered if it was rude to come to a person's home in the country past 9 pm. The TV was loud, an Andy Griffith marathon was on, and the smell of popcorn was in the air. It made me smile and miss home. Finally, after a few moments, Mrs. Reavis came to the door, pleasant and welcoming as always.

"Oh my, that air is getting cold. Come in, honey!" The kind woman wrapped her fuzzy pink housecoat tight around her neck. I had the instant feeling of nostalgia. Mr. Reavis quickly arrived beside her with a puzzled look on his face.

I was quickly escorted to the basement.

"I am so sorry to bother you, but I think I found something interesting." I was filled with excitement but tried to appear composed. I wanted to avoid appearing childish.

Practically sprinting to his working board, I looked up and down, searching for a small piece of the puzzle.

"Come over here. I think I found something." I was embarrassed at how my voice sounded, shaky and uncertain, but as he stood staring at me, I began to feel even more nervous.

"Look at the pictures taken in the hospital rooms." I pointed to the pictures in the hospital rooms, then I pulled up the picture of the General's hospital room. He saw it immediately.

His face transformed in front of my eyes. He went from stern and serious to soft and excited. I was inwardly proud of myself, smiling like a Cheshire cat as I saw the acknowledgment.

Until this moment, no one had noticed that all the deaths were veterans. How was that possible? In reviewing all the room's photos, there was one similarity. On every bedside table, a small red flowerpot, and in the flowerpot, a small flag on a little wooden pole. The interesting thing was, the flag was upside down, in every single room. Under normal circumstances, the American flag should never be displayed in this manner, unless to signify "dire distress." It was conceivable that the General might have felt such distress, but this rationale didn't apply to all the victims. While some were elderly and ailing, others battled terminal illnesses, not every one of them fit this description. The pieces of this enigmatic puzzle were scattered, yet they provided a vital connection— the very first one we had. And the common denominator was my very own hairdresser, Angel.

Chapter 8

I returned to my apartment wired, unable to even consider sleep, despite knowing that in a few hours I would have to be at work. I was proud of myself. I was energized. An FBI agent I was not, but hey, I could pretend, right? I felt like a TV heroine. I had done something good; I discovered a connection no one yet had. I was proud of myself.

"You go, girl! Good job, Layla!" I dorkily cheered myself on as I peered into the mirror. I could feel my heart racing and took some cleansing breaths to calm it. "This is why they sent you here, to investigate, to help determine find answers in a genuine case for the FBI," I told myself. I wondered if Mr. Reavis was calling headquarters right now and telling them. I deeply hoped I would get to stay.

The air had continued to get colder, and the forecast was for snow. I didn't even care; I was on fire and wanted to keep looking for clues and connections. Did Angel kill those people? If so, why? She hadn't been working on some of the other nights, but she could easily walk in without anyone questioning her simply because of her employment.

The American Flag, a symbol of pride in the USA. It stands for more than freedom, and even though there has been controversy surrounding the anthem and the flag, for the most part and for most people, it is the staple of patriotism. Soldiers especially treat it with care and reverence. So, the little flower pots at each bedside with a flag are not an uncommon occurrence. Some hospitals do recognize veterans. At the previous hospital I worked at when a veteran passed away, we covered the body with a flag. This hospital gave them a little flower. But for the flag to be upside down, well, that's a huge indicator of something not right. Did the patient do it? Did a staff or family do it? Is it a person that is anti-American, that has something against our vets? Questions plagued my mind.

Hoping to calm my mind, I brewed myself a cup of tea to soothe my weary mind and body. Exhausted, I decided it was time to lie down for a few hours of much-needed rest. Standing in my petite bathroom, I gazed out of the window, which opened up to a small backyard and then stretched into dense woods. The snow had started falling, blanketing the grass in a pristine white layer, resembling a delicate, gossamer veil spread meticulously over the undulating ground. The porch light cast an ethereal glow on the snow, illuminating the scene.

Suddenly, seemingly out of nowhere, something captured my attention. A figure stood beneath a tree in the woods. Panic began to claw its way up my chest. I doubted myself for a moment, but I was certain of what I had seen. Snow, despite its beauty, doesn't provide much cover. A person standing amidst the snow finds it hard to conceal themselves. I stood there, motionless; it was 2:30 a.m. I could tell it wasn't Mr. Reavis or his son. My eyes locked onto the figure, and it unmistakably stared back at me. I dared not make any sudden movements, feigning normalcy, pretending I hadn't noticed them, although my heart threatened to burst from my chest. With trembling hands, I used my voice to activate my phone, desperate for the lifeline I had in Mr. Reavis.

I voice texted Mr. Reavis and let him know what was happening:

Someone is in the back yard looking at me. I don't know what to do.

...

Will he wake up? He is older. What if the phone doesn't alert him? I then reached with my foot and opened the small cabinet, not bending down. The small, emergency-need Glock was taped inside the door. Carefully, I pulled it up onto the counter. I had originally thought it was bizarre when Mr. Reavis showed me the secret weapons in the apartment, but in that moment, I was beyond glad for the stash.

Trying to act nonchalant, stilly trying to convince my

peeping Tom that he'd gone unnoticed, I decided to brush my teeth. The entire time, I watched the dark ominous figure out of the corner of my eye and it made my skin crawl. I bent down to spit, but when I stood upright, the figure was gone. Like a ghostly apparition disappearing in the night. I saw Mr. Reavis exit the back door and it let me know that he had seen the creeper as well. Not long after, a soft knock came to my door. With my pistol in hand, I opened it. Mr. Reavis had an AR-15, and he looked very agitated. I was taken aback by the gun, but he looked ready for battle.

Confusion was etched across his brow for the first time since I met him. He wasn't his typically calm and collected self. He seemed concerned, bewildered, and I felt the same. Who would be out there? No one is supposed to know who I am, or why I was there. He immediately called headquarters and notified them of a possible breach. I was so worried, not for my life, but that they would pull me off the case. I went from a high to a crashing low. I was so relieved when they decided to keep me on, but they did plan on sending actual undercover agents for backup. They officially opened a case and gave me a bit of a pat on the back for connecting the dots, but they also confirmed that they still needed my services. Relief flooded over me. They would send travel nurses to cover the hospital and help keep an eye on who was stalking me.

Sleep never came that night, which was unsurprising considering the circumstances, but it did leave me in a weird state of mind and I couldn't safely see patients without a clear head, so I called Alisondra and asked her to cover my shift. I offered to work her shift that night in return, so it worked out perfectly. It wasn't the best sleep, but I did manage to sleep that day. I kept my gun beside me and triple-checked to make sure the alarm was set. I needed all the rest I could get for what was ahead of me.

Chapter 9

Night shift in the hospital setting is a different animal. On night shift, the staff numbers are significantly lower compared to the day shift. The atmosphere is gloomy and foreboding. It's interesting how church and hospitals, the main sanctuaries for healing, transform into unsettling places at night. Walking in through the lower-level employee parking is a particular creep zone. I just imagine that a zombie from the Walking Dead series will come toward me at any moment and try to eat my flesh or some knife-wielding psycho will jump out from behind a car.

I tucked my little pistol into my discreet chest holster. A new part of my attire that Mr. Reavis insisted upon. Typically, consultants are not armed, but in the Tennessee hills, it is legal to carry if you are permitted, and he encouraged me to do so, so I complied.

The long halls were empty. Old, abandoned x-ray machines, stretchers, and equipment sat like fossils frozen in time. The items had been neglected for years during building upgrades, with no one bothering to donate or discard them. I ambled slowly, immersing myself in the noises and fragrances in the bowels of the hibernating creature I was enveloped by. A hospital is a live animal after all. I was hoping for a slow night with few admissions so I could ask questions and gather information. As luck would have it, Angel was not working that night.

When you think about it, nurses are powerful beings. From the first breath of a newborn, to the last breath of the elderly, nurses are there to hold life. Patients, to varying degrees, are often unable to defend or care for themselves, making them vulnerable. They rely on nurses for food, comfort, and healing. The simplest of tasks can be a daunting feat when you are very ill. A nurse can save a life or easily take it. I felt guilty for spying on them, my peers, my comrades–like I was betraying a sacred bond. Oh, but I was so in love with the amazing little devices I was given for that purpose. I felt like a character in a novel or a movie.

Armed with a little recorder in my ear and my camera pen, I made my way to the nurses' station. I arrived on the floor to be greeted by the night-shift staff. Some of them I knew, but most were strangers to me. I did my rounds, charted and completed my required work quickly so I could proceed with the true task at hand. I snapped pictures of the nurse's station, the rooms, all the staff I could, without being noticed of course. It was a quiet night; the young nurses stayed glued to their phones, looking on Facebook and watching TikTok. Some even danced to make their own post. Older nurses nodded at the desk and seemed irritated if some poor soul rang out for the bedpan. Not all nurses are good. A nurse on paper doesn't make someone a nurse in their heart. Some nurses were ruled out as the killer simply because of their laziness. If you're too lazy to do the simplest aspects of your job, there's no way you have the energy to be a serial killer.

A housekeeper rolling his large laundry cart down the hall caught my attention. He was surely in his 70s, with advanced kyphosis. He was almost completely bent over due to his degree of spinal disease. But his pleasant smile pricked my heart. It made me terribly sad that he had to work a night shift at his age and in his condition, especially one with such a demanding job. I opened the doors for him and let him pass, snapping a quick pic, just because.

Next, it was time to talk to nurses. I went to the desk and settled in with the cookies I had bought on my way in. Eating is a favorite pastime for nurses, and this instantly warmed them up. There was one face that I did recognize. An RN from the hospital where I live. Heather, in looking at her badge, had become a travel nurse and, because of the nursing shortage, had taken a three-month assignment at this exact hospital.

What are the odds? She was a great ICU nurse, but travel nurse pay is better. She smiled and leaned in to give me a big hug. Unexpectedly, when I hugged her, she wrapped her arms around me in a *real* hug. I immediately recoiled as my holster would be easily felt. Her eye contact let me know that she had felt the abnormal bulge. A wide smile grew across her face, and she nodded ever so slightly. What in the world? What did she think she felt? I was flushed with embarrassment for no reason. What was that grin about? She then took me by the hand and pulled me toward her, looking around as she spoke.

"I want you to meet Mackenzie. We have been working for the same company and we room together. We try to synchronize our assignments. We work a few months, then take a few months off. The money is awesome." She pulled me by the arm while she was talking. She spoke rapidly, always had, like she was naturally caffeinated. I just love nurses like her; high energy, meticulous nurses. Their patients were always well taken care of, bathed, and pristine.

We went into the med room and her body seemed to relax. She kept speaking in a bubbly, audible tone as she casually closed the door behind us. A striking blonde nurse was pulling meds out of a drawer. Her scrubs were far too tight, revealing a hot pink thong when she bent over. This is not uncommon, as nurses *can* have a reputation for being, well, promiscuous. The most surprising thing was not the seemingly intentionally visible panties. It was a tiny pistol, maybe the smallest gun I'd ever seen, tucked discreetly between her scrubs and string-like underwear, right at the top of the neon thong and contrasting with the smooth skin of her low back. The gun was secured in a way that I couldn't comprehend, and it left me shocked. I found the baffling sight amusing and giggled to myself almost involuntarily. I was both amused and completely confused. Does everyone in Tennessee pack heat in their underwear? She stood, gave me a hug, and flashed a smile. The jacket she hastily pulled down over her scrubs concealed the gun. I didn't expect the hug, however, so I'm sure I seemed rigid and awkward.

"Hey girl! Just call me Mac. I have heard a lot about you. The kindness in her southern voice and her warm hug filled me with an unexpected happiness. So many Southerners are huggers, but usually not *before* you've even been introduced.

"It's a pleasure to meet you, Mac." I said tentatively, conscious of the side-eye of confusion plastered on my face. "What's going on?" Turning to face them both, I continued "Why do you have a gun in your underwear?" As I turned to look at Heather, she glanced toward the location of my own weapon and gave me a loaded look.

"We are the undercover agents sent to watch your six."

"Wait, what?" I was genuinely shocked. My mouth hung open.

"I was actually on assignment back when we met for a completely unrelated case. That's why I wasn't there very long. But when we got the call to come here, I was blown away to find out you were involved! I mean, talk about a coincidence!"

I stood in stunned silence for a while, my mouth still open. Heather laughed and looked at Mac, Mackenzie shrugged. "I can't believe it! You're such a good nurse," I said finally.

"No, I'm not. But I am a good agent. I do what I can to play the part when I have one."

"She makes a great hooker, too." Mac laughed.

"I don't even know what to say. It's like all of the sudden I'm tripping over FBI people. And you were on assignment at *my* hospital? The entire time?" The bizarre coincidence of it all was overwhelming. I actually felt lightheaded.

"Girl, yes. There are undercover agents in places you would never imagine. Back then, the case involved one of the patients who had been implicated in a massive shipment of Fentanyl across the border and planned to turn state's evidence on a federal case. And to answer your other question, a case *has* been opened here, but we are also here to keep an eye out for you. They briefed us on the events, and they're not sure why anyone would be watching you."

"So, we got your back, babe." Mackenzie had to interject herself, likely sensing that I could have been knocked over by a feather in that moment. She put her arm around me. It again dawned on me how touchy feely she was.

"Ok, well, um, great. I'll see you ladies later." I was flustered. I tried to sound cooler and more collected than I actually felt. I was way out of my depths. I was literally working side by side with an FBI agent for quite some time and had no idea— and yet, there I was, playing pretend. What ego I had developed over my wins in the case, deflated quickly at the idea that an undercover agent was right under my nose for months and I noticed nothing; not a single red flag. "Some kind of sleuth you are," I said to myself as I considered how intimidating these ladies were. To top it off, they reminded me of Kayleigh. I felt my emotions start to well up. I needed to walk away.

"Stay aware Layla, stay safe." and for the first time, I saw a flicker of concern and seriousness in Heather's dark eyes. For some reason her change in tone gave me a shiver down my spine. But in her voice, I heard a strange assurance that, to her, we were equals. She didn't view me as any less vital to the case than she or her partner. Though my own self-doubts threatened to sabotage my mission, I decided then and there too, "pull my big girl panties up," as they say. I still had work to do.

We discreetly went our separate ways and returned to work.

I cautiously approached the director of the nursing's office. Unlocking the door was a crazy experience, but it turned out well for me. The fact that I could, in fact, pick a lock cracked a tiny seed in my soul, a weird new level of confidence filled my body as I took quick pictures of the schedules, the time sheets, and the file she had titled "Deaths- Past 6 Months." I continued snapping random pictures and noticed that Mackenzie and Heather had stealthily filed in behind me and seemed to be doing the same. They were seasoned agents and, observing them from a distance like a shy teenager pretending to be cool, I admired them. We *were* on the same team. My emotions were all over the map. I felt proud, but anxious at the same time; confident, but completely overwhelmed. Looking back, I can confirm it was one of the most exhilarating and challenging times in my life, second only to motherhood.

The night passed without any excitement, but I was content with the information I received. I thought that among the 250 or so images, I would surely discover something, a clue about the why and who. As I made my way down the long hallway to the back lot, ready for bed, I couldn't help but notice the door to environmental services was open. The feeble man I had witnessed earlier in the shift was finishing up. I peeked into the large room. Initially, nothing appears to be unusual; various cleaning supplies, mops, biohazard bags. That's when I saw it. Little American flags neatly organized in boxes inside a large cabinet. I saw it as my chance to go in and have a discussion with him.

"Hi there... How are you doing?" With a cool demeanor, I went inside and introduced myself. "I am Layla, one of the new hospitalists. I just wanted to introduce myself."

"Well, hello to you! My name is Marvin. Layla, it's a pleasure to meet you." He had the most gentle and endearing personality. I felt my heart melting." Welcome to our little hospital! I have lived in the area my whole life and I've worked right here for forty years. So, if you need to know anything about anything, you just yell at me." He winked and smiled. It was utterly adorable. His voice was dripping with pride, but at the same time seemed weak with age.

"Oh, yes, sir. Thank you so much! I will be sure to do that." I smiled a genuine smile. "Everyone has been very kind and welcoming so far."

"Well, if they're not, you tell them they'll answer to me," he quipped.

After a giggle, I feigned surprise at the sight of the flags and inquired about their purpose.

As he approached the cabinet of small flags, he began

speaking about his veteran father, and his unwavering commitment to treating all those who have served our country with dignity, ensuring they are duly acknowledged. "It's just a little something we do as a thank you.," He seemed so passionate about it; his eyes glistened as he told me exactly how many flags he had delivered over the years. I was amazed that he'd been keeping count for so long. I managed to take a few pictures as he turned away, then I said my goodbye and made my exit.

By the time my shift was over, the temperature had dropped and there was about two inches of snow on the ground. Although I was ready to sleep, I knew I wouldn't be able to go to bed without at least glancing at the pictures. I shuffled along quickly, fueled by the promise of potential clues. While searching for my keys in my bag, I accidentally collided with two men who apparently didn't see me either. The two men, one tall and Caucasian, the other short and Asian, and quite an unusual duo, said they were attempting to find the ER in order to visit their sick friend, who had been brought in overnight. The scent of whiskey and old cigar smoke clung to both of them and I assumed their sick friend likely smelled the same when he arrived. Being new, I had to concentrate on providing directions, but they seemed grateful and I apologized for nearly running them over in my distracted state. I proceeded to my car. I noticed that they were both staring at me, which made me feel a bit uneasy. I laughed it off, thinking they likely had one too many, and I just happened to be female. I couldn't help but laugh as I drove away. As awkward is it is to be obviously ogled, it's still flattering, no matter how old one gets.

Escape Plan

Kayleigh was confined to a small yet cozy room with a TV and bed for the following week, an improvement from her previous situation, but she remained aware of her captivity. She was being pampered and groomed to bring a better price; the auctioneers planned on making a profit from her. There were no windows in her room, so the only information she could gather was from when she was let out of her room for very short times or from pressing her ear to the walls. It was cold, very cold, and the wind blew hard at night. Nightmares and dreams of death haunted her. She had only a thin wind suit on and knew that even if she could somehow escape, she would freeze in the woods without proper clothes and provisions. She had been given the opportunity to bathe daily with clean undergarments, but the same wind suit was all she had as far as her wardrobe was concerned.

One early morning, a petite elderly woman delivered her breakfast and informed her that she would be moved to a different room after eating. After a surprisingly large meal, she was led to another section of the building. She made a conscious effort to observe every detail during the short walk. The older women in the facility seemed occupied, heads down, avoiding conversation. Men, armed and vigilant, guarded specific areas. Through a side room window, she caught a glimpse of Jody, the repugnant man, and his small Asian accomplice, Lam, lounging on a couch, smoking cigars. They exuded an aura of repulsiveness. Among them, there was one familiar face–the blonde vixen from her past.

As they crossed paths in the narrow corridor, their eyes met. In that moment, Kayleigh realized her captor, the venomous Krissy, had recognized her. Krissy placed a hand on Kayleigh's shoulder, her touch like ice, and let out a chilling laugh. The entourage halted, and Krissy's thin, pale fingers, manicured with a pale pink polish, squeezed Kayleigh's clavicle with a sinister grip. Her lips, painted in the same shade, curved into a malicious smile, and a Louis Vuitton purse hung from her arm. The scent of lavender and flowers trailed in her wake. Leaning close, she whispered in Kayleigh's ear, "Don't worry, this will all be over soon, for you and Layla." A sinister grin stretched across her face as she turned away. Kayleigh didn't flinch, maintaining a calm facade while a tempest of emotions raged beneath her surface.

Kayleigh was ushered into a harsh, clinical-looking room, where two older men in lab coats awaited her. One of them, his voice raspy and devoid of emotion, instructed her, "Go take a shower, bathe thoroughly, and remove all body hair with the razor provided. We'll be observing, so don't attempt anything crazy."

He pointed towards an open shower in the corner of the room, devoid of doors or privacy. Already shivering from the room's icy temperature, she complied, albeit reluctantly, hoping the hot water would offer some solace. Undressing in front of the men felt degrading, and she flushed with embarrassment. Hurrying into the shower, she found the water barely warm, but she rushed through the humiliating task, hoping it would end swiftly. As she turned off the water and reached for the towel, she was stopped.

"No, not yet. We need to ensure you've done what was asked of you effectively," one of the men said, scrutinizing her body critically. Tears welled in her eyes as she was informed she hadn't shaved well enough and had to repeat the process. Compliance came with the accompaniment of warm, salty tears that mingled with the cold water.

What happened next didn't shock Kayleigh. A complete medical examination was conducted using outdated yet functional equipment. Tubes of blood were drawn, an EKG was performed, and ultrasounds of various organs were taken. She was being appraised like a commodity for the auction. The men worked methodically, their actions disturbingly systematic. They never met her gaze, exchanging glances with each other instead. Their depraved task seemed to arouse them, adding to the disturbing atmosphere.

Once the examination was over, the older women reappeared, slathering her body with thick, creamy lotions that carried the scent of cucumber melon. Her hair was cut and dried, a brief moment of reprieve as she envisioned herself in a luxurious spa or her local salon. Sadly, reality crashed down upon her when she opened her eyes. The illusion was shattered by the return of her nemesis, Krissy.

Heels clicked on the floor as Krissy entered the room. She addressed the men nonchalantly, "What do you think would fetch the best price? Should we sell her organs individually, or the whole body?" Kayleigh was discussed as though she were a lifeless object.

The raspy-voiced man spoke up, "I believe she's too much of a liability. Keeping her alive poses risks. Her body, despite being slightly underweight and malnourished, is in excellent condition. Organ harvest would yield substantial profits." The other man nodded in agreement.

Krissy's excitement was palpable. "Tell me more, doc. How much are we talking about?" Her voice held a greedy anticipation.

The man began listing figures, "A single kidney can bring $10,000. A liver, $100,000. A heart, a million. Lungs, around $900,000. So, a rough estimate would be close to 2 million plus."

In a moment of surreal absurdity, Kayleigh almost laughed at the sight of Krissy clapping her hands like a seal at SeaWorld in designer heels. It was utterly ridiculous.

"That's all I needed to know! We'll sell her piece by piece," Krissy declared with a cruel smile, her voice laced with sadistic pleasure.

Approaching Kayleigh, Krissy stroked her hair and laughed wickedly. "Nothing would give me more joy than to see your heart ripped from your chest while you're still alive. I never liked you, never liked how close you were to Layla. I think I was jealous-ironic, isn't it?" Kayleigh remained still, refusing to give Krissy the satisfaction.

Krissy's blush-pink nails traced a chilling path along Kayleigh's forearm. "What, no snarky comments? No threats? How disappointing. Well, your time will come. Both you and your precious Layla will be eradicated soon enough."

With those words, she turned and left the room, storming out like a petulant child. Kayleigh knew what she had to do. She had to escape, had to warn Layla. The lingering scent of Krissy's perfume hung in the air, a haunting reminder of her personified evil. Krissy was a malevolent force, and Kayleigh was determined not to succumb to her wicked plans.

Layla needed to know that her closest friend, her "sister," was actually Satan in disguise.

Chapter 10

Despite the struggles in our relationship, I still missed Tripp, so when he called to say he was finally coming for a visit, I was extremely excited. I tidied up my little apartment and decided that I, too, could probably use some tidying up. I reached out to Angel to schedule a wax and trim, which would serve a dual purpose, to get me ready for Tripp's visit and hopefully to get a few more details out of her.

Walking into the beauty shop has always made me happy. You go in looking like a troll, but come out looking like Miss Universe. Covering my gray roots always made me feel prettier. It was a shock to discover Angel's absence. I would be getting my touch-up from Sheree. It was okay, but I couldn't help but wonder why Angel hadn't informed me of the change. Sheree mentioned the unpredictable weather, a factory closure near town, and several snippets of gossip. Finally, I mustered the courage to ask where Angel was.

"So, where is our Angel girl today?"

"Oh, well, she had to attend a memorial service for a friend. Her voice was soft and discreet, as if whispering a secret.

"Oh no! I am so sorry. Who passed away?" I expressed my shock; and it was genuine.

"It was a friend of her father's that passed away a few days ago. I immediately knew the person she was talking about. It was confusing to me that they had a service knowing his body wouldn't be back for weeks. She didn't give me a chance to ask more questions before continuing her explanation.

Instead of a funeral, it's a celebration of life. Mr. Smith was a nice man. I do his wife's hair."

"Oh no, how heartbreaking. How is she doing?"

"Well naturally, she is devastated. It came as a shock to everyone because he wasn't really that sick." Her voice carried a mournful tone. "He was well-loved in our little town, and he was very close to Angel's father before he passed away. They were in the same military company I think he might have been Angel's godfather. So of course, she is hurting, too."

It took every cell in my body to hide my shock. Angel never mentioned she even knew him, let alone that he was her godfather! And she certainly didn't seem emotional when she discussed his death. She was anything but sad. I would have described her as almost cold. The entire situation became increasingly unbelievable.

With other women entering the salon, I couldn't pry more information from Sheree. After my salon visit, I drove out to the Scenic Garden Memorial Park to take a look. I parked inconspicuously and snapped pictures of guests arriving and leaving. The memorial park had a separate section for veterans, with flags adorning many graves.

Once again, I found myself immersed in my imaginary role as an FBI or CIA agent on a covert mission. It was oddly exhilarating, skulking in my car and capturing moments in photographs. I dared to believe that cracking a case might just pave my way into their esteemed ranks. Wishful thinking, I knew.

When the final guest departed, I returned home to prepare for the impending weekend. Although I felt a pang of disappointment at not spotting Angel at the service, I redirected my focus to the moments ahead.

With the anticipation of a pleasant evening, I busied myself with downloading and printing the night's pictures. As the printer whirred to life, I began preparing a lavish dinner for Tripp and me. In the midst of my culinary preparations, I took a moment to call Aubrey. Her cheerful voice resonated from Atlanta, filling me with both longing and happiness. Despite the miles between us, I couldn't help but feel genuinely content for her. She had found her place in the world, even if it was a perilous one.

In the rhythm of the music playing in the background, I

danced around the kitchen, my awkward attempts to mimic those dances I had seen in TikTok videos. I love watching TikTok dancers. My heart swelled with lightness as I peeled potatoes and seasoned the meat. A glance out of the window revealed the Chief wandering in the woods, piquing my curiosity. Yet, my attention was quickly drawn back inside; my husband, unseen for months, was due to arrive at any moment.

When Tripp's soft knock echoed through my door, my heart leaped with anticipation. Our relationship had weathered the storm of the Body Auction ordeal, the Dubai trip, and the imminent threats that had tested our marriage. He still harbored hurt and betrayal, which I couldn't entirely blame him for, but I could only apologize so much. The therapist reassured him it was a consequence of my trauma, but it didn't heal his heart. Uncertain of the future, I feared that my collaboration with the FBI might be the last straw for our marriage. Nonetheless, I loved the man. I always had.

Eager to reconnect, I flung open the door, enveloping him in a warm embrace. Tripp had shed weight in recent weeks, his features sharp and defined. A clean shave and my favorite cologne clung to him, he smelled delicious, and his smile was inviting and genuine. In an unexpected surprise, he seemed *normal*, free from the tension that had gripped our relationship for so long.

"Hey baby! I've missed you so much!" I greeted him passionately, our lips meeting before he could respond.

"Hey honey, I've missed you too. How've you been? I love your cozy apartment," he replied, his smile genuine as he stepped inside.

The evening unfolded smoothly. Tripp inquired about my current case, and we delved into conversations about his recent clients. Inevitably, our daughter became the topic of discussion, and we eagerly planned a family vacation. While I tidied up the dishes in my compact kitchen, Tripp relaxed on the couch. The printer's low ink beeped, prompting me to ask him to replace it. He graciously complied; his attention captured by the pile of over 200 photographs laid out on the table. This keen interest struck me as unusual; he typically grew annoyed at the mere mention of an FBI case and would never have dared joined in.

Having not shared the details of my investigation, Tripp was oblivious to the significance of the photos. Nevertheless, I enjoyed his earnest attempt to feign interest. My mind, though, wandered to the bedroom, anticipation simmering. Yet, he stood there, engrossed in the pictures like a statue. Just as I was about to lead him away, he spoke up.

"I think I see something odd," he said, his eyes fixated on a few pictures before holding up one featuring Angel, her father, and Dr. DeWhite, and Mr. Smith.

"What do you see, Mr. Detective?" I teased, intrigued.

He pointed at the pictures, comparing the tattoos on their right forearms. At first, nothing registered, but then it hit me. My eyes widened, and I gasped, "Oh my Lord! How did I miss that? The Tattoo!" A sense of embarrassment washed over me, barely softened by the fact that I hadn't even reviewed those specific photos.

"They all have the same tattoos on their right forearms," Tripp confirmed, a sense of pride evident in his discovery.

I gathered more photos, and indeed, the same tattoo adorned all their forearms—a fusion of mystical symbolism and military imagery. In that moment, I felt like an idiot, unable to discern the connection that had eluded me until my husband, who hadn't so much as a clue about what was happening, brought it to light. However, this revelation was not without a tinge of defeat; my excitement waned, and the once-tangible sexual tension dissipated.

Sensing my disappointment, Tripp reassured me, "Oh honey, it's okay." He enveloped me in his arms, his warmth a comforting presence. "You hadn't even taken those photos off the printer yet. How could you have seen that? But who knows, maybe I should join the FBI too. I think I did something good!"

He chuckled and playfully teased me about joining the FBI before whisking me off to the bedroom.

Thankfully though, despite my sulking and self-doubt, the effects of the wine did the trick, allowing me to fully enjoy my husband's presence. After a passionate rendezvous, my throat felt parched, leading me into the darkened kitchen for a drink. Gazing into the inky night, I once again noticed movement in the yard. I stood still, my senses alert, waiting for further signs of life. Moments later, a different tall figure strolled along the yard's perimeter. The clock read midnight, and as the figure approached the light, I saw that it was the police chief conducting what must have been a late-night inspection. Relieved, I returned to bed, finding solace in Tripp's embrace. That night, my sleep was undisturbed by haunting dreams, yet I knew the morning would usher in new challenges and with them, lots more work to be done.

Chapter 11

I only had Tripp for two days, so I didn't want to spend the entire time working. I told him I'd run to Mr. Reavis, inform him about the tattoo, and be right back while Tripp showered. I planned to show him around town and unwind. Excitement bubbling within me because of the new revelation, I carried the fresh photos down to the basement. Instead of going through the house, I decided to take a detour and explore the backyard area. With very little snow left, I couldn't distinguish footprints, but there were many sets. I could see far into the woods, noticing signs of multiple trips made by someone, evident from the broken trees and shifted branches.

Entering the basement, both men greeted me. "Hey guys, good morning! I've got something you might want to look at," I said, leaving out the part about my husband making the connection. I took the photos and pinned them up on the board.

"Okay, great. What are we looking at?" Mr. Reavis appeared confused and shocked when I hung up the housekeeper's picture. "Why is his picture up there? What does he have to do with any of this? He's an old man. Are you trying to be a detective now?" he asked, his tone condescending, and he patted me on the back.

"Well, I met him the other night and noticed the little flags he had. I took pictures of everyone. It's just a coincidence," I explained.

The picture seemed random. In my hand, I also held pictures from the memorial. Since I was already downstairs, I began pinning them up as well. I hadn't had time to review them, but I noticed that certain groups of people appeared in multiple pictures, engaging in conversation and embraces. It was clear they shared a close connection.

"I'm sorry to interrupt, but I wanted to update you. My husband is here to visit. I'll be back at full capacity when he heads back home," I informed them. They nodded politely, and I left. Tripp was waiting for me, and I hoped for a wonderful weekend.

"Wow, this is a small town, but it's beautiful," Tripp said, affectionately rubbing my knee and upper thigh as we took the scenic route.

"Yeah, it is, but the people are nice."

"Well, not all of them. I mean, someone is a killer, right?"

I laughed. "Touché!"

We explored the little town, visited antique stores, and

dined at small restaurants. It was an amazing time.

The next 48 hours passed quickly, and we had a relaxing time. I was genuinely sad to see Tripp leave. As he was packing up, his phone vibrated. Curious about why the ringer was off, I picked it up.

"Hey babe, someone is calling you. Want me to get it?" I yelled into the bedroom.

"No, it's fine. I'll check it later."

The call went to voicemail.

Message: "Hey, how's it going? Have you left yet? Everything is on track, I hope. Call soon."

The voice was female, distant yet familiar. As I was about to replay it, Tripp emerged. Not anger or irritation, but a flicker of emotion in his eyes that I couldn't quite place. He quickly took the phone from my hand.

"I told you I would check it," he said, his voice dripping with irritation.

"Wow, what's the big deal, and who was that? Should I be jealous?" I joked; my tone nervous.

"It's a new work contract. I'm behind on some deadlines because of this trip. Good grief, Layla."

"Okay, sorry, I didn't mean to upset you. I've had a great weekend and don't want to end up in a fight. I love you," I said, trying to diffuse the tension.

"It's okay. Sorry I was rude. I just have a lot to do. I need to head out. I love you too. Please be safe." With an odd kiss on the forehead, he left, and the entire vibe of the weekend vanished with that call.

As soon as he pulled out of the driveway, I went straight to the workroom. I needed to focus on work, not my strange marital situation. Mr. Reavis was sitting at a computer desk, a smile on his face. He had a scheduled call with HQ and had already logged in. I was allowed to stand in the corner and listen as he updated his superiors. To my shock, Mr. Reavis explained the tattoo connection in detail.

"The tattoo we've discovered is a mark of an elite unit of Marines. The Navy has their own–it's called Swallow tattoos, where each swallow represents 5,000 nautical miles in a sailor's career. This one is called The Cerberus, meaning protector or guardian. They're considered somewhat fanatical, believing they're protected by a warrior spirit. There are rumors of secret initiation rituals to join the group. They believe they're chosen by God and can defeat enemies others can't. The group has secret ceremonies and procedures that they're not allowed to discuss, even with family. Their activities aren't sanctioned by the military," Mr. Reavis explained, seeming uncomfortable discussing the group's oddities.

This revelation provided insight into the closeness I observed in the photographs. But if they were this close, why weren't they upset about someone targeting them? Mr. Reavis informed me that the forensic report should be back by the end of the day before signing off.

"I want to thank you for getting those agents sent to the hospital. I feel safer knowing they're there," I said, noticing a fleeting expression in Mr. Reavis's eyes. I hadn't imagined it–he knew something I wasn't privy to. He was the type of man who met your gaze, but at that moment, he never stopped looking at his shoes.

I blushed with embarrassment. They were keeping details from me, but why wouldn't they? I was just a consultant, but not knowing grated on me. I was a control freak and felt anything but in control at that moment.

"I know I'm just a consultant, but please tell me what you can. I hate being left out of the big picture, especially if it involves someone watching me," I said, using the sweetest country voice I could muster while tenderly touching his arm. "I'm a little scared, you know?" I knew the "protect me big strong man, I am a weak female" approach would work, because it works every time..

He tried to downplay it, but he knew he would lose the battle.

"We found out that someone had been in the woods even before the night you saw them. Someone had been following you," he said, his tone uncertain.

"Why? Why would I be watched?"

"We're not sure, so we've placed cameras in the woods and around the perimeter. But we haven't been able to capture a face. We can't figure out who would know you're here. We're concerned about a leak within the agency. But it's okay, Layla. I won't let anything happen to you."

I stood frozen. I hadn't considered this–I was too preoccupied with the case.

"I want you to tell me who knows you're here. I mean everyone–don't leave anyone out."

"Tripp, and Aubrey, of course. My best friend Krissy, Agent Johnson, and you guys. That's it."

"Okay, I'll inform them, and I'll keep working on this. We need you to keep gathering all the information you can. Report back what you find and let me handle the big stuff. Remember, you're here to get information, not to take action. It's the way to stay safe."

"I know, I know, but it's hard. I like to pretend I know what I'm doing," I said, nervously laughing, feeling foolish.

"I feel like we're finally making progress. I think you've found a connection. You're doing a great job," he said, chuckling and patting my arm. "Just make sure your doors are locked, be aware of your surroundings, and keep your weapon with you at all times."

"I sure will. Thanks again for your help and patience with me. You're the best," I said, scurrying back into my little workspace.

Slightly rattled but feeling secure that he would uncover the truth, I tried to focus on what I needed to do. I wanted my own work board. Over the next four hours, my walls were covered with pictures (so much for not pretending to be an actual agent). I researched all the military personnel in the area, their branches, and the groups they were affiliated with. My efforts paid off—every unexplained death had a connection to the same military group. I had to conduct several searches to find pictures of the first victims, but they all had the same tattoo.

I knew I couldn't tell anyone I was a consultant for the FBI, but a part of me just wanted to go to Angel and say, "Hey, I'm helping the FBI. What's up?" Something felt off about her, but a killer? No, I didn't think so. But let's face it, my intuition hadn't been great up to this point. While I pondered my next step, my phone rang. It was Mr. Reavis.

"Hey, I have the medical examiner from the forensics team on the line. I'm going to conference you in since you understand the medical stuff better than I do."

"Okay, great," I said, trying to sound calm but secretly thrilled to be included.

"Sorry for the delay, but I wanted to call you myself instead of relaying this through an email," the medical examiner began, his voice carrying a hint of a Middle Eastern accent. "Initially, I found nothing. But after removing a superficial layer of skin and placing the body under a black light, I used a special radiopaque liquid. This was when I discovered a tiny injection site. It would never have been noticed under any other circumstance. Under the hallux nail, there was an area where something had been injected–some substance potent enough to stop the heart and remain undetectable in postmortem blood samples. Potassium Chloride in a large enough dose, when injected, will stop the heart and be undetectable. It could have also been a large dose of insulin. This is your cause of death–an injected lethal dose of something."

"Thank you so much. So you can't determine what was injected?" I asked, hoping for more answers.

"No, I'm sorry. All toxicology tests came back normal. If you have any questions, feel free to call me. I'll email the full report now. Good luck, Agent."

"Okay, thank you very much. Layla, do you have any

questions?" Mr. Reavis inquired.

"Not right now. I'll look at the report and decide if that's okay," I replied.

The call ended, and I decided to run down and check if Mr. Reavis was actually going to let me read the report. It took me about five minutes to put on my jogging pants and shoes, but something significant happened in that time. I overheard a heated conversation between Mr. Reavis and another agent. The man was in a suit, red-faced, with an abdomen that revealed he was a beer connoisseur.

I crouched on the stairs, not proceeding to the backyard veranda, and eavesdropped on their conversation.

"Who knew she was here? I need all the names, and I need answers now. This is a severe breach of protocol!" The agent's voice resonated with depth and authority.

"I provided you with the list. Layla assured me these were all her personal contacts who knew she was here. I understand the gravity of the situation. There's no need for a lecture. I am actively working on it," the response came, although it was unlike any tone I had heard before; stern and resolute.

In a slightly less accusatory tone, the agent continued, "I apologize for my initial tone. We've received reports of heightened activity in the Tennessee area, especially in Nashville. It's quite peculiar—several affluent individuals have flown in and are staying in the vicinity. Ordinarily, this wouldn't raise suspicions, but these millionaires from Boston and Europe aren't typically country music enthusiasts. The FBI watch list was alerted."

Recalling my readings about FBI protocols, I knew there were specific instances when the FBI and CIA monitored trends: clusters of drug dealers, mafia gatherings, or misplaced wealthy diplomats. They detected something amiss and were on high alert.

Mr. Reavis didn't conceal his concern and confusion. "I have no idea what this could mean, but I've bolstered security measures and will remain vigilant. Thank you for the update. I'll stay in touch."

After a firm handshake, he departed. As he left, a sinking feeling settled in the pit of my stomach. I knew...

Chapter 12

I refused to neglect my task, pushing other pressing issues to the back of my mind. My focus returned to my quest. The next step was obtaining the hospital videos. I had the police chief request them, and until they arrived, I continued my search for connections in the deaths. So far, military service seemed to be the common thread holding this puzzle together. Some of the older men had served together, but the key connection was their involvement in a specific group. After extensive research, I managed to locate the local chapter of veterans who were still part of this group. The organization's level of secrecy astounded me.

Task Force 88/Task Force Black was a highly specialized unit, as per internet sources, though it was uncertain whether it was still operational. Comprising elite members from the Seal team, Delta Force, and British SAS, their operations were shrouded in top secrecy. Some members were known to be radical and fanatical. My research hit a dead end there; all further information was heavily guarded. I made a note to have the Chief look into it.

At work, I collaborated with Angel as much as possible, but she seemed different, distant. She was quiet and appeared distracted, lost in her thoughts. My days were spent attending to patients, and my nights were consumed by work. My board, once small, now covered the entire wall after weeks of relentless effort. I would sit and stare at it for hours, growing increasingly obsessed. "I am not an agent, this is not supposed to be easy," I repeated to myself, attempting to anchor myself in reality. Yet, I found myself getting drawn into the investigation, losing sight of my purpose here.

At times, I felt as if someone was watching me, trailing my every move. Paranoia washed over me in waves, my spidey sense tingling. Despite my scrutiny, I saw no one—only looming, imaginary shadows.

The middle of the night in the darkened hospital haunted me the most. Memories of my past horrors resurfaced, triggering occasional flashbacks. However, I managed to control my panic; those were my past battles. I had two FBI/RNs with me on every night shift, and I knew the Chief of Police was looking out for me. I tried to focus solely on my job, ignoring the other unsettling events. That was my biggest mistake; I should have taken the situation more seriously, given my history. I had made countless enemies, dismantled numerous wealthy individuals. Retribution should have been expected.

I was so immersed in solving this case, which wasn't even actually *my* case, because consultants don't even *have* cases, that I lost all awareness of my surroundings. A colossal mistake...

After what felt like ages, the video footage arrived. We decided to watch it together to discern what had happened that night. Armed with pizza and copious amounts of coffee, we settled in for a long night, grateful that I was part of the investigation once more.

The initial hours seemed ordinary—nursing assistants came and went, and Angel made her rounds. Then we reached the hour before the victim was found. Angel entered his room, empty-handed, closed the door, and turned off the light. Shortly after, that familiar, sweet, elderly man went in and emptied the trash. From the video, it was evident that the patient was alive, sitting up and watching TV when the door closed. And then, nothing. No one entered the room before he was discovered. It seemed impossible, yet the video appeared intact and unaltered. We replayed the footage repeatedly, but nothing made sense. Frustration boiled within me; what we were witnessing defied all logic.

"Do you notice anything unusual, Layla? Anything off about the night shift?" the question came from my colleague.

"I'm sorry, no. Nothing seems out of the ordinary. I can't watch this again. I'm going to bed," I admitted, defeated, and bid goodnight.

As I ascended the stairs, worn out and disheartened, my phone rang. It was Krissy. Relief washed over me at the sound of her voice. I had grown attached to her and missed her terribly, and my mood instantly lifted.

"Oh, it's so good to hear your voice. I miss you. We went from talking every day to just once a week. How are you? How's work?" I inquired eagerly.

"I'm good. I miss you too, babe. How's the case? I can't believe you're there on assignment. I'm so proud of you," Krissy replied.

"Not exactly an assignment, just consulting, but it's not going well. People are being targeted at the hospital, and I was supposed to find out if it's an FBI case. I'm trying my best to be helpful so I can stay, but they could send me home any day. I'm giving it my all, though. Have you heard anything? How's work going?" I shared my frustrations with her.

"Oh, that sounds like quite the first case. They should keep you there. I mean, who knows the hospital better than you? Show them how valuable you are. Don't let them even think about sending you home," she encouraged, chuckling. "Have you received any updates about the Auction or any leads on

Kayleigh?"

"Nope, not a word. And I haven't asked. I'm sure he knows who I am, but all that stuff is way above my pay grade. Agent Johnson updates me sometimes on the down low, but there's nothing really new. They have no leads that I know of," I replied, feeling a heavy sadness settle in my stomach. The mere thought of my friend weighed heavily on my heart.

Krissy sounded disappointed about the lack of progress. After briefly catching up on her job, we agreed to talk more often and ended the call.

I went to bed that night disheartened. I had hit a brick wall with my current case, and with each passing day, Kayleigh slipped further away from us. I felt defeated, so engrossed in the investigation that I had become oblivious to my surroundings. This was basic modern-life stuff: always be aware of your surroundings, because when you aren't bad things can happen.

The Cold

Kayleigh was acutely aware that her survival depended not just on her ability to escape, but her ability to weather the elements. The cold, thin walls of the metal building served as a constant reminder of the harsh and brutal weather outside. The long drive had taken her deep into the woods, a place where she could potentially survive, but the biting cold posed an entirely different challenge. The pressing question was the timeline she was up against; her captors could return at any moment to take her away. She'd been fed and cared for. She had gradually regained some of her lost weight. The groomers ensured she was kept in decent appearance, but it was the meals that arrived on trays that provided her with an unexpected opportunity.

Each meal, served on a tray with a plate, plastic utensils, and wrapped in plastic wrap, gave Kayleigh a glimmer of hope. The elderly attendants didn't seem to notice the missing pieces of plastic and wrap, or perhaps they didn't care. Hidden away meal after meal, these pieces became essential tools for her escape. Under the cover of darkness, she would reinforce the inside of her thin wind suit with these makeshift insulators. It was her only *defense against the elements.*

One night, a bowl of chicken and Gnocchi soup arrived. It wasn't as delicious as the one she had once enjoyed at the Olive Garden, but taste was secondary to what she saw. It was the Gnocchi, those little dough balls, that captured her attention. Squishy, soft, and slightly rubbery, they held a peculiar charm. Kayleigh held one of these pasta morsels in her fingers, contemplating its significance. It was probably made by one of the women serving her, a meticulous creation formed from dough, milk, water, flour, and seasoning. As she rolled it between her fingers, she murmured her meager future aspirations aloud, aspirations that seemed massive in a setting like hers. "Someday I want to make Gnocchi."

Unbeknownst to her captors, this innocuous little ball held the key to her escape.

As the food was served, Kayleigh moved toward her door and leaned casually against it, prompting the attendant to spring to attention, fearing an escape attempt.

"Whoa... it's okay, I am just walking around, I am not going anywhere," she assured, raising her hand in a gesture of peace. She positioned her back against the door, her hands resting behind her. Seizing the moment, she discreetly used the tiny ball of gnocchi to manipulate the lock. "Thank you for the delicious food," she added with a hint of gratitude, as the attendant silently returned to her

task.

That night, as they closed and locked her door, nothing seemed out of the ordinary and she breathed a sigh of relief that her Gnocchi effort would escape unnoticed.

She anxiously awaited the night, until the silence in the building was palpable, to see if her plan had succeeded. Slowly pushing the door open, relief washed over her when she realized the tiny dough ball had worked perfectly. Every move had to be careful, slow, and quiet; the metal box amplified even the slightest sound. Staying close to the walls, shrouded in shadows, she avoided the gaze of the cameras that dotted the hallways. She hoped the guard on duty, likely Jody, was in a deep slumber, unaware of her nocturnal activities.

Luck was on her side when she heard a resonant snore echoing down the hallway. Recognizing it as a snore, she felt emboldened to explore her surroundings. Down numerous hallways, she cautiously examined closed doors, peeking through any cracks she could find. Finally, a dim light at the end of a long, dark hallway caught her attention. Curiosity piqued, she ventured forth, her adrenaline surging. A red light marked an exit, a tantalizing promise of freedom. Yet, she knew rushing out would mean certain death; she had no supplies, no idea of her location, and her suit was not adequately prepared. She needed more time, a plan to ensure her survival. But now she knew where her escape door lay.

Retracing her steps cautiously, she returned to the room where the guard slept. He reclined in a chair, feet up, emitting sounds that hardly seemed human. In a moment of desperation, the idea of cutting his throat crossed her mind. She could steal his coat and keys, making a hasty escape. However, she knew impulsive decisions could lead to failure. She needed a few more nights to solidify her plan. Just as she turned to leave, her eyes fell on a knife resting by a small sink in the room. It was dangerously close to the sleeping guard. Moving with painstaking precision, she approached, her ears tuned to the rhythmic sounds emanating from his nostrils. With a swift and silent motion, she grasped the knife and made her way back to her room. Concealing it among her belongings in the mattress, she finally experienced a night of restful sleep. The knowledge that she could escape fueled her determination.

Chapter 13

Days passed, each one blending into the next, and the investigation remained at a frustrating standstill. Doubts crept in; maybe there was no investigation after all. At times, I found myself forgetting the purpose of my presence in that town. I followed the routine, working at the hospital and returning to my apartment. Angel remained distant, but Alisondra and I grew closer with each passing day. Our camaraderie deepened as we shared laughter, meals, and anecdotes from our respective careers. We became confidantes, bonded by our shared experiences. So much so, that at one point, I almost blurted out my true purpose over a glass of wine. There was a noticeable chill between Angel and Alisondra, an unspoken tension that hung heavily whenever they were near each other. I resolved to learn more about it during my next hair appointment.

The breakthrough came unexpectedly. While assisting a patient in a hospital room, I discovered an adjoining door leading to another room—a shared bathroom, a relic of a bygone era. Realization dawned on me. This explained how someone could enter a room undetected. I immediately contacted the Chief, requesting new video footage, my excitement palpable. This discovery was the breakthrough we desperately needed.

My elation only grew when my phone rang, and I saw Krissy's name on the screen. "Hey, my BFF, I know you're busy, but I've got good news. I'm coming to see you. I've snagged us Luke Combs tickets in Nashville. You can't say no. You need a break, and what better way than a concert with your bestie?"

I couldn't help but squeal with delight. "Oh my goodness, thank you! I really need that. I can't wait. Text me the details. I can't talk right now. I've got a lead in the case, so I've gotta run."

"No problem, good luck, and see you soon!" Krissy's voice echoed with enthusiasm, matching my own excitement.

As I drove back to my apartment, I glanced around the small town, taking in its quiet streets, the cold nights, and mild days. The sense of unease crept in when I attempted to call Aubrey, but she didn't answer. A pang of anxiety flickered within me, quickly dismissed. I refused to let paranoia spoil my triumphant day.

As I pulled into my driveway, I received a text from Alisondra. She wanted to ensure I'd arrived safely and had a somewhat desperate request for me to join her as her wing woman at a club. Another buzz from my phone revealed a playful picture of her in a backless dress, striking a seductive pose. It elicited a chuckle from me, but something caught my eye—a peculiar irritation arose in my gut as I noticed the pink thong hugging the curves of her lower back, reminiscent of Mackenzie and her pink thong.

It suddenly dawned on me that I hadn't seen either Heather or Mackenzie during the past couple of shifts. Initially, I thought they were just off-duty, but if they were supposed to keep an eye on me, they were doing a terrible job. Hastily, I dashed up the stairs and phoned Mr. Reavis. Due to my lack of clearance, he had to make several calls. After several redirects and a slightly raised voice, he confirmed they had been missing for six days. Anger surged within me, eclipsing any progress I'd made. I hadn't even noticed their absence or missed their presence. I kept forgetting the potential danger I was in. My eagerness to be involved in the case and establish connections had pushed my own safety to the back of my mind.

Fury mingled with panic. "Why am I just hearing about this now?" I demanded, my voice betraying my anxiety.

"They didn't want to cause unnecessary alarm if there wasn't a reason, Layla. Apparently, these agents have a history of missed check-ins, but when they didn't report in yesterday, concern grew. They're sending more agents as we speak. But,

Layla, we need to talk..."

I felt my heart skip a beat. The dreaded moment I feared had arrived.

"Your job was to assess the situation, determine if the FBI was needed. You've done that. You've made connections we couldn't without your access to the hospital. But I'm worried for your safety. I think it's best if we pull you from the case and you go home."

Panic set in, followed by desperate pleas. "Please don't send me home. I'll be careful, I promise. I can still help, get information. I can still make a difference."

Mr. Reavis, his hand absentmindedly rubbing his bald spot, sighed in apparent inner turmoil, obviously feeling my palpable sincerity. "Okay, fine. But if this continues, I'm pulling the plug on you."

"Thank you. I'll be safe, I promise." My voice shook with relief and determination. From now on, I vowed inside that I would keep my fears to myself.

Late at night, I wrestled with guilt, wondering how anyone knew about Heather and Mackenzie's FBI status. They had been excellent, and I hadn't shared the secret with anyone but my regular select few. The blame gnawed at me, but perhaps they themselves had spoken to the wrong person? Alisondra did mention spending time with them at a local bar. Somehow, though, I felt it was all my fault.

As I sent one last text to Aubrey, I attempted to push aside my worries and prepare for a long day ahead. I would be scrutinizing new video footage and searching for two missing agents, determined to unravel the truth.

Chapter 14

Early morning light filtered through the window, casting a warm glow in Mr. Reavis' office. He greeted me with a steaming cup of French coffee, his smile reminiscent of a kind grandfather, always inviting and reassuring. The rich aroma enveloped the room, creating a sense of comfort deep within me. It was a day meant for progress; we had video footage to analyze, a crucial task that demanded our full attention.

The room fell into silence as we focused on the screen, hoping to catch a detail that could provide a breakthrough. I felt the weight of my role as a consultant; I needed to contribute meaningfully, or my time in this investigation would come to an abrupt end. I blinked, struggling to maintain focus. On the screen, a nurse aide entered the room and retrieved a food tray. The seconds passed, the door remained ajar, and then it happened—exactly what I had been praying for. My breath caught, and Mr. Reavis tensed beside me as we witnessed a petite figure, shrouded in dark leggings and a hoodie. The hood obscured any chance of glimpsing facial features. A female, unmistakably. This had to be the killer.

Thirty minutes later, the CODE BLUE was called.

While phone calls were made and pictures were dispatched to FBI headquarters, Mr. Reavis focused on obtaining footage from the parking deck and all hospital entrances and exits. We needed to know how this person had left the scene. Adrenaline surged through my veins; finally, a breakthrough. The body type and size of the figure would allow us to narrow down the pool of suspects. I returned to my workspace, adjusting my board in anticipation of the forthcoming footage.

During this interval, I attempted to gather information about Heather and Mackenzie. I called the hospital to confirm their last shift and then sent a casual text to Alisondra:

> *Hey there! Hope your day's going well, not too many admit, I hope?* ◆◆ *I have a bit of a weird question. Have you seen those two travel RNs recently? I think one of them might've taken my stethoscope by mistake. Need to catch up with one of them. Luv ya!* ♥

Alisondra responded promptly, her message reflecting weariness and camaraderie:

> *Hey love! Ugh, this day's dragging. I am ready to be done. Yeah, we went out about a week ago. I can send you their numbers. Haven't heard from them this week. They were pretty hammered, haha. Luv u 2! C U soon.*

With a sense of urgency, I drove to the bar, my heart

pounding. I knew I shouldn't be taking matters into my own hands, but what harm could a brief investigation do? "You got this," I told myself in the mirror before striding in to make bold requests. I reasoned with the manager, even flirted a little, but received a firm refusal. Left with no choice, I called the Chief.

"You're doing what?" His disapproval reverberated through the phone. "Why are you getting involved? We've discussed this, Layla. Stay out of it."

"I was just waiting on the footage, Chief. I was curious, that's all. I found out where they went and thought I'd check it out. I have a hunch, a feeling. You know, women's intuition. Something's off."

Silence hung in the air, followed by an exasperated sigh, so I continued. "Please don't be upset with me. I'm just trying to help, to assist you in the legwork. I thought getting you the footage would save you time."

He hung up on me.

My pseudo-agent antics were clearly pushing him to his limit. Nevertheless, within a few hours, I found myself scrutinizing grainy bar footage, attempting to identify familiar faces.

The footage played, and I made meticulous notes. Alisondra entered, exuding confidence with every step, her presence commanding attention. Mackenzie and Heather followed, blending into the crowd. Men approached, conversations ensued, and the atmosphere grew thick with desire and anticipation. Mackenzie danced, Heather maintained a serious demeanor, intimidating those around her. Eventually, the night wound down, and the women prepared to leave. Two shadowy figures followed them out—men in dark clothing, their faces obscured by UNC Tarheels caps. A sense of familiarity gnawed at me, but their identities remained elusive. As I was about to switch off the footage, I spotted Alisondra—she was dancing closely with a man. Their intimacy was striking, not like a typical bar encounter; they seemed familiar. It puzzled me because she had repeatedly claimed to be single. The closeness of their embrace and the way she moved against him suggested otherwise. Perhaps an old boyfriend, but they left the bar together. As he enveloped her in his arms, something caught my eye. He was muscular, wearing a snug t-shirt. When he raised his arms to help her with her jacket, I noticed a tattoo, and despite the poor video quality, I recognized it.

I forwarded the videos to headquarters and updated the Chief.

Given the small-town setting, I aimed to leverage this to my advantage. I headed down to the basement, and luck was on my side—they were both there. I accessed the footage and presented them with both videos. They had no clue about the identities of the two men following the agents. However, as I unveiled the video featuring the man with Alisondra, their surprised expressions immediately revealed that they recognized this man.

"Yeah, I know him," the Chief spoke up. "He's Colton, an ex-military man dishonorably discharged a few years ago. Severe mental illness, extreme mood disorders, and a history of violence. He's been affiliated with all the victims in some way. I did not know he was back in town."

Confusion and hurt swirled within me. Why had Alisondra kept this information from me? The Chief made calls to his military contacts while I struggled to focus on the videos. The dual investigations, each more intense than the other, left me drained. I excused myself to the restroom, my hands trembling with nerves. In the midst of my turmoil, Krissy's text appeared, a lifeline in my chaotic world:

>*Hey, babe, don't forget our plans! Luke Combs concert, laughter, and drinks!* ♥ *Girls' trip!*

I responded, my voice laden with uncertainty.

>*Hey girl, I remember, but I'm not sure I can make it. Something's come up. I'll keep you posted. Love ya!*

An angry call followed my response,

"What?? You are not canceling on me! I mean it. I miss you;

I need and want to see you."

"I know, I am not sure yet. Trust me, I want to go. I will try my best. But I cannot talk right now. I'll 'll call later," but before I could even process the conversation, a voicemail from Aubrey pinged on my phone.

"Hi, Mom. Look, I don't have all the details, but things are getting weird here. I overheard talk about two missing agents, a lot of chatter about the Body Auction case. Please be safe, stay alert. I love you."

Aubrey's tension-laden voice hung in the air, adding to my mounting anxiety. I resolved to call her later. The emotional roller-coaster took its toll, but I couldn't afford to show weakness. I returned to the room, determined to maintain my composure.

"His name is Colton. He's been back in town for almost a year, keeping a low profile. Looking closely at his records, he's been linked to all the victims in some way, sharing the same military background," the Chief shared, excitement and dread clashing within me. The high of progress was tinged with the crashing low of the possibility of Alisondra's involvement. I felt my energy waning, exhaustion seeping into my bones.

"Okay, guys, I'm heading up. You do your thing. I need a shower and some sleep. See you in the morning." Their nods mirrored relief; they needed me out of their way. As I left,

I suppressed my fragile emotions, determined to regain my strength for the battles yet to come.

The Plan

Days had passed, and in the silence of her captivity, Kayleigh meticulously fortified her suit, stuffing it with every available material to create a thicker lining. Her determination to escape this infernal pit burned fiercely within her. She refused to succumb to the icy clutches of death; she had devised a plan and hoped to execute it in the coming days. The atmosphere in the building had shifted, palpable even within the confines of her prison. The air carried a different weight, laden with tension. Louder noises echoed through the once-muted hallways. A few nights prior, she had sworn she heard screams and the clash of a struggle, but the source remained elusive. Each night seemed busier, with additional people infiltrating the building. The opportunity she had been waiting for seemed to slip further away with each passing moment.

Then, one morning, as Kayleigh sat upright, savoring her breakfast and knowing she needed all the energy she could gain, the door burst open, shattering the fragile peace she clung to. The demon herself, Krissy, stormed into the room, her usual arrogance replaced by an unsettling flush of panic. Kayleigh found a flicker of amusement within her as Krissy, who had exuded confidence until that very moment, displayed her vulnerability. Something had gone awry; something had changed.

Krissy settled on the bed, her gaze fixed intently on Kayleigh, who remained outwardly composed, masking her internal turmoil. With a nervous smirk, Krissy hissed, revealing the twisted workings of her mind, "Things have changed. We're moving forward sooner than planned. Enjoy your last few days, for soon, I will carve you and your dear friend Layla into pieces. Both of you have cost me millions and been nothing but a thorn in my side!"

For the first time, Kayleigh spoke, her voice steady, "I am equally impressed and disgusted by you. Your ability to deceive Layla, the FBI, and everyone who knows you, astounds me. Yet, you disgust me as a woman. You sacrifice the lives of so many young, beautiful women for profit. I can't decide if you're brilliant or merely foolish. Perhaps both. Brilliant in your execution of this plan, infiltrating Layla's life, cultivating a friendship to gain access to the inner sanctum of the investigation. Everyone trusted you, and perhaps they still do. Foolish, however, to believe you can continue this charade indefinitely. Tell me, how did you gain Layla's trust?"

A sinister smile curved Krissy's painted lips; she seemed poised to revel in her perceived victory. "Rest assured, I am far from stupid. I. Am. Brilliant. I suppose I can share, given that you will never live to share it with anyone else. I have ensured that," she sneered, her condescension dripping with malice. A swift text on her cell phone summoned a shorter lady into the room, a woman Kayleigh recognized from her initial arrival—a woman with coal-black hair, delicate features, and an aura reminiscent of Snow White. It all clicked into place. She knew who this woman was, a vital piece of the puzzle falling into its rightful place.

As the pieces of the puzzle came together in her mind, Krissy reached over, cupping the newcomer's bottom, and planted a long, affectionate kiss on her lips. Their smiles, though loving, held a sinister undertone as they locked eyes with Kayleigh.

"It was surprisingly easy," Krissy chuckled. "I spun Layla a tragic tale about my best friend, Whitley, disappearing. She was more than eager to help me. You see, Whitley never died. That was one of our initial tests, to see if we could fool everyone and truly pull this off. When Layla escaped and survived, we needed an insider to provide intel. I cared little when the other Auction members were arrested or killed because I craved control. In a way, the FBI did me a favor by putting the operation in my hands. I appreciate it, thank you! With their help, I've amassed even more wealth, and no incompetent men can lay claim to what is rightfully ours. I am always kept informed of the ongoing developments because I am Layla's 'BFF.'"

The revelation was a crushing blow to Kayleigh's understanding *of the situation. Krissy had been present during the meetings, part of the search for the Auction members, deeply involved at every stage of the investigation. Her brilliance in deception deserved accolades, and yet, it left Kayleigh with a bitter taste in her mouth. Looking at the raven-haired beauty, Kayleigh's voice was laced with a mix of incredulity and pity, "You know, she will turn on you too. She is a sociopath, narcissistic to the core. She cannot comprehend true love and compassion. It's only a matter of time before you become a threat."*

Blind rage flared in Krissy's eyes, and without warning, her hand collided with Kayleigh's cheek, the sharp sting echoing in the room. "You shut your mouth, or I will kill you now," Krissy hissed, her threat hanging heavy in the air. Beside her, Whitley stepped forward, her touch gentle as she offered her reassurance, "It's okay. She can't intimidate me. I know you, and she's just trying to get under your skin. Don't let her."

In an instant, Kayleigh had witnessed the brutal eradication of all her allies, leaving Krissy firmly in control. They had all believed in Krissy's façade, trusting her implicitly. The one who had trusted her the most was Layla. All Kayleigh could do was pray that Layla was far, far away from this dreadful place, wherever it might be.

Chapter 15

Colton Farmer was indeed a member of Task Force 88, just like the other victims. After some digging, Mr. Reavis was able to access his closed military files. Farmer was a combat veteran who had served in multiple special ops. He was a sniper and was the one they sent in for top-secret assassinations.

The record was very vague. No details were provided, only that he had an *"Other than honorable discharge due to excess violence toward a fellow Marine."* There were, however, documents that were so classified we could not get access to them. The chief reported that the US government could not release them due to national security concerns.

The next record was his chart from a psychiatric hospital in Black Mountain. These records were also very vague and gave little details about the admission. This had been no help at all. I was working a night shift and needed to head out. Saying my goodbyes, I left, promising to touch base the next day if I had any new information.

I tried to clear my mind on my drive to the hospital. It was dusk, and the sky was absolutely beautiful as the sun slowly disappeared behind the mountains. The pink and light blue colors looked as if a child had painted the scene haphazardly. Trying to calm myself and think of the new information, I could not shut down the anxiety welling inside of me.

Who is killing these people and why? What do they all have in common? Who is watching me and why? Where are the missing agents? What did Aubrey's call mean?

My heart was racing, and nothing seemed to help. I literally screamed when my cell phone rang. My tone when I answered was anything but welcoming.

I was embarrassed that it was Krissy, and I apologized as best as I could.

"What in the world is wrong with you, Layla?" Concern was thick in Krissy's voice.

"I am so sorry. It has just been a very hard few days. I am stressed beyond words, and now I have to work a night shift, and I am exhausted. It isn't your fault. Please forgive my attitude."

"Ok, you have a few minutes. Tell me what's up. Maybe it will help to talk about it."

"I would love to, but you know we aren't supposed to discuss cases. It's too much, anyway. I have to get inside soon."

"Really, Layla, it's me. I have been in meetings with the FBI, I have been in the workrooms. I am practically one of you guys.

You know they ask me to be a consultant too? I am not some random nurse you met. I know everything there is to know about you and your past. Now dish!"

"You're right. Okay, well, let me see. I don't know who is killing these people in the hospital. I am being followed by someone. Two agents sent to protect me have disappeared, and Aubrey says something is up. Do you want more?" My voice was shaking as the emotions that had been hidden were determined to come out. Talking to Krissy made me feel better. I could be myself. I could cry, laugh, whatever with her. She had been so good to me when I struggled to deal with Kayleigh missing. She was like a sister to me. And once again, she was right. That felt good to say all of that out loud. Her support was never-ending, but maybe I was saying too much. I decided to focus on myself, not the case.

"I had no idea I was being followed, and Tripp actually made the only real breakthrough I have had!" I took a deep breath as my rant came to an end.

"Okay, Layla, they would not have sent you if you could not handle it. Second, how do you know someone is following you? Third, what do you mean, Tripp found it?"

I went on to explain briefly, but I had to get inside the hospital. I promised I would call Krissy with more details in the next few days. She had been right. I did feel better getting it off my chest, even though I knew I should not be discussing it with anyone. But she is from another state, and it's not like she would tell anyone. Newly optimistic, I walked in, hoping for a breakthrough of my own.

I was happy to see that because of the high number of admissions, I would be working with Alisondra and Angel. This may turn out to be a better night than I thought.

Angel was on the third floor. After Alisondra and I started working on admissions from the ER, things slowed down. We got coffee and had a normal conversation about our day. Acting completely nonchalant, I asked if she had heard from Heather or Mackenzie. Trying to read her body language as best I could, I waited for an answer.

"No, I really haven't. We all went out that night, but we split up when we got there, and we did not leave together. I met an old friend and hooked up with him." A sly smile crossed her face.

"Oh really? An old friend, huh... Who is this old friend? Tell me all about him." I tried to act excited and ready for some good girl talk. I was relieved that she was being honest about the situation.

"Well, I have known him forever. We grew up together. He went off in the military, and when he came home, he was different. You know what I mean, a lot of military guys go off in combat, and it does something to them. He is a great guy, and I try to be there for him. He has been through a lot."

Her voice had a tone of kindness and compassion. She seemed very sympathetic and loving to this man.

"Oh, that sounds so sad. I am glad he has you to be there for him. Are you guys romantically involved?"

"Well, I wouldn't call a booty call now and then being romantically involved!" Her sweet laugh filled the room. "But I wouldn't worry too much about the travel nurses. Those chicks come and go. I cannot imagine their contract was over, but maybe they got a better offer somewhere else. Well, I have to go check on the little sweet man I admitted earlier. He was not doing well, and I think he may need to go to CCU. I'll catch you later!" A little shocked that she changed the subject so fast, I was left sitting there alone.

I barely noticed Marvin roll by with his cart. His sweet smile beamed at me and snapped me from my trance. He exchanged pleasantries, and right as he turned the corner, I saw it. A little American flag pointed up from the supply cart. That's when I realized one of the new admits must be a veteran. Maybe it was the break I needed.

Without consent, it is illegal to install cameras in a patient's room, unless their life is at risk. This is typically used in cases of child or elder abuse. So, I quickly texted Mr. Reavis to let him know we would need some cameras set up:

> *Hi, it's Layla, new admit. I think a vet. If we can, let's try*
> *to place the equipment in the room. I'll get details and text*
> *asap!*

Since the last death, there had been no veterans admitted, no little red pots and flags placed. I had to find the man before his flagged was placed. His life may depend on it.

Chapter 16

Mr. Marion was a proud man who had served his country with honor, receiving multiple medals. He had been admitted with weakness and left-sided numbness. I looked into his record from the ER and noted his stay seemed to be an arbitrary ER admission to rule out a stroke.

I was confused because Alisondra thought the patient might need the CCU, but he seemed fine on paper. His head CT was negative, so he would be observed overnight and discharged the following morning if there were no new issues. All labs were normal, and all deficits had resolved. Why did he need to go to the CCU? Typically, patients aren't moved to the Critical Care Unit unless they are unstable or at very high risk of decline. These patients require more intensive care, like 1:1 nursing. So why would she move him and take a CCU bed?

I decided to go to the floor and investigate. Angel was one of the nurses on the 3rd floor, the telemetry floor, always busy with the constant beeping of monitors and the scurry of hospital staff. Spotting her, I went over to initiate a conversation. She seemed stressed.

"Hey, I haven't talked to you in a few days. Are you doing okay? I missed you at my last hair appointment."

"Yeah, just working. You know how busy it can get. I'm sorry I missed you. Hey, I got to run and move this guy to CCU. I'll text you later."

"Oh, okay, can I help you? I am on tonight. What's up with the patient?"

"Sure, yeah, that would be great. It's so hard to roll these beds down by myself. He seems fine, really, just a rule-out CVA. I have no idea why Alisondra is moving him," her voice thick with irritation.

It was the break I needed. I could see the patient for myself. He would be safe in the CCU, no one could sneak in or out because of the glass doors and constant monitoring.

I was shocked and agreed with Angel; the man seemed fine. He was awake, alert, and relayed to me that his symptoms had resolved. As we rolled the huge, difficult bed down to the elevators, I talked to the patient as much as I could. I also noticed that on his left forearm he had a tattoo, The Cerberus. So I took that opportunity to mention it.

"Oh my goodness! I love that tattoo. What does it mean?" I was starting to get an odd feeling of dread and trepidation within my soul.

"Oh, thank you, honey. It was from my military days. I was

in a group that was very close, and we all had the same tattoo. Over the years, many of us have come and gone. We may not have served at the same time, but we know each other from The Cerberus. I'm not sure if younger men still do that."

"Oh, I see. Do you get to see your friends often?" I kept pushing.

A small reaction crossed his face at the question; his eyes darted for a split second. "Well, the ones of us that are left, yes. But we are getting older, so of course, some have passed on." His eyes met Angel's, and she took his hand and offered comfort. Sensing the emotion from them both, I changed gears.

"Well, I hope you feel better soon. It was nice to meet you."

Sensing his discomfort at my questioning, I decided to stop pushing. We rolled into the CCU just in time to see Alisondra waiting at the desk.

For the first time, I saw a side of her I had not seen before. The sweet, kind demeanor was gone. The soft eyes of kindness were replaced with small, angry orbs. Her normal huge pink-lipped smile was now a thin straight line. A coldness seemed to radiate from her. I tried to swiftly soften the mood.

"Hey girl, I was up on 3N, and Angel needed help rolling this patient down. He seems to be doing okay."

"Okay, well, whatever," she quickly went into the room and

closed the door in my face. I was taken aback and just stood there in shock. What was wrong with her? Angel's expression also showed great shock. Our eyes met right as the door slammed.

Irritated, I decided to check on my patients, knowing the guy would be safe tonight. Nothing was going on, and as the night went on, things slowed down. I checked emails, texted Aubrey, and called Tripp. It was midnight, but he typically stayed up late, especially when he was home and not out of town on business. I regretted the call as soon as I heard his voice.

"Hello... Hello? Who is this?" His voice sounded like he was still deep asleep.

"Oh gosh, honey, I'm so sorry. I didn't mean to wake you up. I figured you would be up watching the ball game."

"I went to bed earlier. I'll call you tomorrow."

Click.

I didn't even have time to say a word. Deflated, I just sat there. It was a really strange night, to say the least.

Sitting in a deep trance and letting my mind run wild, the door opening to the dictation room startled me. Alisondra came in, and instant ice formed in the room. Walking over to the fridge to get her expensive spring water out, she didn't even acknowledge me.

"Hey, are you okay?"

"Yes, I am fine. Why do you ask?" Her voice was stiff and harsh.

"Really? Don't be sassy. You are acting like you are mad about something. I am not sure what I have done, but whatever it is, I am sorry. I just helped Angel take the patient down. I wasn't trying to do anything to upset you."

Her face, once hard and cold, softened almost instantly. She came over and sat down, putting her face in her hands; her shoulders started to convulse. Taken aback, I just sat there a moment, then I realized what was happening. She was crying. I immediately wrapped my arms around her. "Oh my gosh, what's wrong?"

"I am just stressed. I'm sorry. I didn't mean to be so rude to you. I know you were only trying to help. You haven't been here long, so you don't know what has been going on. I think it is all starting to affect me." Tears poured down her face, creating black lines from her mascara and eyeliner. Mucus dripped freely from her nose and fell to the table. I was a little repulsed that she didn't even try to wipe her nose. Awkwardly, I handed her a napkin. She went from a porcelain doll, essentially a perfect appearance, to something out of a gothic horror movie.

"It's okay," I tried to reassure her as I awkwardly rubbed her back, handing her another napkin as the mucus was now a steady stream along with saliva that had begun to drip from her open lips. Man, she was an ugly crier. "What do you mean? What has been going on?" This was the perfect time to pry.

"Well, we have been told not to discuss it with anyone, but there have been some deaths that are odd. Patients that aren't really that sick just... die. The police were even involved for a while. We were all questioned. I have no idea what happened. You know how small towns are. The police are old and dumb. So I guess they just gave up looking. Well, that patient, he is a great friend to my family. I practically grew up at his house, and I cannot let anything happen to him, so I moved him to keep him safe. I want to rule out a stroke and then get him out of here. I don't know who to trust. I only am telling you because it cannot have anything to do with you as you weren't here."

My mind was racing. I could not help but chuckle to myself at the comment about the local police—if only she knew. "Oh my goodness, that is horrible! Of course, you can talk to me. This all sounds very bizarre. Do you have any theories? Ideas of what happened?"

"Well, I do watch a lot of crime shows and CSI, so I feel like I may have an idea."

She straightened in her chair and seemed to realize she had

literally fallen apart as she started to wipe her face and calm down. She seemed excited to be able to talk about it with someone. I was anxious to hear her thoughts.

"I cannot figure out what they have in common, but they all died in their sleep. All of them had been fine and were actually close to discharge. I have a good friend over at the medical examiner's office, and she says the autopsies have all been negative. So, I think some type of poison maybe, that was undetectable in the blood. I will tell you this: I have noticed that Angel is always working or has worked. So I just don't know. I mean, I know she's your friend. But you haven't been here that long. Be careful, Layla. You don't know how crazy some people can be."

She had gone from sad and distressed to almost giddy describing the possible murders.

"I mean, think about it, Layla, things happen in hospitals all the time, medical malpractice and such, but this is different. I looked at it. These patients were absolutely fine, no reason to die suddenly. I feel certain they were murdered. But the who and why I am unsure of."

"You really don't think Angel would murder someone, do you? I mean, she seems so sweet and cares for her patients with such passion?" My mind was working through these accusations. I was not sure which thing shocked me the most—her accusing Angel or someone giving out information about autopsies in an ongoing case. "Maybe it is just something coincidental, like a heart attack in one, and a blood clot in another. Why do you think MURDER? I know what you said about small-town cops, but small-town medical examiners miss things too. Maybe that's it." I tried to deflate the situation and for one second, I thought I should tell her who I am and why I am here, but I held off. Not right now, soon, but not yet.

"Trust me, it's murder, and I will not let anyone hurt him!" Tears started to well up again. "You are as bad as these hillbilly cops, not taking these deaths seriously. It is murder, Layla, MURDER!"

Here comes the mucus again... Kleenex anyone?

"Okay, okay, let's go get some coffee and try to calm down. We can talk more later."

Cleansing breaths and coffee fix everything.

After a little touch-up of her makeup, we strolled out of the office, just in time to hear...

"CODE BLUE CCU! CODE BLUE CCU!"

The Devil Herself

Kayleigh found herself lost in a sea of thoughts, unable to shake off the disturbing information that had recently come to light. Her mind kept reverting to the time when she had first encountered Krissy. Back then, Krissy had seemed sweet, kind, and innocent, qualities that had shielded her from suspicion even among the seasoned agents. Kayleigh pondered whether Krissy's gender had played a role in her deceptive facade or if it was her act of pretending to mourn a loved one lost in the auction that had thrown everyone off.

Her mind drifted to a story Layla had shared during a casual lunch, shedding light on Krissy's troubled childhood. Layla had revealed how Krissy's quiet demeanor stemmed from childhood trauma, inflicted by her demanding mother. Forced into beauty pageants at a young age, Krissy's childhood mirrored the dark side of reality TV. The hours spent on elaborate makeup and hair routines robbed her of the simple joys of childhood play. Kayleigh learned about a particularly harrowing incident when a fellow contestant, the girl who had defeated Krissy, had tragically drowned in a pool right before her eyes. The traumatic event had *left an indelible mark on Krissy, shaping her into the person she had become.*

Krissy's mother had met an equally tragic fate years later, succumbing to a freak accident in her bathtub. The details surrounding her mother's death remained unknown to Kayleigh, but she couldn't help but speculate, was it an accident after all?

The pieces of the puzzle began to fall into place as Kayleigh contemplated Krissy's motives. She realized that Krissy was a sadist, harboring an intense hatred for beautiful women. In her twisted mind, she sought to subject these women to the same judgment and scrutiny she had experienced in her childhood beauty pageants. Krissy wanted to see them tormented, paraded in front of others, and ultimately sold off piece by piece—a horrific reenactment of her own childhood experiences. The meticulous care taken to present the women for sale was a macabre emulation of her past, reflecting the deep-seated traumas that had shaped her twisted desires.

Kayleigh's sense of hope was rekindled when she learned from Krissy that Layla was still alive. With renewed determination, she prepared herself for an imminent escape. Time was running out, and the changing weather hinted at the approaching winter cold. Kayleigh meticulously lined her wind suit with whatever insulation she could gather without arousing suspicion. Every day was spent in rigorous exercise, building her muscle strength in anticipation of the escape ahead.

One night, a night that would ultimately change everything, Kayleigh decided to make one final attempt to gather supplies before her planned escape. Waiting patiently for the building to fall into a hushed silence, she stealthily made her way out, retracing her steps with caution. Luck was on her side; her captor, Jody, lay asleep, a half-smoked Gurkha cigar dangling from his mouth. The sight of the expensive cigar in his possession puzzled Kayleigh, adding another layer of intrigue to the enigma that was Krissy.

Careful not to make a sound, Kayleigh approached the table, finding another dirty knife. It was a crude tool, but it would serve her purpose. The sight of her assailant in such a vulnerable state fueled her determination. She ventured further, exploring drawers until she discovered a precious stash of matches and an old plastic fork. Gathering her newfound treasures, she retreated to her room, heart pounding with the anticipation of her impending escape.

As she reached her room, ready to stash away her newfound supplies, Kayleigh overheard whispered voices emanating from a nearby room. The voices were unfamiliar, different from the women she knew worked there, and certainly not Krissy's. Eager to make contact, she took a calculated risk and tapped lightly on the door. The voices hushed momentarily, then resumed.

"Shhhh, Mac, be quiet. I heard something!"

"Hello, can you hear me?" Kayleigh whispered back, her voice barely audible.

A tense silence followed, broken by the hesitant response from the other side.

"Who are you? How are you here? It's me and my friend. Some psychos kidnapped us. How did you get out of your room?"

A sense of relief washed over Kayleigh as she realized she wasn't alone in her struggle. The connection with these strangers brought a wave of emotion, and for a moment, she couldn't find her voice. Finally, she managed to speak, her words quivering with a mix of fear and hope.

"I'm not sure how long I've been here. But I was already being held somewhere else. I was moved here, and I know it's cold, but I have to try. I have a little food hidden. I will take you guys with me, but you have to figure out how to fix the door so you can get out."

The voices from the other side were cautious yet hopeful, expressing gratitude for the newfound alliance. Kayleigh, lying on the ground, felt a profound connection through the crack beneath the door. For the first time in what seemed like an eternity, she had found allies—people who shared her plight and were willing to fight alongside her.

As the conversation continued, Kayleigh's fingers found solace in the gentle touch of the strangers on the other side. Their shared vulnerability bridged the gap between them, offering a glimmer of hope in the face of despair. With newfound allies and a renewed sense of purpose, Kayleigh retreated to her room, her mind buzzing with plans for their escape. The knowledge that she wouldn't face the impending danger alone filled her with determination, propelling her forward with an adrenaline-fueled courage she hadn't felt in a long time.

Reviewing her meager supplies, Kayleigh felt a mixture of pride and apprehension. She knew the wind suit, the limited food, and a handful of matches wouldn't be enough to guarantee their survival in the unforgiving wilderness. Yet, her resolve remained unyielding. She was willing to face the harshness of the forest, preferring the prospect of dying in the wild over the horrors she faced within those walls. Armed with newfound allies and a flicker of hope, Kayleigh prepared herself for the upcoming night—a night that held the promise of freedom and the possibility of reclaiming their lives.

Chapter 17

The overhead announcement of the Code Blue sent shockwaves through us, leaving our mouths agape for a split second. We raced to the CCU as fast as our legs could carry us. My mind raced at a tempo that rivaled that of my heart, thunderous beats reverberating in my ears. As we burst through the doors, the chaos of a CODE BLUE unfolded before our eyes. The crash cart was hastily pushed to the side and cracked open. The small room was packed with a motley crew —lab technicians, physicians, CCU nurses—all striving to bring the man lying in the bed back to life. The man I had spoken to mere moments ago looked unrecognizable now. A male nurse, identified by his badge as KYLE, RN, fervently performed chest compressions, each thud causing the man's entire body to jerk. I could hear the unsettling snaps of ribs breaking every few minutes. Beads of sweat dripped from Kyle's face as he exerted himself, utilizing every ounce of his arm, shoulder, and back muscles. I knew he'd be sore in the morning.

Once strong and proud, his tattooed arms hung lifelessly. Another nurse pushed medications into a small port at the doctor's request. The patient, a once heroic military man who had fought for our country, lay naked, tubes protruding from various openings, shattered and exposed for the world to witness. I found it difficult to process the scene unfolding before my eyes.

Summoning my composure, I surveyed the room and the CCU more thoroughly. I needed to discern if anything was amiss; if it was another murder, we were witnessing it unfold in real-time. Amidst the frenzied atmosphere, I caught sight of a person peeking around the corner, attempting to remain unnoticed. Only one eye, filled with apprehension, peered around the wall that separated them from the patient. I approached the mysterious figure and was astounded to discover it was Angel.

"What are you doing?" I asked, trying to steady my voice.

"I heard the code called and ran back to see what happened. He was just my patient. Do you know what happened?" Her voice trembled with anxiety and nervousness.

"We heard the code and rushed back down. I don't know what happened. Maybe he did suffer a stroke. Who knows?" We stood there, watching in silence.

"PULSE CHECK!" someone yelled. The line on the monitor appeared flat when the compressions halted. Asystole. No pulse.

"Restart compressions!" the next voice commanded. "Why are you lurking around back here? I barely saw you."

"I just wanted to stay out of the way. I hate codes; they make me really nervous. I just can't understand. How could this have happened?" For the first time since I met Angel, I saw emotion in her eyes. A solitary tear rolled down her cheek, her chest heaving with panic.

Before I could respond, she turned and fled from the CCU. I stood there in shock. When I turned back to the Code, I noticed Alisondra had witnessed Angel's emotional departure. Her icy stare returned. As our eyes met, she mouthed the words, "I told you."

The code persisted for over 45 minutes, but the man never regained a pulse. Finally, the code was called, leaving the room in complete disarray. One by one, the staff exited the room, leaving only the primary CCU nurse, Dr. DeWhite, Alisondra, and me standing there. The nurse began cleaning up the debris —papers, needles, and bloody gauze—scattered around the room.

"I will go call his wife," Alisondra's voice quivered.

"Are you sure? I don't mind doing it. I know this is horrible and incredibly difficult for you," I offered.

"No, I need to call her. He was my patient."

"Okay, let me know how I can assist you. I'm going to the

restroom, and I'll be right back."

I excused myself and called Mr. Reavis.

"Hey, sorry to bother you, but I need you to come over to the hospital now. There has been a death. This will be the freshest crime scene your team has had."

"I'll be right there."

Click.

As I returned to the CCU, I was stunned to find the nurse removing lines and cleaning up the patient. Aware that she might be tampering with potential evidence, I intervened, cautious in my approach.

"Hey, I don't think you should be doing that yet. They will probably want an autopsy."

She shot me an irritated look over her thick-rimmed glasses. "Dr. DeWhite just came in here and told me the family didn't want an autopsy and instructed me to clean up the body. Alisondra agreed, so I'm doing what I was told. I have other patients to care for, so if you don't mind..." She turned back to her task, clearly frustrated.

"I understand, but please wait a moment. Let me speak to them first."

After a dismissive eye roll and an exasperated huff, the nurse removed her blue gloves and left the room, leaving the deceased man exposed. I gently pulled up his sheet before I exited.

I interrupted a heated conversation between Alisondra and Dr. DeWhite. "Excuse me, but don't you want an autopsy? Don't you want to know the cause of death?"

"We know the cause of death. Are you stupid?" The physician's words were sharp and rude.

"Do we? He was admitted for a possible CVA, and we aren't sure if that's what caused his demise. Do you know something I don't, sir?" I spoke firmly, challenging his certainty.

"Of course he had a stroke. What's the point of putting his family through an autopsy? I said no, and I mean no!" With that, he stormed away, leaving Alisondra and me behind.

"Well, isn't he just delightful? What do you think? What did his wife say?" Alisondra seemed stunned that I had that I could be so direct with a physician.

"She was understandably upset. I didn't even ask her about the autopsy."

I replied in a hushed tone. "Don't you think we should have one? Especially after what you told me earlier. Don't you want to confirm if he really had a stroke?"

Her eyes, pale and tear-streaked, glazed over. She weakly muttered, "No, it's okay. He probably did have a stroke."

"Alisondra, what's wrong with you? He needs an autopsy. This might be the same thing that happened to the others.

With no response, she turned and walked away. Just as she opened the door to leave the CCU, the police officials led by Mr. Reavis walked in. I couldn't hide my astonishment as he confidently passed me and headed straight for the charge nurse's desk. While he spoke to her, other officers began cordoning off the room and its surroundings with yellow tape. Fortunately, the patient was situated at the end of the CCU, allowing them to secure the area without disturbing other patients.

"This area is now a possible crime scene. No one can enter from this point onward," Mr. Reavis declared, his voice echoing through the CCU. Every nurse stopped and listened. "All nurses on duty this shift will be questioned after their shift ends. Any personnel who had contact with this patient must return to this area immediately," he continued, igniting hushed whispers among the staff.

A police officer with a camera meticulously documented every corner of the room. The nursing supervisor complied with Mr. Reavis's instructions, summoning staff back to the CCU one by one. The atmosphere became charged with concern and irritation. Some complained of fatigue and questioned what was happening.

Suddenly, the CCU doors swung open with tremendous force, scattering papers from the desk. "What in the world is happening here? I demand to speak to whoever is in charge, and I mean right now!" Dr. DeWhite's face was crimson, a throbbing vein pulsating on his forehead. He looked like he was about to explode with anger.

"That would be me." Mr. Reavis's voice, calm and adorned with a gentle southern accent, cut through the tension as he walked across the nursing station, nearly toe to toe with the fiery cardiologist.

"What exactly are you doing? This is not a police matter. This man passed away from a CVA. Why are you here?" Dr. DeWhite's tone was sharp.

"We have reason to believe this may not be as straightforward as it appears. An investigation is underway. I will need to speak with you and all staff members who had contact with this patient. After processing the scene, we will transport the body to the medical examiner's office," Mr. Reavis responded, his voice maintaining its calm and smooth demeanor.

"No. You. Will. Not." Dr. DeWhite punctuated each word with a jab of his finger into Mr. Reavis's chest. "This is my hospital, my CCU, and this will not happen under my watch. Who informed you? How did you even know to come?" Dr. DeWhite's gaze darted around the CCU, his accusatory eyes scrutinizing everyone present.

Everyone was focused on the escalating situation. An eerie silence settled over the CCU. Addressing the staff, Dr. DeWhite continued his tirade, demanding to know who had contacted the police. His rage only subsided when Mr. Reavis put an end to it.

"Firstly, let me make this clear: do not touch me again, or I will charge you with assaulting a police officer. Secondly, either cooperate or be charged with obstruction. Thirdly, sit down and keep your mouth shut, sir, before I do it for you. Do we understand each other?" Mr. Reavis's voice, though still calm, now carried a forceful undertone.

"How dare you speak to me in such a manner?" Dr. DeWhite's tone grew more timid. He had met his match. "I will be contacting your superiors, and I will have your job. I make significant annual donations to local law enforcement, and you have just made a grave mistake, sir."

With that, the humiliated physician slinked away, feverishly dialing his cell phone. I chuckled softly. Next in line was Alisondra, her appearance disheveled and her nerves frayed. She approached me directly.

"What in the world is happening? Why are the police here?"

"Are you serious, Alisondra? You were the one who informed me about the unusual deaths. I suppose they suspect foul play, and I agree with them."

"Yeah, but this just occurred. How did they know to come? Who alerted them? And how can you remain so composed? We are in a terrible situation and will be scrutinized. I am panicking right now.

"Why? You haven't done anything wrong." Or had she, I wondered silently. "I am calm because I have nothing to hide. If something nefarious happened, they need to uncover the truth. I'm unsure how they were notified, but it's a small town. Word spreads quickly."

"Okay, you're right. I shouldn't be upset, and I genuinely want to know what happened." As Alisondra finally regained her composure, I attempted to absorb the scene once more. The lifeless body, the monitors, the IV poles, the crash cart, the used supplies, the opened wrappers, the needles, the trashcan. The bedside table pushed aside, the ultrasound machine, the bedside table again… and there it was—a small red flower and an upside-down flag….

I jolted upright before I could restrain myself. I despised merely standing by. I yearned to be inside, gathering information and evidence, but I couldn't. I was only an onlooker. However, my abrupt movement caught the attention of the Chief. I glanced at him and then at the table. His eyes followed mine, and he comprehended my unspoken inquiry. He approached and indicated for the items to be collected as evidence. As time wore on, the staff members were called into an office for questioning. Finally, it was my turn.

"Is there a Layla Matthews here?" the officer called my name.

I entered the office, immensely relieved to converse with someone who grasped the situation. Mr. Reavis sat with a pad and notes on the desk.

"Okay, tell me precisely what transpired and what you know," he said, seemingly glad to see me as well.

I recounted the events to the best of my ability. "Did you notice the flower and flag? Isn't that peculiar?"

"Yes, it is. I'm grateful you contacted us. You're right; this is the first fresh crime scene we've been able to process. You're doing an excellent job maintaining your cover, by the way. That doctor, though—isn't he a character?" Mr. Reavis chuckled, his deep laughter filling the room. "Is there anyone else we haven't spoken to?"

"Wait, have you interviewed Angel? I haven't seen her. She was the patient's nurse prior to his transfer to the CCU, and she left looking quite distressed."

Mr. Reavis checked his notes and shook his head. He stepped out, inquiring about her whereabouts from the nursing supervisor. To our surprise, we learned that Angel had departed the hospital before the lockdown took effect. I found it hard to believe, considering her ongoing patient duties on her floor.

"Let me go find her. I'm certain she's still upstairs. Good luck, and inform me when they transport the body. I assume it's going to the FBI lab, not the on-site medical examiner, correct?"

"Absolutely, *not* here. I'll text you."

Chapter 18

I searched everywhere for Angel, but she was nowhere to be found. She had gone back to the floor, told the charge nurse she was sick, handed off her assignment, and left. I immediately tried to call her, and it went straight to voicemail. I couldn't fathom that Angel could be the killer. Why? What motive would she have? She was a part of this private group and seemed close to them. What reason would she have to kill anyone?

Walking back down to the CCU, the small hospital was abuzz with gossip. Whispers circulated about the CCU happenings and police presence. I tried to clear my mind take in the scene.

Police detectives were still taking photos and putting everything they could find in evidence bags. Everyone had been questioned, and the video from the security cameras was being uploaded to the FBI server. Alisondra sat in a corner, almost in a trance. Once again, she looked defeated and devastated. Dr. DeWhite was speaking to hospital administrators who had come in, and a man who I assumed was the hospital attorney. Tension seemed to hang in the air. I needed to speak to Mr. Reavis but could not appear suspicious, so I texted instead:

Make sure they get the needle box off the wall. All of those syringes will need to be analyzed. Also, someone needs to go get Angel. She left the hospital and will need to be questioned. I have to go to the ER for an admission. Text me if you need me. I'll see you back at the house.

I went over to Alisondra and hugged her.

"Are you okay? Why don't you head home? I can take the rest of the night. The ER isn't busy. You are in no condition to work, babe."

With only the nod of her head, she was up and out of the CCU.

I went down to the ER to admit my little old lady with a UTI (urinary tract infection) and tried to wrap my brain around what had taken place. The patient had been fine: I talked to him, walked upstairs, had a conversation with Alisondra: he coded. Very little time had passed. I needed to see that footage; I wanted to know who was in that room.

I texted Mr. Reavis:

Hey, I thought of something. Get the footage from the floor before he was moved to CCU, please. Send it to my laptop, and I'll start reviewing ASAP!

Crap, I said that wrong, too bossy:

Sorry, that sounded wrong. I know you are slammed right now. I would be glad to help out and review footage if that's okay.

He replied:

Gotcha! Sending as soon as I get it. I can use the help.

Trying to finish one last admission and focus on my other job, I went to the lobby to grab a drink. Something caught my eye. Alisondra was in the parking lot, in an embrace, with a man. Even though it was not light yet, I could tell by his shape and size who this man was. Colton. He seemed to be comforting her, I assumed, due to the death. I am sure since she was so close to the deceased that he had known him as well. I walked over to the window to get a better look. She was only about 5'2", he was at least 6" tall. Her small frame was engulfed by his muscular arms. He was caressing her head with one hand while the other arm snaked around her waist. This encounter definitely looked like they were more than "friends with benefits" like she had alluded to earlier. I took a few photos with my phone and decided to start wrapping up for the night.

As I walked back up to the office, I passed a few officers in the hallway, then the gurney with the body on it rolled past me. The black bag was zipped, and only a tag marked its contents. How sad. Just a few hours ago, this man was fine. He was talking and hoping to go home in the morning. Now he is only a shell. A lifeless bag of flesh rolling down the hall in a big ziplock bag. A few hours ago, he was eating dinner at the local Thai restaurant. A few hours ago, he was laughing with his wife of 45 years. A few hours ago, he liked his daughter's photo on Facebook. A few hours ago, he was planning a golf trip to Myrtle Beach. A few hours ago, he had a little numbness in his arm and face. A few hours ago he was alive, now he is not. That fast.

Emotion filled me, as life is so uncertain. A person never knows if they will take one more breath, if they will have one more day, tell someone I love you one last time. Life is so fragile, and someone took this man's life away from him. I had no doubt that this was another murder, and I was determined to find out who was responsible for this. Who snuffed the light of this man's soul out too soon? It wasn't his time to go; a horrible thief stole from him his time.

Waves of exhaustion seemed to crash over me from nowhere. Being a hospitalist is exhausting in itself, but the added stress of this case was wearing me down physically and mentally. I hurried home, took a quick shower, and decided to rest for just a few minutes before starting my review of the events.

Right before I fell asleep, my phone beeped:

Hey babe, sorry I missed talking to you last night. I crashed. I ♥ U! Text me later, headed to work.

But I did talk to Tripp; he just didn't remember. A restless sleep crashed over me in waves, I was finally on my way to actual rest, only to be awakened by my phone ringing in under an hour.

"Hey, sorry to wake you. I know you are exhausted, but I need you to see something. Come to my workroom now, please."

I knew by the sound of his voice something had happened. Splashing water on my face and throwing on a pair of pants, I went to the basement. What awaited me was truly a shock to my system.

New Friends

Kayleigh could barely sleep; the excitement of meeting new people, especially those also being held captive, had given her renewed hope. Being out in the woods would be challenging, but being alone would have been even worse. Having someone else with her would make things better. She just hoped she wouldn't have to babysit them or constantly take care of them. Not that she didn't have compassion for them, but she didn't have the energy to be in FBI mode; she was in self-preservation mode at this point. She tried to nap during the day, which was unusual for her, but with no idea when she would sleep again, she attempted it. Multiple times she took inventory of her meager supplies. They were modest, but better than nothing. She turned the small knife over and over in her hands. It was old and worn, but anything could be a weapon, right?

Just as she had placed her matches deep inside her pocket, the door opened. Krissy and Whitley walked in, hand in hand, sinister smiles on both faces making a chill go down her spine. She took a deep breath; she had been careless, almost caught. She needed to be more careful; she was too close to escape to screw up now.

"Well, how are you feeling today? Did you sleep well?" Krissy's voice was smooth and sweet. Kayleigh's mind raced; did they know she had been out? Why did she ask that? Stay calm...

"Yes, thank you. The accommodations are lovely. Room service is not up to par, however." The smile quickly disappeared. "You are a comedian, aren't you? Well, you will think this is a 5-star resort soon because where you are going is much worse." The sweet voice transformed into a venomous hiss in an instant.

Her heels clicked loudly on the cement floor as she walked over to Kayleigh. Whitley followed obediently behind like a little Pomeranian on the heels of its master. Shoes... Kayleigh stared at her shoes, then down at her feet. She had no shoes...

"In a couple of days, this will all be over. You will be dead, Layla will be dead, and I will be free of you troublesome women. I will carry on my business without another thought of you crossing my mind. You have both been the proverbial thorn in my side since this started." As she spoke, she stroked Whitley's head, rubbing her little puppy with affection.

"I am sure I will be dead soon; I have no doubt. I will never see my family again or be free, but I know in my heart someday you will pay for what you have done. You are a disgrace to women. You are a traitor, a murderer, and an evil soul. I know for certain you will be eternally damned to Hell for what you have done to so many innocent people..." The slap across her face was so hard and fast

Kayleigh was knocked to the floor. Krissy's eyes now revealed her true evil side. The bright blue eyes had changed to narrow slits. Her face was one of terror and anger.

"You shut your mouth. You don't know me; you know nothing about me!" She was shrieking in anger as she yelled at Kayleigh. "I will kill you now, RIGHT now. Don't push me." She began to pace; Kayleigh had hit a sore spot, so she kept going.

Laughter... Kayleigh wiped a tiny drop of blood from her mouth. Getting up slowly from the floor, taking a moment to clear her head, she was pleased. She had rattled the beast's cage.

"What is there to know? You sell women to men... There is no other way to spin that. You can call it whatever you want, but that is the truth. Someone will catch you, someone will stop you, and I hope you get the same thing that the poor souls you sold have received."

"Well, you are getting ready to get exactly what you deserve. I promise you that. And the money I get from you, well, I plan on buying myself something special. I deserve it, having to deal with you. Come on, baby, I am bored. I have a concert to get ready for." Her face had softened again, the face of a true chameleon.

With that, Krissy exhaled and walked out of the door. Whitley stood staring at Kayleigh for a moment then followed her, closing the door.

Kayleigh, despite the sting of her face, felt good about what had just happened. She had upset Krissy, exposing a weakness. She might need this at some point.

Looking down at her feet, she had no shoes. Why had she not thought of that? How could she survive in the woods in the cold with bare feet? Panic began to well up within her. She sat on the floor and took deep breaths, trying to calm herself. "It's OK, you got this, it will be cold, but you don't know how far you will have to go, you can do it..." Aloud she tried to soothe herself and give herself a pep talk to calm her nerves.

Finally, she came to the realization that she had better chances out in the cold woods than to stay here, shoes or not. Pulling herself together, she once again organized her stash of snacks, two little knives, one bent fork, and one small book of matches. "I think I have OCD; how many times have I done this? And why am I talking to myself?"

She could do this, she had to do this. She had no idea where Layla was and knew she probably wouldn't be able to save her, but she had to try to save herself and the two other women being held.

Time seemed to pass so slowly, but finally, the supper tray was delivered. Like always, the elderly lady held the door open long enough to carry trays in. Kayleigh peeked at her door lock to be sure she could still get out, pretending to help carry the water in. Everything was in place. As she stood near the door, she was able to see into the hallway and noticed the extra trays on a small cart.

That must be dinner for her new friends. She hoped they would be smart and plan to save some food for their escape. When her door closed, she sat down on her little bed with her last meal tray. A smile crossed her face, and she knew this would be her last meal in captivity. One way or the other, she would be free. Free in life, or free in death; either way was fine. But she would not be held captive any longer.

Opening the little sandwich, she ate it all but crammed the carrots and celery sticks into her pillowcase/supply bag. The napkin and plastic wrap were stuffed into her pockets, and she waited. Typically, it wasn't long until she would hear the doors close, lights would be dimmed, and she would know the staff had left for the night. The only one left would be the guard, and if this night was typical, he would sleep right through her escape.

Just like clockwork, the night was like all the other nights. She waited a few extra moments, trying not to be so anxious that she prematurely acted. When she was sure she heard no movement, she slowly opened the door. Pausing... waiting to hear any sounds... her heart was pounding so loudly in her ears she was afraid someone would hear it. Putting on her jacket, she stuffed her pillowcase up to her chest and zipped it up, making sure both arms were free. With her little knives in one pocket and the broken fork in the other, she ventured into the hallway. Slowly retracing her steps, she found her way to the door that held the other women.

Stop... listening...

Snoring...

Just as she had hoped, the bear of a man was already in his nighttime slumber. Stopping at the door, she listened. No sounds. Were they still there?

Tap.

Tap.

Tap.

"Hello?? Are y'all there?" A too loud whisper.

Silence.

Tap.

Tap.

"Yes, we are here. Hold on; we are coming."

Finally, some noise from inside. Whispers, but she could not make out what they were saying. Slowly, the door opened.

Standing in front of her were two women: one tall, blonde, and the other shorter. Serious looks on their faces as they looked at each other and at Kayleigh.

Kayleigh was shocked as they did not look like typical prisoners or victims, so to speak. They seemed ready to fight, defensive stances, and not timid at all. She was relieved. She felt like the weak one now. She wanted to cry, hug them, and talk to them, but there was no time. That would be later.

"Get what you are taking... let's go. Stay close behind me; we don't need to get separated. We will have to walk right by the door where the guard is, but he is already asleep, so it's fine. Just go slow and be quiet." They nodded and started down the hallway slowly.

Kayleigh noticed they had on normal street clothes; it looked like they had been at a club or something. They both had on cowboy boots, so they had to go very slow to avoid being heard. She wished she had shoes...

The closer they got to the exit sign, the louder the snores. Kayleigh held her hand up, signaling that she would cross in front of the door first. As she walked by, she could see the man in the recliner sleeping. Next came the tall blonde, then the other lady. They seemed to know how to handle themselves and continued to impress Kayleigh.

EXIT.

The red sign was like a lighthouse in the middle of a midnight storm. It was hope, it was a chance for freedom, it meant life. As her hand, shaking, reached out to push open the door, she heard it. Suddenly, the crash of the recliner slamming shut, heavy feet hitting the ground, the snores stopping, and heavy steps...

All three women froze when the man came out of the room like a bulldozer.

"And where do you ladies think you are going?" The man named Jody was standing before them, Kayleigh's hand still on the door, a smile on his face with some type of old food particle stuck between his front teeth. You could smell his body odor when he moved. The other two women were also staring at him in disgust.

Her mind raced; she could push open the door and run. Surely they could outrun him. She had no time to react until she heard another voice.

"Well, what is going on here?" The second guard appeared from a different hallway. Lam stood next to Jody. "You ladies going out for a little stroll, are you?"

"I say we just have a fun night with them now; I mean, we can tell the boss they were trying to escape, and we had to kill them. She hates them and won't care. I want to have some fun. It's been a long time for me." As Jody spoke, he walked over slowly toward the tall blonde. She stood tall and had a look on her face that scared Kayleigh. As he took his brown, crusty finger and rubbed it on her cheek and all the way down to her cleavage, he was talking in slow, breathy tones, like a man about to explode with desire. She did not flinch; no emotion but pure and simple hatred. "Yeah, I *want this one first. She's hot, and I want to rip her apart from the inside out." He was up in her face now; her friend was close behind her. Kayleigh's hand never left the door. Before anyone knew what had happened, the tall woman, in one fast movement, grabbed the disgusting excuse of a man by the scrotum. Her hand gripped his genitals as tight as she could, and through gritted teeth, she said, "You will never touch me, you disgusting tub of lard." As she was talking, her wrist contorted to the side as the man crumbled to his knees. His once arrogant, deep voice now screamed out like a little girl. His manhood was still in her hand; she continued to twist and contort.*

Lam never moved.

Why did he not move?

Kayleigh made eye contact with the other women; then they both looked at him.

As he slowly reached into his jacket, he pulled out a 9-millimeter pistol. He did not raise it but held it down at his side. Everyone was frozen in place; the only noise was from the man crumbling on the floor.

Who are these women?

"Let him go, please. We need to talk."

The voluptuous blonde now stood up and released her grasp. He continued to whimper until he finally recovered. Moving to a kneeling position, he growled and with one fast movement punched her in the stomach so hard she was knocked up against the wall.

At that moment, the shorter lady responded by kicking him in the face. It seemed to happen so fast, as he once again was on the floor moaning.

Kayleigh's hand was still on the door; she was thinking about just running. In all the commotion, she could make it... couldn't she?? Suddenly, the man jumped up to retaliate; Lam reacted, the gun up now. Once again, everyone froze. The gun was not pointed at either lady, or Kayleigh; it was pointed at Jody.

"What are you doing, man? What is wrong with you? Kill then now!" He continued to curse and defame until his fear forced him into a different approach. "Don't do this."

Ignoring his partner, he looked at the smaller lady, "Here, take these keys and go about 5 miles north of here through the woods; there is a truck there. Take it and get out of here. Do not stop until you are at least a few hours away. Go as fast as you can; as soon as they realize you are gone, they will have a lot of people looking for you, and you cannot trust anyone!"

For just a moment, no one knew what to do or what to say, then finally, the tall blonde spoke.

"Hey, can we get our guns back? When you guys took us, you took my 9MM, and we are going to need something to defend ourselves."

"Take his." Motioning toward the battered Jody, confusion etched across his face. *"I have no idea where yours is."*

"Bro, you're making a huge mistake. What the heck, man? What are you doing? Why are you helping these whores? You're going to die. She's going to kill you; you know that? She's going to kill you."

"Shut up, man. Just shut up," Lam said firmly.

The shorter woman retrieved the gun from Jody's pants and tucked it into her boot. Taking the keys from Lam, she looked at the group and said, "Let's get out of here!"

Kayleigh's hand still on the door, she had been a bystander during this entire event. Just as they were about to escape, Jody made one last attempt and lunged at the smaller woman. Before anyone could react, Lam shot him in the back, and Jody crumpled to the floor.

"You have to go! Go now! They'll be here soon, but first, you must help me," Lam said, his voice weaker than before.

"Why are you helping us?" Kayleigh finally found her voice.

"That doesn't matter right now. There's no time to discuss this. The gunshot will bring more men; you need to get out as fast as you can," Lam urged. Grabbing a knife from his waistband, he handed it to the tall woman. "Here... take this too; you'll need all the help you can get. But first, stab me right here," he pointed to his right flank.

"No! You're helping us; come with us, please!" Kayleigh pleaded.

"Please, just do it, and fast. It won't kill me, but it has to look like I put up a fight, or I'm as good as dead too."

"But..."

With one swift motion and not a word, the large knife went into Lam's right side. He yelled in pain, but the woman showed no emotion.

"Okay, it's done. Let's go," he said.

"Who are you people?" Kayleigh asked, her mouth agape. These women... where had they come from?

The shorter woman didn't hesitate. "Let's go!" Pushing past both Kayleigh and the tall woman, she opened the door. The cold night air rushed in, and within 30 seconds, a shrill alarm pierced the silence.

Kayleigh had anticipated having to be the strong one, taking care of the two women, but the opposite had occurred. She stood there, watching the scene unfold. However, when the cold night air brushed against her face, she snapped out of her trance. Glancing back at Lam, lying on the floor, she wondered if the stab wound would be fatal. He was losing a lot of blood, and their eyes met. In a voice weaker than before, he said, "Go... I'll be fine. Hurry, and I'm sorry... Good luck, now run!"

Chapter 19

Walking into the large workroom always took my breath away, but this morning it was even more awe-inspiring. The walls were adorned with hundreds of pictures from the CCU, displaying faces, the room, the body.

"Good morning," he said, handing me a hot cup of coffee without wasting a moment. "Sorry to wake you up, but I think we need to move sooner than later. This was the break we needed. I want you to watch this video. Good call on getting the footage from the floor. The footage from the CCU was no help. Whatever happened occurred before he was transferred."

"Okay, great. What do we have?" I could see that he had spent the entire night piecing together this massive puzzle. The coffee pot in the corner was full, and a plate of muffins sat on the table. He had such a sweet wife. I followed him to the corner of the room, where large screens displayed the footage.

"Okay, watch this."

I observed the footage from the 3rd floor unfolding on the wall. It appeared to be a typical night: nurses passing by, med carts rolling, nursing assistants carrying linens, and a few random visitors. Thankfully, the camera had a perfect angle on the room's door, allowing us to see everyone entering and exiting.

Angel arrived at the door with her med cart. She stood there, checking the medications and glancing at his record, before entering the room. She stayed for about 12 minutes. Then Marvin approached, holding a small flower and a flag. As Angel left, he entered the room. They didn't exchange words, but their eyes met, and they nodded at each other. He stayed in the room for only 5 minutes. After that, Alisondra came into the picture.

"Watch this closely. Pay attention here," he said, standing up, eager to show me what he had discovered.

Angel's med cart was positioned at the door. As Alisondra approached, she forcefully pushed the cart and Angel aside. The two women confronted each other, inches from each other's faces. Alisondra said something heatedly, her emotions palpable, before she entered the room, slamming the door shut behind her. She stayed in the room for 14 minutes. Angel had moved on to the next room. Alisondra returned to the desk and made a phone call, likely the one to transfer the patient to the CCU. At that point, Angel approached the desk and said something to Alisondra. Alisondra didn't respond, but turned away. Angel grabbed her by the arm, forcing her to face her.

This time, it was Angel who displayed aggression. The other nurses watched the encounter in silence. And then, that's when I walked in. At that precise moment, the altercation ceased abruptly.

Within the next 30 minutes, he was transferred to the CCU.

I stood there, my mouth slightly open. I had spoken to both of them before this incident, and neither had mentioned a word about any issues between them. Alisondra had mentioned moving him to protect him, but nothing more.

"So, did you have any idea this had taken place?" he inquired.

"No, neither of them mentioned anything about this. You can clearly see they stopped arguing as soon as I arrived on the floor. We need to question the nurses about the nature of their argument."

"I'm already on it. I've contacted the Director of Nursing and scheduled a meeting with all of them this afternoon. So we've narrowed it down to these three people. Our suspects are Marvin, Alisondra, or Angel."

"I agree this is a significant breakthrough, but we should really wait for the medical examiner's report before we jump to conclusions about murder. Perhaps he genuinely suffered a stroke. I can't fathom any of them wanting to harm this kind man or any of the other victims. Alisondra seemed devastated,

Marvin is as innocent as they come, and Angel... well, let's just proceed with caution," I cautioned, instantly regretting my words. It wasn't my place to speak to him this way. This was his case, and I had overstepped my bounds.

"I concur. I'm baffled by this whole situation," he responded, a hint of irritation in his voice.

"As for the argument between the two women, it could have been about anything. He was a close friend of Alisondra's, and she was emotionally invested. She can be quite moody, and Angel, well, she has a peculiar personality. They clash frequently, so it could have been something trivial. Nothing necessarily indicative of murder," I added, attempting to clarify my position.

"I've contacted the forensics lab and informed them that I need answers today. This case takes precedence, and we should have a preliminary cause of death by 1400 hours."

"Any other red flags? You spoke with the entire staff and Dr. DeWhite. Anything noteworthy?"

"Nothing substantial. Aside from being insufferably arrogant, I don't think he had a clue that this could be a murder. I suspect he was avoiding an autopsy out of fear that he had missed a heart attack."

"Okay, well, that's what we really need. Let me reach out to Alisondra and see if I can cover her shift tonight. I'll speak with the nurses and try to find out what happened last night. They might open up to me more than a police officer. Anything else catching your attention?"

"Nothing else for now. I just have this feeling that it's one of them. Trust me, Layla, I've been doing this for a long time, and something just doesn't sit right here. The motive may not be clear, but sometimes it's the least obvious person."

"Oh, I understand that. I'm just completely clueless at this point. But I did notice Alisondra talking to that guy, Colton, outside, and they seem much closer than she admitted to. And you're right; their behavior is bizarre. Especially since I spoke with both ladies right after that altercation, and they seemed fine. Angel appeared a bit anxious, but she claimed she was just busy. I'm wondering if it's tied to all of this. There's definitely a connection somewhere, but what is it?"

"Go get some rest. I need you at the top of your game tonight. I'm sorry for waking you up."

"No problem. I'll text you when I'm up." Grabbing a muffin, I headed back to my place.

My mind was spinning. What had I just witnessed? What was going on? Standing in my room, I stared at the photos on my desk. I hadn't added anything to the mix. But maybe that's what I needed—more context about what happened before last night.

Colton... Why does he keep showing up? Why does he bother me so much? There's something about him... The sound of a text message made me jump. I needed to sleep:

Hey, babe! I'm so excited about this weekend—concert time! Luke Combs! We need to decide what to wear and where to eat, etc. I need to meet you. Call me later. Love ya.

Krissy... the concert... Well, at least it was still a few days away. Hopefully, the situation would calm down by then. If not, I might have to cancel. I didn't respond. I'll text her back later.

Finally, after what felt like an eternity, I drifted off to sleep. Dreams haunted me, but that was nothing new. My phone ringing woke me up, and I gave up on trying to get any decent rest.

Before I could even say hello...

"Mom, are you okay?" Aubrey's voice sounded different, strained... tense.

"Yes, baby, I'm fine. Why? What's wrong?"

"There's lots of chatter in that area. Nashville has had a lot of wealthy people flying in, and weird rumors are starting. They won't tell me much, and it probably has nothing to do with you, but I know you're in Tennessee, not far from Nashville, so it gave me a weird feeling."

Should I tell her that someone has been following me?

I hadn't even thought of that with my case consuming my thoughts. Mackenzie and Heather crossed my mind. I hope they're okay.

"I don't know, babe. I haven't heard anything, but then again, I wouldn't. I'm focused on the hospital where I'm consulting. You can't panic when you hear stuff like that, sweetheart. You're in training, so you'll probably only get bits and pieces. Don't let it stress you out. I'm sure it has nothing to do with me. Don't worry, baby. What have you been working on?" I changed the topic, using my mom voice to soothe my daughter.

"Okay, Mom, just be safe. Don't get so wrapped up in what you're doing that you don't pay attention to what's going on around you. That's a big mistake. I'm working with a group of people dealing drugs on a college campus. It's been a good learning experience for me. I'll fly out to see you when I get a break. Have you talked to Dad?"

"Not today. I'll probably call him after we hang up."

"Okay, well, I love you. Please stay safe and remember to PAY ATTENTION, be on alert. I think I'm getting paranoid." She let out a nervous laugh. "Call me soon."

"Okay, I promise. You be safe too. Hope to see you soon!"

Still lying in bed, I dialed Tripp's number.

"Hey, good-looking, what are you doing?"

"Oh, hey, honey, working. What about you?"

"Just getting up. I worked last night and have to do it again tonight. I'm pooped. My old booty can't handle the night shift. How's your work going? I'm sorry I woke you the other night when I called. I just knew you'd be up watching the game."

"It's okay; I fell asleep early and barely remember the phone ringing. How's the case? Can you please come home? I miss you. I thought once you found out there was foul play, you would come home. I don't like this. I want my wife back."

Emotions welled up inside me. "I know, baby, I'm sorry. Soon, very soon. I think we're close. Technically, I could come home now, but having access inside the hospital is really helping the investigation. Please understand. I just spoke to Aubrey. Why don't we plan a family vacation when we have a break?"

"That sounds good, babe. I'd love that. But seriously, Layla, we need to talk. I don't like this. Well, I have to go. I have a meeting at 5. Call me later. Be safe. Love you."

"I love you. Have a good rest of the day."

What did that mean? I knew he didn't like the consulting work, but I couldn't focus on that now. I had to get to work. I had some time before I had to be at the hospital.

I sent a quick text to the Chief:

Any updates on who was following me or the missing nurse/FBI agents?

His reply was quick: No. Why, has something happened?

No, just asking. Don't want to be caught off guard.

Quick on the draw again, he returned: As far as we can tell, whoever was following you has stopped. We're still looking for the agents. You're safe.

Okay, thanks.

With that reassurance, I stepped into the shower, preparing for my night ahead.

Chapter 20

After relishing in the hottest and most invigorating shower imaginable, I made my way downstairs, eager for a quick update before my impending visit to the hospital. Mr. Reavis, visibly drained and clearly sleep-deprived, stood before me, his exhaustion etched across his face.

"Dude, you need to go to sleep! You look like you can hardly stand up," I exclaimed, genuine concern lacing my words.

"I know. I am going to update you and then head that way. I spoke to the nurses on the floor, and they swore they didn't hear anything, even when I pointed out we have them on video. So maybe you can get something useful tonight. I've sent the video to forensics for closer analysis. And here's the best part... the medical examiner called me. No stroke, no heart attack. No natural cause of death. This is definitely a homicide case. No illegal drugs in his system. Labs were normal for a dead person. They used a black light and looked for needle sticks, and sure enough, found a small puncture right behind his left earlobe. If that body had gone anywhere else, it would have never been found. Since the death was so fresh, he was able to excise the skin from around the puncture. It appears someone injected a lethal dose of insulin. He wasn't diabetic, so no one checked his glucose level during the code," Mr. Reavis divulged, his words leaving me stunned.

"Oh, my Lord! So you are right. It's probably one of those three because of the timeline. By the time he was moved to the CCU and the CODE happened, the insulin had time to take effect. OK, here's what I can do to help if you think it's OK. I can question those nurses, but I can't waste a whole night working. I will meet with them and then around midnight, I'll 'get sick' and have to leave early. I will come straight back here and get back to work. You sleep, and let me handle this tonight. I know it's not my job or why I'm here, but I can try. What will it hurt? I hope the video footage will be ready by then. I think we're about to solve this. I mean, you are," I suggested, a mix of excitement and trepidation filling me. The realization that people I liked could be capable of murder weighed heavily on my heart.

"OK, sounds good. I'm about to pass out. Good night, and good luck," he said with a yawn, turning to leave. Just before he left, he added, "One last thing, Layla, be safe. We're getting close, and that means things can get more dangerous. Be on the lookout. And remember, I'm letting you look over things, but I don't need to keep reminding you why you're here."

"Yes, sir, I sure will, and thanks!" I replied, acknowledging his concern for my safety as I prepared for my night's mission.

Driving to the hospital was exhilarating; a palpable sense of anticipation filled the air. The feeling that this was coming to an end sent shivers down my spine. However, in the midst of my excitement, I remembered I had forgotten to reply to Krissy's text.

Hey boo! Sorry I had to sleep, night shift. I am working in a little town outside of Nashville, so I can just meet you. There may be a restaurant close to the venue. No idea what I am wearing, but I'll call you tomorrow. Love ya. I can't wait to see you. ◆◆

I pulled into the hospital parking lot just in time to witness a car screech up to the ER, recklessly discarding a body before speeding away. Shocked, I hurried over, shouting for help. The ER doors flew open, and the medical staff rushed out. Two muscular male nurses quickly lifted the injured man onto a stretcher. He appeared young, Asian, and was bleeding profusely from a stab wound. It was clear the police would soon be involved, but my focus had to remain on my own investigation. I couldn't afford to be distracted, not now. After ensuring the man was in capable hands, I proceeded to my call room. There was a nagging sense of familiarity about the injured man, but I couldn't quite place it. Nevertheless, my duty was clear—I had nurses to interrogate. Armed with donuts, the ultimate icebreaker, I headed to the third floor where the gossipers resided.

"Hey, ladies! I hope everyone slept well today. I got donuts! Last night was rough, so I thought food might help!" I announced, attempting to lighten the mood and win their cooperation.

Smiles spread across the faces of the nurses gathered around the nurses' station. One older nurse, stationed near the Telemetry monitors, caught my attention. I strategically settled down beside the chatty group. A young brunette nurse was expressing her intense excitement over the night's cafeteria fare – walking tacos.

"What in the world is a walking taco?" I asked, laughing, trying to steer the conversation, away from food and somehow toward the events of the previous night.

"Girl!! They are great. They give you a bag of Fritos or Doritos and put meat and cheese on it, and you shake it up. I usually don't eat in the cafeteria at night, but we were all called in early, so I didn't have a chance to pack my lunch," explained one nurse, her enthusiasm infectious.

"That sounds absolutely disgusting! Who invented that?" I chuckled, joining in their laughter. "Why did you all have to come in early? Was there a staff meeting or something?"

"They are really good; you should try them. No, there was

an argument between the hospitalist and one of our nurses last night, and they wanted to know details. I mean, why would we tell them anything?" Donut-filled-mouth nurse interjected between bites, her hunger apparent.

"Oh no! It sucks you all had to come in early. Who was arguing?" I probed, feigning innocence, hoping to extract some useful information from their gossip.

"Alisondra is a hospitalist here, as you know, and she and one of our nurses hate each other. They always have. I heard it goes as far back as high school, but who knows? They were all up in each other's faces last night, and Alisondra actually pushed her! We lost it. I mean, Angel is ex-military and would beat Alisondra's skinny ass!" one nurse eagerly shared, her excitement palpable.

"Yeah, it was awesome. I like a good cat fight," chimed in another nurse, her eyes sparkling with enthusiasm.

"What would make them argue like that?" I continued to probe, skillfully guiding the conversation.

"It was something about the patient. Alisondra didn't want Angel to be his nurse, and Angel pretty much told her to kiss her ass, that she didn't have the authority to change a nurse's assignment without a good reason. But like I said, this isn't new. They argue all the time. Last night was the worst. I also heard they were both hooking up with the same dude at one point, so who knows? OK, ladies, let's just order out. I don't think I want hospital food tonight. Those walking tacos always give me the walking farts!" announced one nurse, steering the conversation away from the tense topic.

I had garnered as much information as I could from the nurses, learning about the ongoing feud between Alisondra and Angel. Their complicated history only added fuel to the fire of my investigation. Hanging around a bit longer in an attempt to extract more details, I eventually decided to continue my rounds.

Upon entering the CCU, I noticed police officers. They had arrived to investigate the stabbing victim I had seen earlier. Since that had nothing to do with me, I steered clear of the drama altogether. I needed to check on a woman who had been admitted earlier, so I tried to ignore the commotion. While walking past the large glass doors, I couldn't help but glance at the patient inside. He was awake, sitting up in bed, with an officer by his bedside asking questions. As I passed by, our eyes met. He suddenly sat upright with a jolt, mouth agape, motioning for my attention. I assumed he was confused and kept walking, he caught me off guard. But I couldn't escape the nagging feeling that I knew him from somewhere, although I couldn't recall where. He seemed oddly familiar to me.

Feeling restless and anxious, I knew I had to get out of there.

I messaged Dr. Harris, informing him of a "sudden bout of vomiting" that necessitated my departure. He was not happy with me, but under the circumstances, he had no choice but to find coverage for the remainder of the shift. Under normal circumstances, I would never have fabricated an excuse to leave work, but this was a unique situation. I couldn't wait to go back and analyze the intricacies of the case. Despite Tripp's desire for me to return home, my determination to see the case through was unyielding. I was emotionally invested in the investigation, making it essential for me to uncover the truth.

The drive back to the house passed in near silence. The charming town I had grown accustomed to was now a backdrop to my life. My impending and inevitable conversation with Tripp loomed in the back of my mind, but I pushed it aside, refusing to be swayed from my mission. I needed laser focus.

Arriving home, I quickly changed into a comfortable pair of jogging pants and a sweatshirt. The night air still held a cool edge, prompting me to prepare a large pot of coffee, seeking solace in its warmth. Armed with my coffee mug and notebook, I retreated to my designated workspace. *Layla Matthews, FBI Wanna Be*, reporting for duty, ready to immerse myself in the case that had consumed my thoughts.

The night was dark and eerie, a dense fog hanging over the

valley, giving me a foreboding sense of something amiss on the horizon. I hastened my pace, entering the basement and swiftly locking the door behind me. I found myself panting, not from fatigue but from anxiety.

Craving more coffee, I brewed a substantial pot and settled down to review the footage again. While I worked on the remedial task, my eyes roved over the expansive working board. One image stood out—a picture of Colton. Curiosity gnawed at me. Had he and Angel truly been together at some point? I hadn't heard from her since the CODE. I resolved to text her the next morning.

As I awaited my coffee, readying myself for the expansive video review, I pulled up the online yearbook from the local high school. Angel and Colton were older than Alisondra, yet they had all attended the same high school. Angel was a basketball player, the athletic type, while Colton was an All-American football player. Alisondra, the quintessential cheerleader, hadn't changed much. None of this startled me. I found only one photo of Angel, Alisondra, and Colton together, at a party, nothing seemed out of place.

Surveying some military photos on the board, the delightful aroma of coffee filled the room. Just as I turned to pour myself a cup, something grabbed my attention. In one of the groupings of Marine companies, I spotted Colton, his arm around a handsome young man. He seemed incredibly familiar, reminiscent of someone, but I couldn't pinpoint who. I took the photo down and brought it over to the table.

The coffee was comforting, warming me from head to toe. I took a sip and settled in front of the computer, ready to review the enhanced video footage.

Angel at her med cart, Alisondra approaches, an argument ensues, and Alisondra shoves Angel, who stumbles into the med cart, pushing it backward. Over and over...

The footage didn't reveal much during my first ten viewings, despite the improved resolution offering a clearer look. It was an exhausting process, but one I knew to be vital.

As I stood to stretch my back, I paused the video, with no forethought or planning. That's when it happened. That moment led me to the most crucial piece of this puzzle – not because of my skill, but because I just happened to pause at the right time. Zooming in further, I saw it—on top of the med cart, a tiny little bottle. A syringe.

Angel? But why?

Run

"Run," that's what he said, and run was exactly what they did. The alarm screamed, echoing throughout the woods like a banshee in a horror flick. Just as she had imagined, the metal building stood in the midst of a dense forest. They all headed toward the edge of the woods but paused at the entrance. Out of breath, the shorter lady gave orders, while the taller one had fallen behind. Finally, she came running out of the building.

"What were you doing?" The smaller one's voice was angry, yelling over the noisy building.

"I had to get her some shoes!" The taller one held up a pair of Nikes, tossing them to Kayleigh. "He is Asian, his feet are small, and I figured you would need them!" She wore a smile as bright as the sun. How could anyone be so perky in this situation?

"Good Lord, you are crazy! Okay, they will be coming after us; we need to throw them off. Let's each go a different way. You go 2 kilometers east, I will go 2 kilometers west, and you go 2 kilometers straight ahead. Then cross inward to meet in the middle." Looking at Kayleigh, she asked, "Do you understand? Do you know how much that is?" Kayleigh stood in shock. "Yes, yes, I do."

"Then let's go!" Before Kayleigh could say anything, the two ladies disappeared into the dark woods. She slipped on the shoes, secretly rejoicing, and ran as fast as she could. All the while, she wondered who these people were. They had to be military because no one uses or knows what a "klick" is but the military. She set her pace to measure her distance precisely and ran.

The air was cold on her skin, but the adrenaline and her insulated wind suit kept her warm. Her survival instinct had kicked in, and she was just happy to run. She was free. Tears streamed down her cold face, and at the same time, she was laughing, running, and crying all at once. The branches lashed out at her, and the forest undergrowth bit her ankles and legs, but she didn't care. The pain did not bother her. Despite her attempts at exercise in the small room, her leg muscles revolted with pain and spasms. Her lungs burned with the cold air, but she kept pushing. At that moment, she was unstoppable, never having been so happy before.

Free.

Finally, when she met back up with the other women, it took a moment to catch their breaths. The first one to speak was the woman who had given her the shoes. "Hi, I am Mackenzie, and this is Heather. Are you okay? I hope you like the shoes," she said, laughing amidst her gasps for air.

Kayleigh laughed, too. "You have no idea how much I

appreciate that."

"You are an idiot, Mac. You could have gotten us all killed for a pair of Nikes," Heather scolded her friend, her tone sharp.

"Ah, shut the hell up. She needed them; how far could she have run with no shoes? Stop being so rude. She helped us get out."

"I didn't see her do anything but open a door, but whatever!" Kayleigh was shocked at Heather's harshness.

Mackenzie continued to laugh, unfazed by the lecture. "Well, I can tell you what I am pissed about; they kept my gun. My Baby, she was my favorite. I had Bertha for years!"

"Okay, who are you guys? You are not just normal women who were kidnapped. Are you in the military or what?" Kayleigh asked, her curiosity piqued.

"Look, we can talk and get to know each other, and braid each other's hair for heaven's sake, but can we get to that truck first? We need to get as much distance as we can between us and them. Now, let's go!" With that, the running resumed and didn't stop until they reached the truck. Heather, being in charge, jumped in and started the engine.

For the first few miles, no one spoke. They really couldn't. They were all so out of breath from running that they needed a few minutes to catch up. The road was deserted; the clock on the radio said 11:00. Kayleigh was so happy. Her lungs burned from the night air and exertion, and she was fairly certain she had numerous cuts on her legs and face, but she didn't care. She laid her head back on the seat and was just so happy. She had feared never getting free, she had feared the woods, she had feared freezing to death, and none of that was going to happen. She. Was. Free. The sound of the tires on the rough road was loud, an old back road not maintained well. She bounced in the back seat. Any other time it would probably have been annoying, but it seemed to soothe her. The steady cadence of the road relaxed her. Leaning her head back, she closed her eyes. Heather had gotten a little chilly and turned on the heat. The warm air flowed over her face. She would not have been happier at a five-star resort at that moment.

"Okay, what's the plan?" Mackenzie asked in a low, hushed voice.

"Well, we have to do something with her; she is going to slow us down, and we cannot put a civilian in danger. We will need to call ASAP and let someone know where we are and give her to them. Our goal is the same as it always has been. We have to get weapons and get back before it all goes down."

"I agree; stop at the first store you see, and I will grab a burner phone. Wait, we have no money."

"Maybe someone will have a landline, and we can call headquarters."

Kayleigh kept her eyes closed, not moving, breathing slowly, listening, heart racing. Who are these people? That was the *question she kept asking over and over.*

"From what that psychotic slut said, this is all going down soon. If she had not helped us get out, we would be dead. So I really want to be sure she is okay. She said she had been held for a long time. She looks like she has been through hell, so let's make sure..."

"Mac!" Heather's voice was louder than she intended. "She is NOT our priority; she is NOT who we are here to protect. You are so emotional; stop. She will be fine; she survived; she is free. We will get her to the bureau; she will be debriefed, and we will do our job. Our only job is Layla!"

Eyes popped open. Before the ladies in the front even knew what had happened, Kayleigh was practically in the front seat, yelling, "What did you just say? Who are you? Tell me now!" As she was yelling, she was feeling around in her pocket for her little knife.

"Whoa, whoa, calm down, sister!" Mackenzie was shocked and confused at the outburst.

"Pull over! Pull this truck over now!" Kayleigh's yells replaced her earlier raised voice.

"Okay, okay, calm down..." Heather seemed unfazed. She slowly pulled the truck over to the side of the road. "Look, we can talk for a few minutes, get a plan, but we cannot sit here long; it's too dangerous."

"Okay, who are you? Tell me now. You are not two random kidnapping victims. And who are you calling, and who did you say

you were protecting?" Kayleigh's voice shook with a mix of fear and anger.

"Wow, that is a lot," Mackenzie said, laughing amidst the tension.

"Okay, we are FBI agents. We were working undercover in a hospital near here. We are going to call our agency headquarters and have you picked up. You will be safe, we promise. I don't know what you think you heard; you were half asleep, but we cannot tell you why we are here or what our assignment is."

Kayleigh could not believe what she was being told. She slid back in the seat, shaking, tears starting to come. They had said Layla; Layla was close. Of course, Krissy went to where she was. Heather, in a more compassionate tone, reached back and put her hand on Kayleigh's leg.

"Hey, it's okay. You're safe now. We got you. You can tell our superiors what happened and how you got taken. We really appreciate all that you did for us. We won't let anything happen to you."

"Yeah, boo, we got you! We owe you. If you hadn't helped us, that crazy, skinny blonde, she-devil would have killed us. You were great back there; don't cry." Mackenzie reached back and rubbed her hand. Kayleigh looked at that hand. The hand she had held under that door, lying on a cement floor. That soft hand was the first ray of hope in so long. She reached down and grabbed the

hand.

Swallowing the huge lump in her throat, she wanted to find words but felt mute. She almost couldn't find words. Finally, in what sounded like a croak, not a word, she managed to speak. "You said Layla; I heard you. I am Kayleigh." Tears flowed steadily now. Silence, total silence. The two ladies in the front seat sat frozen, mouths gaping, and for what seemed like forever, no one said a word.

"Wait, you are Kayleigh? THE Kayleigh? The agent that was taken?"

"Yes." That is all she could manage to get out.

"Dear sweet baby Jesus!" Mackenzie's southern tone was thick with shock.

"Okay, well, we have to go; they will be right behind us, and knowing who you are means they will be Hell on wheels!"

With that, Heather hit the accelerator, and they sped into the night.

Chapter 21

I stood there frozen, staring at the med cart in disbelief. Why would Angel kill those people? She knew them; she was close to them. Determined, I meticulously reviewed the files of all the deceased patients once more, compiling a spreadsheet that linked Angel to each one, either providing direct care on the same shift or the shift prior to their death. The gravity of the situation hit me as I observed the murder weapon, clearly visible on her med cart. That was the evidence we needed.

Hoping Mr. Reavis had gotten enough rest, I sent him a text: *Hey, I think I found it. Come down when you wake up.*

Aware that Angel had five other patients she needed to administer medications to that night, I wanted to ensure that the insulin wasn't missing for any of them. I accessed those records and began reviewing. I had to remain useful, there was no way I could leave at that point. As an RN, you have your own med cart, so I was desperately trying to find anything that would exonerate Angel. Unfortunately, I had no luck and was reviewing the medication for her third patient when Mr. Reavis walked in.

He brought a smile to my face. Despite having only about five hours of sleep, he had shaved, dressed, and smelled of Old Spice. He headed straight over to the coffee pot and asked, "What do you have?"

"Sorry to wake you, but I knew you'd want to be notified right away. Look at this." I pulled up the video, freezing the frame and zooming in. He leaned down, his eyes fixed on the screen.

"Well, I'll be darned! So it was Angel?" His words hung in the air, a mix of question and statement.

"Yes, I believe you have to assume that. I'm currently reviewing her assignments for that night to confirm this couldn't be another patient's meds. But so far, no one on her assignment was diabetic. Moreover, she was directly involved in all the deaths. But why? What could be her motive?"

Mr. Reavis pondered the situation, his voice thick with uncertainty. "Well, great work, thank you. I wouldn't have thought of that. Remember, she took her father's death very hard. Then she was discharged due to the distress she experienced. Maybe it took a toll on her mentally. I have no idea, but I suppose we need to bring her in. Her behavior has been erratic, but I never imagined her as a killer. I'll make the call."

The excitement I had anticipated never came. Instead, a

wave of sadness and disappointment washed over me. I felt like a poor judge of character, questioning my abilities. I had even considered telling Angel about my true identity at one point. As I sat there, listening to Mr. Reavis make phone calls, I couldn't help but berate myself for my oversight. How had I missed it? There were likely signs all along, and I realized she likely should have been at the top of my suspect list. That moment screamed of the fact that I was "Layla the consultant" and not "Layla the agent."

Reflecting on the entire investigation, I recalled seeing Marvin and Angel together at the very first murder scene. They had been in and out of the room, leaving a trail of suspicion.

"My son is on his way here to collect the list of evidence so he can bring her in for questioning," Mr. Reavis said, his voice filled with distress. "You keep going through the files to ensure no other patients were on insulin that night. We need to eliminate any excuses she might have for having insulin outside the door, on that patient, at that moment. I can't believe I missed this. I've known her since she was a little girl. I was good friends with her dad. She's very military-oriented and loyal, so this is quite a shock to me. But I guess you never truly know what goes on in people's minds. There was definitely a change in her after her dad died. She was at the top of her military command, very successful. The discharge from the military was hard on her. It hurt her."

"I'm sure she was let down, but she had to know why, right? I mean, if she had that much emotional toll and mental stress and she wanted to take care of her dad. Surely she understood why she was discharged." I listened, nodding sympathetically, though my mind was elsewhere. I examined pictures from the previous crime scenes, scrutinizing the military groupings. Mr. Smith had been Angel's godfather, and I couldn't fathom her killing him. Looking at the images from the memorial, I noticed Angel's absence. None of it made sense to me.

I discovered that Dr. DeWhite, Marvin, Mr. Smith, and Angel's dad had all belonged to the same military company. An old photograph revealed a younger version of these men, standing tall and proud in their military uniforms, ready to defend their country. I stared at the picture, captivated by their youthful vigor and determination. It saddened me to think that the youth of today had little understanding of the sacrifices made by our military. Many secrets remained hidden, known only to the higher echelons of government. The youth of today have no concept of war, and some of them are so sheltered by their parents that they have no idea of real life outside of their own home towns.

Mr. Reavis's voice pulled me back to reality. He continued, his words a jumble of thoughts and emotions. "I know what you're thinking. It's hard for me to wrap my mind around it too. Like I said, I've known Angel my whole life. But I'll tell you, she wasn't the same after her father died. That military company is incredibly secretive; we don't know the details of their operations. They undertake many clandestine missions, things only the upper levels of the government are privy to. I just don't know if we'll ever find out the truth. We looked through those files, but many of them were confidential, and we couldn't access them. Let me make some calls today and see if I can dig deeper into her psychiatric records. She wasn't dishonorably discharged; it was a medical discharge, at least that's one thing. If I can petition the Attorney General to unlock some of those files, perhaps it'll shed light on why she might be so mentally unstable as to murder her own colleagues. I know it's hard for you to grasp, Layla. But believe me, severe trauma, loss, death... it changes you."

"Maybe ease up on the coffee; you're talking a mile a minute," I suggested, attempting to calm him. "It'll be okay. You'll figure it out. Trust me when I say I understand how trauma and death change a person. I live with the constant fear and uncertainty of my friend Kayleigh, who was taken while trying to save me. Not a day goes by that I don't wonder what's happened to her. Is she being tortured? Is she dead? Is she enslaved somewhere? It haunts me. So I understand what you're saying. It's just hard for me to fathom why Angel would have a motive to kill these people. I might not be an agent, but I thought motive was a crucial aspect."

"Yeah, Layla, it is," he replied, his tone heavy with the weight of the situation. With that, he hung his head and returned to the computer.

The room fell into a somber silence, uncertainty and dread hanging in the air. The chief barged in, slamming the door open, snapping us back to reality. Hastily, we updated him, showing him the incriminating video. None of us wanted to act prematurely, risking the arrest of the wrong person, but the evidence was overwhelming. There was no choice but to issue a warrant for Angel's arrest.

I excused myself to head upstairs for a quick shower; dawn had broken. As I emerged from the basement and turned the corner, I caught sight of the breathtaking sunrise. The valley was still shrouded in fog, but the sun's rays illuminated the sky, dispelling the mist before my eyes. It was a surreal sight, almost ethereal. I should have been ecstatic in that moment, but instead, all I felt was sadness. I had missed it. There was no other way to see it—I had missed it.

Yet, if I continued consulting after this case, I would learn from the experience. I realized that when I came in to consult and gather information, I couldn't afford to truly befriend everyone. One of my biggest flaws was becoming too attached, wanting to be close to all my coworkers. I needed to maintain a professional distance, which I failed to do with Alisondra and Angel. I vowed to learn from it and do better on my next assignment.

I should have been excited. I wanted to be excited. But instead I felt down, mourning the loss of someone I considered a friend.

So, when my phone vibrated, it was just what I needed in that moment. I smiled at the text from Krissy:

OMG, almost time! I am soooooo excited! See ya soon!!!!!

My reply was a simple smiley face. Before stepping into my hot shower, I decided to send Tripp a message:

Good morning, have a great day. Luv ya. Be home soon, case almost over. I have missed you!

The three little dots indicated he was reading my texts, but they disappeared. Perhaps he was on the road. The hot water felt heavenly, and I let it wash away the fatigue and sadness. I stood there, lost in my thoughts. I was ready to go home, ready for the nightmare to end. I longed for my large, hot bath, a bit of normalcy, and the upcoming vacation with Aubrey and Tripp. Perhaps I should just go home; there was no obligation to stay any longer.

As I contemplated my future plans, I realized I needed a

hair appointment, outfits for the concert, and time to pack my belongings. My job here was done; the FBI had been brought in to solve the case and identify the killer. The local police had control now, knowing who the perpetrator was. They no longer required my help. Although a nagging feeling persisted, I had to let go of the situation. Once again, my job was done. Besides, Mr. Reavis was more experienced and capable; he could handle it from here. I planned to stay in Tennessee a few extra days after the concert, ensuring all loose ends were tied up before heading home.

Standing in my towel, my wet hair still dripping onto my shoulders, I thought about my next steps. My case was closed, and it would soon be time for me to return to my normal life, leaving that dark chapter behind, still undecided about the path I would take in the future.

Chapter 22

I had nothing to do with what happened next; the chief and Mr. Reavis would handle the arrest warrants, search Angel's home, and oversee all the final steps. In our small town, gossip spread like wildfire. Everyone knew of the arrest, and the Police Department was inundated with calls and complaints. Families of other deceased victims came forward, some furious that it had been missed, while others staunchly defended Angel.

Amidst the chaos, Alisondra reached out to me as soon as the news spread throughout the hospital. I hesitated but eventually decided to answer her call.

"Oh, my gosh! Why haven't you been answering my calls? I am dying! Have you heard? Have you heard? They arrested Angel. I told you. I knew it was her. I knew it."

Her voice was shrill, excited, and obnoxious. I couldn't help but feel irritated. Why was she so jubilant that someone she had known her whole life was a murderer? I tried to make sense of it.

"Yeah, I heard. I'm relatively new in town, so I don't know

the ins and outs, but it seems odd that Angel would have killed anyone. Aren't you a little shocked, Alisondra? You've known her your whole life, right? Didn't you mention you knew each other before the hospital?"

"We were in high school, but we were in completely different crowds. I was never really friends with Angel. We never got along, so no, I'm not shocked at all. Anyway, at least the nightmare is over. When are you back at work?"

"Well, I was only here on a short assignment while they needed help, and it looks like they have all the empty shifts filled now. I won't be coming back. I need to finish up my orders and charts at the hospital in a couple of days, but then I'll be heading home. We'll have to stay in touch. I've enjoyed working with you and appreciate your help."

"Are you serious? We don't have enough help. Why are they letting you leave? This is ridiculous. I'm going to complain to Dr. Harris that I want you to stay at least six more months. This is crazy! It's hard to find a hospitalist who actually knows what they're doing and is fun to work with. I really want you to stay. Do you want to get dinner tomorrow?"

She seamlessly shifted topics, her words tumbling out without pause, a talent of hers.

"Sure, I have a hair appointment tomorrow because I'm going to the Luke Combs concert with a friend from my hometown. I want to look good. I also need some fashion advice. I don't have any concert-worthy outfits, and there's not much shopping here. I don't want to shop when I get to Nashville either. Do you have any suggestions?"

"Girl, please! You're welcome to come to my house and raid my closet anytime! I'm smaller than you, but I'm sure there's a cute halter top or blouse you could borrow. And I have awesome boots because you have to wear boots to a country concert in Nashville. You know that, right?"

I wondered if she realized how rude she sounded, but I needed cowboy boots, and I accepted her offer.

"Okay, great. It's a date. I'll have my hair appointment, we'll meet for dinner, and I'll come raid your closet. Hopefully, I can find something to wear. I'm sorry I can't continue to work here, but hopefully, I can fill in now and then if you need help."

"Sounds good. I'll be in touch. I've gotta run. The hospital is a complete nightmare today. Everyone's all up in arms over Angel. We're short-staffed. You're not here, so I *really* gotta go. Plus, there was a guy who got stabbed, and the police are here. It's just a nightmare. If you get bored and want to do some work, come on over." With her typical laugh, returning to her usual self, she hung up.

Certain that the hospital was a disaster zone, I decided to stay far away. I still had to maintain my cover; they couldn't know that I had consulted with the FBI. I could only be an agency staff member who had come to fill in. Working in healthcare for the FBI meant being strategically placed in hospitals nationwide to gather information about ongoing crimes. It made me wonder if I had ever worked alongside FBI agents without knowing it. My thoughts drifted to Mackenzie and Heather; I wondered where they were and if they were okay. I texted Aubrey:

Hey, babe. What's the latest? My job is done here; I'll be heading home soon. Have you heard anything?

I wasn't sure what to do next. Should I start packing up the photos and information I had gathered? Should I begin packing my stuff? I felt uncertain, so I decided to lay down and rest for a bit. I had a splitting headache, and neither the shower nor the phone call with Alisondra had helped. As I lay down on the couch, intending to rest briefly, I fell asleep and woke up four hours later to my phone ringing.

Before I could even say hello, Mr. Reavis spoke, his voice anxious and stern.

"Hey, are you okay? I've been trying to text and call."

"Oh, gosh, yes. Sorry, I fell asleep. I think I'm just exhausted. What's up?"

"I wanted to let you know we got Angel down at the station. She denies all charges, of course. She's furious that she would even be considered. She insists she didn't put the insulin on the cart and claims it wasn't hers. As you've probably heard, the hospital is in an uproar. The press is here. It's a complete nightmare, which we expected. I mean, one of their own has murdered multiple people, so it has stirred up a lot of issues within the hospital. But like you, I can't wrap my head around the motive. That's what she keeps harping on—motive. Why would she kill these people? She's insulted that we would even consider that she would kill people who meant so much to her."

"I get that. I've been saying it all along. I just don't understand. What could she gain from killing these people? Unless, like you said, it's some sort of trauma or psychological revenge? Shouldn't we investigate more? Talk to people who served with her? I was looking at photos, and I noticed that Dr. DeWhite, Mr. Smith, and her dad were all in the same company. Maybe you should talk to Dr. DeWhite, just to be thorough."

"That's a good idea. Let me talk to him and see if he has any insights into why she would do this. If he served with her dad, he might have more information. By the way, I'm still trying to get results on her files, why she was discharged and the details. Hopefully, I'll have that by the end of the day. Many of those records were marked confidential by the military, and it's nearly impossible to obtain them, but I'm working on it."

"Okay, good. Let me know if there's anything I can do to

help."

"No, you've done enough. I was just venting to you. You're easy to talk to, and you know how us Southerners are. We never shut up." With a hearty laugh, we hung up.

He had reservations, just like me. No one wanted to put the wrong person in prison; no one wanted to accuse the wrong individual. Furthermore, if they had the wrong person, the deaths wouldn't stop. The fact that he and I both had the same gut-wrenching feeling—that we had the wrong person—was concerning. But with the evidence literally in front of us on the med cart, who knew?

Disappointment enveloped around me. I didn't experience the expected surge of adrenaline. Instead, I felt a dull ache in the pit of my stomach, a sickening knowing that my first case hadn't really been cracked.

Freedom

Mackenzie kept repeating, over and over, "It's her, Oh my God, Heather, it's her."

Kayleigh just sat in the back seat, piecing things together. Of course, it made perfect sense. If Layla was still alive and Krissy wanted to kill Layla, she would get them in the same place, a nice dramatic flare. She had made multiple comments that it was almost time for Layla to be disposed of.

Heather seemed to be quiet. She was processing. She was very serious and a very intense agent. Knowing they were FBI, Kayleigh absolutely understood. It all made sense now. The way they handled themselves, the terms they used, the way that Mackenzie could crack up laughing over stealing shoes, it made perfect sense.

Heather started the questions first. "So do you know where you were? Do you know how long you've been gone? I know this is a lot. I know you've been through hell. But just know that the agency has not stopped looking for you."

Her once harsh, thick tone was one of compassion now, one of camaraderie, one of sisterhood. Heather did not look at Kayleigh as an outsider now. She didn't look at her as a weak person that was just rescued. She looked at her as an equal; she admired her for her survival. Kayleigh's heart instantly softened toward Heather; that tough shell of demeanor was just a shell. Heather had a warm, gooey center like us all.

"All I know is in the very beginning I was captured by Dr. Ricardo. I'm sure you all know the story well. I was placed in some type of basement. I honestly can't tell you how long I was there. At one time I thought I was going to be rescued. I had heard gunshots and commotion, but no one ever came for me. I'm not sure how I didn't starve to death. Finally, they came and got me and I absolutely could not believe it was Krissy."

"Wait, who's Krissy?"

"The blonde you guys were talking about."

"How in the heck do you know who that is? So wait, you mean she was involved with you from the beginning? Oh my gosh, this is so confusing. I am so confused right now. I need a drink. I need a Shirley Temple, I need something." Mackenzie's personality was absolutely funny. Kayleigh couldn't help but chuckle.

"Will you shut up, Mac? Will you let her talk? I mean, good Lord, the woman's been held captive for so long, and you can't shut up, just shut up."

Heather snapped at Mackenzie. Their relationship was hilarious. You could tell they were sisters to the core. The way they barked at each other was like a 60-year-old couple that had been *married for 40 years. They went back and forth, but you knew that if anything ever happened, they would lay their life down for each other. Kayleigh missed that. That's how the friendship she and Layla had. They loved each other that much. Seeing them banter back and forth, seeing the relationship they had, their sisterhood, made tears start again. What had happened? Kayleigh used to never cry, and now she seemed like a blubbering idiot.*

"It's OK, Mackenzie. I understand it is a lot. So you know about the Body Auction? You know who I am? Krissy is actually Layla's best friend and was very deeply involved in cracking the case. Supposedly they are looking for her friend who had been a victim, so Layla has no idea that Krissy is involved."

"Oh, good Lord. So Krissy knows Layla?"

"Yep... So tell me how you guys know Layla? Why are you here, and where is Layla?"

"Well, Layla is consulting with the FBI now, and she was working undercover at a hospital in a small town in Tennessee. That's where we are, by the way, Tennessee. We're very close to Nashville. She was up here working on her first case, and someone was following her. The agency always has surveillance on her. There's a whole arm of the agency still looking into the Auction. And I know since you were captive, you really don't know what happened or what took place. And there's no way we can debrief you on all that right now. We just don't have the time. But I can

tell you that we were brought up here to also be undercover nurses to protect Layla and watch over her. The agency wanted Layla to focus on her case, and then we were supposed to focus on Layla. However, those two goobers kidnapped us and brought us here. So Krissy had figured out that we were here to protect Layla and had us removed."

"Are you kidding me, Layla, consulting with the FBI? That's absolutely ridiculous. I know you guys can't tell me all that happened. I only have one question, what happened to Dr. Ricardo? Is he still alive? I truly don't want to know all the details. You're right; I need to be debriefed. But I really want to know because if he's not dead, I've got to kill him."

Eerie silence hung in the truck before Mackenzie turned around, and their eyes met. "Girl, he's dead. He's dead, and up until recently, we thought the Body Auction was dead. We thought it had ended, but evidently not. The agency was only trying to tie up loose ends and find buyers and sellers that were left out there and try to rescue any victims, but the Auction is still continuing, and they have no idea."

"Oh, yes. Krissy had no intention of me surviving, so in her arrogance and stupidity, she word-vomited all the information. There's evidently a huge auction happening here, and I was supposed to be auctioned for organs. She was excited about making money off me, so they fattened me up and got me into selling shape

so I would look good and bring a better price. It's supposed to be happening soon. That must be when she plans on taking Layla. So we have to get there and warn Layla. Knowing her, she has no idea what's coming." Secretly, her heart skipped a beat hearing that her demon was in Hell where he belonged.

"Bless her heart. She was so focused on her first case; she had no idea people were following her, and me and Heather kept a close eye until we were nabbed. It's really not our fault. We were at a bar just hanging out. Layla was tucked in at home and fine. We came out of the bar, and these two guys grabbed us, quite embarrassing actually."

"Oh, OK well, we can't go over everything now. There's too much information to go through. We'll play catch-up later, but right now, we have gotta get to a phone. I have literally no idea where we are, and this road seems endless. We're out in the middle of nowhere. The little Asian dude did us a little favor, but his truck is about out of gas."

After about another 20 miles of talking and trying to catch up as much as they could, with a sputter and a jerk and a loud pop, the truck died. They were stranded on the side of the road in the mountains of Tennessee. They had no idea where. Luckily, it wasn't freezing cold, and this was an old hunting truck, so there were some supplies in it, but to their dismay, they had to start walking.

As the sun started coming up over the horizon, it was absolutely *beautiful. Kayleigh stopped and just stood there for a moment. She couldn't remember the last time she saw the sunrise. She couldn't remember the last time she smelled fresh air. She couldn't remember the last time she had been around people that didn't want to kill her or take her organs from her body. She was still worried for Layla, but once again, she had a feeling of euphoria. She could die right now, and at least she would die happy. Heather grabbed her hand for the first time, and they started walking.*

It was a good thing that she had been trying to work out and exercise a little bit in her tiny room because she was able to walk pretty well and keep up with Heather and Mackenzie. Heather was constantly scolding Mackenzie while Mackenzie laughed. Their banter back and forth was so entertaining; even though the mood was serious and their mission intense, it added levity to the group.

"I'm freaking starving. My fat 'a' doesn't go this long without eating."

"Oh, good Lord, Mackenzie. It's not even been 12 hours; you're not gonna starve."

"Here, guys, I have a few snacks in my little bag I packed."

Kayleigh unzipped her windbreaker and pulled out her pillowcase of goodies. An apple and a few carrots. They were very excited just to have a few bites of anything. As they continued to walk, there were no signs of life anywhere, no cars passed. This was a very secluded area of Tennessee. Eventually, they would have to come to something. All roads lead to somewhere, but time was of the essence. Some of the inclines took them forever as their thighs ached from the exertion. Finally, after about two hours, Heather said, "OK, I got to stop and sit down. Just a minute, guys. I'm worn out; we've had no sleep, I'm exhausted. My quads are killing me; you're so much taller than me. I'm having to run to keep up with you."

"OK, let's just sit and rest for a few minutes. We're going to be no good to anyone if we pass out from exhaustion. We have to be getting somewhere soon. Can anybody remember when they brought us here how long it took?"

"Yeah, I was awake. I was tied in the back of a car with the two guys. But it did seem quite a while. It was a long ride... I wonder who that Asian guy was? I mean, he helped us. I haven't even thought about him. I hope he's OK. It seemed like you stabbed him pretty badly."

"Well, he asked for it." Mac smiled. "I don't know. I don't know who he was. But we would definitely be dead meat if it wasn't for him. I hope I get to see him someday and thank him."

"So you guys didn't know him? He was not agency? I mean, why would he help us? That's very, very bizarre. Krissy runs a very tight ship. She has to be absolutely brilliant to be able to take over the body auction. She had told me that the FBI had killed everyone in charge, but I really didn't know whether to believe her or not. She *told me that the FBI had done her a favor by getting rid of the top people, but when she was talking about that, I really didn't know if it was true or if it was all a lie."*

"Well, it was true; they did take out all the top people. They thought, just like we told you a little while ago, the Auction was over, and we were just tying up loose ends. Obviously, we were wrong. Before Heather and I were taken, there was chatter about something big going down in Nashville. So now this all makes sense, but the little Asian dude? Yeah, I have no idea where he was from. He did have a nice pair of Nikes though." Laughter, always laughter with Mackenzie. This time Heather couldn't help but chuckle.

Kayleigh could see how Layla probably really liked Heather and Mackenzie. Layla just had that type of personality that she wanted to be friends with everybody, everywhere. These thoughts made Kayleigh wonder how successful she was being as an FBI consultant. Layla was very naive. She never wanted to see the bad in anyone. She always wanted to give everyone the benefit of the doubt. With that thought crossing her mind as they sat in silence, she had to ask; she had to know.

"So you guys are pretty familiar with the body auction case? So just out of curiosity, and once again, I know you can't go into every detail, it would take us forever, but did Layla's husband, Tripp, ever get arrested for being involved in the auction? Or do you guys

know?"

"I don't know. I never heard that. We're pretty up to date on all the happenings of the auction. We know the ins and outs. But as far as we know, Tripp still works the same job, and they are still happily married. He visited Layla a while back and stayed with her at her apartment that she has here. Whoa, wait, was he a suspect? Oh my gosh."

"Well, not really, but at one point we had our suspicions. He just does some weird stuff, but you know, I would have never thought Krissy would have been behind this either. I'm beginning to question my own FBI judgment at this point. Hell, I was taken captive by the main person. I fell in love with the head, had an affair, and was captured, so who am I to judge on FBI talents?" Kayleigh laughed uncomfortably.

"Well, it's OK. You couldn't have known. From what we've read and what we were told in the briefings, no one had any idea of the magnitude. These guys were great; they were calculated, and since you were captured, you have no way of knowing this. It had actually spread all over the world; multiple intelligence agencies from all over the globe have been involved in this. The Body Auction was a global operation. People want to ignore sex trafficking. People want to ignore organ harvesting. People want to ignore sexual slavery, but it is a huge industry. Women are sold daily, women are kidnapped, tortured, and handled like cattle.

People want to live in their nice suburban homes, have cookouts on their back decks, swim in their pools on weekends, and turn a blind eye to what's going on right under their noses. It is actually quite sad." For the first time, Mackenzie was not smiling but had a coldness in her eyes that gave Kayleigh a chill.

"What you guys were able to do made a difference; it probably saved hundreds of lives. But there are still plenty out there that need saving. So the FBI, CIA, and multiple agencies from other countries have joined together to try to stop this. But the problem is, a lot of our government is involved, and I mean high up government officials are part of this and know what's happening, but they are on the payroll. So don't blame yourself, girl."

Kayleigh appreciated the pep talk, but she just wanted to sit on the side of the road and find out the entirety of what had happened since she had been held. Some of the things Krissy had said made no sense to her, and now they're telling her pieces of the story. She wanted to hear exactly what happened from the moment she was taken up until right now. But she knew there was no time for that.

"Ok, ladies, break time is over; let's roll. We've got a lot of walking to do. If my calculations are right, that auction is going to take place soon. And from what we've discussed and what Krissy said, Layla is number one on that menu. So, we've got to get back. Kayleigh, get those Nikes moving, babe." Heather was already on her way up the road.

Chapter 23

Upon receiving a text from Mr. Reavis that he was questioning Dr. DeWhite, I decided to observe before my hair appointment. After much pleading, I gained permission to listen in, hidden behind two-way mirrors. It astounded me how this physician continued to exude such arrogance.

"I have absolutely no idea why that psychopath would have murdered all of those people. Why am I here? What do I have to do with any of this? You are wasting my time," he snapped, sitting at the desk with his shoulders back, hair thinning and face round. He kept spinning a gold ring on his right pinky finger. He was insufferable.

Mr. Reavis, always polite, but firm, responded to Dr. DeWhite's defiance, "We have concerns about why she would have committed these murders. As you are well aware, Doctor, you, some of the victims, Mr. Smith, and Angel's father, were all part of the same mission when you served overseas. Can you shed some light on the mission? I want to hear about Angel's father and their relationship from your perspective. Regarding motive, I suspect it might be related to PTSD and some trauma that drove her to this."

The atmosphere shifted dramatically after the question. Dr. DeWhite's demeanor transformed almost instantaneously. He slouched, his once arrogant posture replaced by one of meekness. He stopped fidgeting with his ring and placed both hands flat on the table, his head hanging low. In a blink, he appeared to be an entirely different man.

After a few minutes of uncomfortable silence, Mr. Reavis asked, "Are you okay? Do you need a moment? Can I get you some water?"

"No, thank you. I'm fine. I don't think any of those things had anything to do with what Angel did. Yes, I served with her father. Yes, I was close to him. I also served with Smith, but these events are unrelated to the current situation. I'm not allowed to discuss those missions, and you know that. Our group operated independently within the Marines, bound by secrecy. I'm sorry, I wish I could help," Dr. DeWhite's once booming voice had diminished to a meek whisper.

"I understand it's top secret. But we're puzzled about why she would do this. Do you have any idea? Please think hard. Do you know her state of mind when her dad was sick? Did you care for him? Did you care for her? We've requested her military records, but as you said, it's classified information. If there's anything you can share without violating government protocols, I would appreciate it, Doctor. We want to ensure we have the right person. If she's not the culprit, these murders could continue, and you know that," Mr. Reavis pressed.

Silence hung in the room. Dr. DeWhite avoided eye contact, his shoulders slumped, his head nearly touching the table. Finally, he spoke, "The only thing I can tell you is that her father was very sick. He suffered immensely, and it deeply affected Angel. The whole situation was horrendous, but he wasn't the only one who suffered. Everyone in our group experienced some form of trauma—mentally, physically, emotionally. We did things, things we buried deep in the recesses of our minds. Some of us cope better than others. Some survive, some don't. We were a close-knit group. You may have noticed our matching tattoos. But it feels more like a curse now. I can't look at it without remembering, and some days, I just want to forget. Forget that chapter of my life, forget about the military, forget what the government did," his voice quivered, filled with a mixture of anger and pain.

His hands, once occupied with the ring, now trembled. If Mr. Reavis had persisted, it seemed Dr. DeWhite might have broken. However, for reasons unknown, Mr. Reavis halted his inquiries, perhaps out of compassion or a sense that he had reached the limit of what he could extract. The two men shook hands, and the tense interrogation came to an end.

Dr. DeWhite, looking defeated, silently left the office.

"Why did you stop? I think you were about to make a breakthrough. He looked like he was on the verge of tears. I'm not even kidding," I interjected.

"I could see he had been through a lot. We're about the same age, and I've known him for years. I've never seen him like that. I didn't want to push him too far or cause any psychological harm. We need more details about their missions. I strongly believe Angel's murders are connected to her father's illness. If we can prove temporary insanity, it could help her case. I need to understand why she killed those people. It might be revenge, maybe for something her father experienced. I know it's not our primary responsibility to find the motive, but for my peace of mind, I need to know," Mr. Reavis explained, his voice tinged with sadness and uncertainty.

"I understand. Just let me know if you need my help further. My job here is done, and I don't want to interfere or violate any protocol. I'll be in touch before I leave town," I assured him.

"Yeah, sure. I'll keep you posted. I have to go to the hospital now. There was a man stabbed and brought into the ER, and there was another attempt on his life overnight. I can't fathom what's happening in our small town. Who would want to harm an Asian man in our hospital? I need to handle that. These incidents seem unrelated, probably gang-related or drug-related. If I require your assistance, I'll reach out. Enjoy yourself, and thanks for everything. We truly appreciate it," he said, growing increasingly erratic, his words tumbling out rapidly. He hugged me tightly, a gesture that felt both appreciative and desperate.

I felt a mix of emotions as I left Mr. Reavis and headed to the beauty shop. Excitement about my impending hair appointment warred with a sense of foreboding about the grim developments in the case. I wondered what kind of drama I would walk into at the salon. Upon entering the familiar salon, I was greeted by the usual sights and sounds—the smell of hair products, the laughter, and the chatter of the patrons. However, today, Angel's station stood empty, devoid of both her presence and customers.

Sheree, my hairstylist, welcomed me with a smile, her hands already bustling with preparations. "Hey, how are you?"

"I'm good, thanks. I need a touch-up and a trim. And a waxing, my mustache is getting out of hand," I said, trying to lighten the mood.

"Of course, I've got you covered!" Sheree responded, wrapping me in the customary plastic cape.

"Oh my God, have you heard? Have you heard what happened?" she exclaimed, her hands shaking as she mixed my hair color.

"About what?" I replied, deciding to let her share whatever information she had.

"They arrested Angel for all those awful deaths at the hospital. It's absolutely ridiculous! I knew our local police weren't great, but this is the most absurd thing I've ever heard," she said, her distress evident.

"Well, they must have had some evidence, right? They couldn't have arrested her without a reason," I reasoned, attempting to make sense of the situation.

"Believe me, there's no way Angel could have committed those murders. She's one of the most loving, dedicated people I've ever known. I've known her my entire life. The military changed her, yes, but she would never kill anyone. There must be a mistake or something. I'm just a hairdresser in a small town," Sheree insisted, her voice filled with conviction.

"I agree," chimed in a blue-haired lady from across the room, her face covered in black goo during a beauty treatment. "I've known Angel since she was in diapers, taught her in Sunday school. I warned her never to join the military. After what they did to her dad, I told her to stay away. But she went and served in the same company as my nephew, and he came back different too. He had to be hospitalized. She's not a killer. That group changed her, but she wouldn't harm anyone. They've got it all wrong, and there might just be another killing at the hospital because of it. By the way, can you trim a bit more on the top?"

The mention of the blue-haired lady's nephew, Colton, being in the same group as Angel struck me. I hadn't considered their shared military background. I quickly texted Mr. Reavis:

Hey, maybe talk to Colton. He served with Angel. He might have insights.

There was no response, probably due to his preoccupation with the hospital issues.

"Well, I heard there had been multiple deaths at the hospital, even before Angel started there. But these idiot local authorities haven't looked into that. I hate to see an innocent person go to prison," another lady in the salon remarked, her face smeared with black goo.

"Have you heard much at work?" Sheree asked me, realizing my connection with the hospital and the ongoing investigation.

"No, not really. Just that she was arrested, and they claim to have evidence. I try to stay out of it. My assignment here is over, so I'll be leaving soon. I came in for my hair because I'm attending a concert in Nashville tomorrow night. It's heartbreaking. I like Angel, and I can't imagine her doing this, but I've only known her for a short time," I shared, attempting to divert the conversation.

After an awkward silence, my phone buzzed with a text from Krissy:

OMG!!! Concert tomorrow night! I am soooo excited! Can't wait to see you!

Girl, me too! Getting my hair done now. I'll text you back in a sec.

Changing my mind, I decided to inquire further. I turned to the blue-haired lady, expressing my condolences, "I'm so sorry to hear about your nephew. How did he get hurt? Was it during a mission?"

"Oh, thank you, hon. Yes, he was badly injured, both physically and mentally. He was never the same. There's a group of military guys in our small town, acting like a cult. They have secret meetings, and they're just peculiar. None of us ladies appreciate it. That's why I told Angel not to join. But you see, her daddy loved it so much. She wanted to follow in his footsteps. She just wanted to do what her daddy did. But you see what they did to him, you see what happened to her daddy. After that, she distanced herself, dropped out. It was all a mess back then. And my nephew, he's never been right in the head since, if you catch my drift," she confided, her voice filled with concern as she shook her head and kissed her own teeth.

I was taken aback by her revelations. *"The FBI should visit local beauty shops for crime intel,*" I thought to myself. This information contradicted what we had been told. I probed further, "What exactly happened to her dad? I thought he had cancer."

"Oh, that's what they said, and he did have cancer. But do you know what caused that cancer? They had been on some type of secret mission, and it was things that he inhaled and then they made him drink something. That's what I heard anyway. I mean, you know, small town gossip, but that's what I was told. But after all that went down, they were told they couldn't talk about it at all with anyone. It wasn't long after Angel had to take care of her dad dying that she went a little bit crazy too. I mean, if you serve your country and they turn their back on you when you need it the most, it would make you go crazy. It was very sad."

Wow, I instantly regretted not coming here days ago. This is absolutely new information that we had no idea of. It actually does make Angel look 100% guilty. These were all revenge killings. Her father died from something that happened on a mission, and these men had lived, so her way of punishing them is to take them out. This definitely makes Angel confirmed in my mind because there's the motive. The mental stress of taking care of her dad, the fact that they were other survivors makes it look like this was definitely some PTSD.

"Oh, I am so sorry."

"Well, enough about that. It'll all work out. Tell me about the concert you're going to in Nashville. What are you wearing?" Sheree tries to brighten the mood.

I quickly texted the chief:

Just FYI, Angel did it. You're right, PTSD. Will update you later.

I absorbed the revelation, a mix of relief and sorrow washing over me. The pieces of the puzzle were falling into place. After quickly responding, I settled back, listening to the salon chatter—a blend of mundane gossip, jokes about avoiding the local hospital, and typical banter. Amidst the ordinary conversation, a reply to my text came in:

OK thx, tied up here, Asian has disappeared???? TTYL.

Chapter 24

After my hair had been expertly styled, I rushed home, eager to freshen up with a quick shower before meeting Alisondra for dinner. Just before heading out the door, I decided to return Krissy's call.

"Hey girl, what's up? Are you all set for the concert? I'm thrilled! Just had my hair done," I exclaimed.

"Oh my gosh, yes! I'm beyond excited too. What time do you want to meet? Should we grab dinner before? There are some fantastic restaurants near the venue. And what are you planning to wear?" Krissy's enthusiasm was contagious, and I felt a surge of joy talking to her again. I had missed her terribly, and the prospect of our reunion filled me with excitement.

"Girl, I'm up for anything. I haven't decided on my outfit yet. I'm going to visit one of my friends here, raid her closet, and figure it out. But I'm definitely wearing boots, don't worry. As for dinner, I'm fine with any place. Eating before the concert sounds perfect; I don't want to pass out midway through the show. How about this? You look up some restaurants, and I'll do the same. We can meet up and then walk over to the venue.

And are we staying in a hotel tomorrow night so we don't have to drive back?" I suggested, eager to make plans for our exciting night.

"I've got that covered already. There's a charming Airbnb close by that I've rented. So, make sure to let Tripp know we'll be at the concert and out late, so he doesn't worry unnecessarily. If you don't tell him, you know how he can get all anxious," Krissy said, her laughter echoing through the phone.

"Absolutely, I'll give him and Aubrey a heads-up right after we hang up. I might do a three-way call to get it done efficiently. You're right; if they text me and I don't respond, they tend to get nervous. I can't wait to see you! I've missed you so much, and the good news is that my assignment is over. I'll start packing up and head home in the next couple of days," I shared, the excitement evident in my voice.

"That's fantastic news! I'm counting down the hours until I see you! So, you assisted with your first case, huh?" Krissy inquired, her curiosity piqued.

"Yep, I sure did. I'm not thrilled about who it was, but at least it's over now, and I'll be heading home," I confirmed, feeling a mix of relief and accomplishment.

"Okay, let's both do some restaurant research. I'll check in with you in the morning. Love ya!" Krissy said, her voice filled with anticipation.

"Love you too, bye!" I replied, my excitement building as our conversation came to an end.

Deciding to finish getting ready, I made my way to the car and called Tripp and Aubrey. Alisondra and I had plans to meet at a quaint Mexican restaurant up the road. As I dialed, a sense of accomplishment and relief washed over me. The adrenaline I had been searching for had finally hit me. I had done well on my first case, and the information I had gathered had contributed to making an arrest.

"Hey guys! I wanted to share some good news with both of you. Are you both available to talk?" I asked, a mix of excitement and pride in my voice.

"Hey mom, hey dad, I'm here. I'm good. Are you okay?" Aubrey responded, her voice filled with concern.

"I'm here too, baby! Hey honey. I can talk, yes, but I'm in between meetings," Tripp chimed in, his voice steady and reassuring.

"Great! Well, first things first—I'm coming home! There's been an arrest, and I'll be heading out in the next couple of days!" I exclaimed, unable to contain my joy.

"Yay!" Aubrey and Tripp cheered simultaneously, their pride and happiness clear.

"I just wanted to give you guys a heads-up. Krissy's coming

up, and we're going to the Luke Combs concert tomorrow night. So, I might not have a signal inside the venue. After the concert, we'll be staying at an Airbnb nearby, so don't worry if you can't reach me overnight," I informed them, eager to share my plans.

"Oh my gosh, the Luke Combs concert! I'm so jealous. How on earth did Krissy manage to get tickets to that? It's in Nashville, right? Those tickets sold out within an hour after going on sale," Tripp said, his voice filled with awe and slight envy.

"I don't know, Dad. I told her you might be upset. But I'm just excited to have some fun and even more excited to get back home," I replied, feeling a sense of accomplishment in being able to surprise him.

"Alright, just go and have a blast, and please be careful. I can't wait to have you back home with me. Aubrey, we're thinking about planning a family vacation. Send me some dates when you can take time off work, and I'll start looking at places today. Maybe we can go back to the Virgin Islands or somewhere and have a week of solitude. Just the three of us!" Tripp suggested, his excitement palpable.

"Sure, Dad, I'll text you the dates soon. Okay, Mom, have a fantastic time. I've gotta run. I have a briefing coming up. Enjoy yourself, but stay vigilant. Remember what I told you about Nashville? I love you. Call me when you can. Have a great rest of the day, guys. Love y'all, bye," Aubrey said, her voice filled with affection and concern.

"Bye, baby, be safe!" I called out, my heart swelling with love for my daughter as the call ended.

"Aubrey mentioned something about Nashville. What's going on? What aren't you telling me?" Tripp inquired, his voice laced with worry.

"Oh, it's nothing to worry about, honey. Aubrey is just being cautious since she's in training. Big cities make her nervous, I suppose," I replied, trying to brush off the concern.

"Alright, just have fun and make sure to text me or call me when you can. I love you, baby. Text me before you go into the concert," Tripp said, his tone softening with affection.

With those words, our conversation ended. Oh how I missed them.

I eagerly pulled into the Mexican restaurant just in time. The building, painted in vibrant shades of yellow and orange, stood out boldly against the backdrop of the rural surroundings. Despite its eccentric appearance, the locals swore it was the best Mexican food in the area. Stepping inside, I found Alisondra seated at a table, nursing an obscenely large margarita that dwarfed her petite frame. She had a talent for alcohol consumption, that much was certain. As I approached, she launched into a conversation about outfit choices for the night, and I couldn't help but feel a surge of excitement. It was exactly the distraction I needed.

Nashville

After a seemingly endless amount of time, they finally arrived at an old, dilapidated service station. Kayleigh wasn't even certain if it was still operational. A single, lonely pump stood in isolation, yet a flickering "open" sign hung on the door. Upon entering, they were greeted by a frail elderly man behind the counter, sporting a warm, toothless smile. The store seemed frozen in time, resembling something out of the 1970s. Dusty shelves displayed outdated snacks, their expiration dates long forgotten. The air was thick with the stench of decaying food, mold, and mothballs, making their eyes water. Despite the grim atmosphere, there were drink machines, which immediately drew Mackenzie's attention. She hurried towards one, opened it, and started gulping down the contents. Kayleigh gently reminded her that they had no money.

"Excuse me, sir, we are in desperate need of using your phone. This is an emergency. We would also appreciate it if you could provide us with some drinks and snacks. We've had a rough night. I assure you that if you let me use your phone, I can provide you with a credit card number, and you will be fully compensated for anything we take," Heather stated assertively, her voice carrying *authority.*

"Is it a long-distance call? I ain't paying for no long-distance calls, little lady, no matter how important they may be," the elderly man responded, his thick country accent filling the air.

As they conversed, Mac leaned over, her flirtatious charm in full swing. "Hey there, honey. My name's Mackenzie. Please excuse my friend; we are utterly exhausted from a very long walk. It will be a long-distance call, but, as my friend mentioned, we'll ensure you're reimbursed and compensated for your trouble. We work with the government, and we were stranded when our car broke down over those mountains. We've been walking for a really long time, and we're tired because, you know, us women can't handle these kinds of stressful situations very well. So, we'd really appreciate it if a big, strong man like you could help out a couple of damsels in distress, okay?" Mac's statement elicited an eye roll from Heather and laughter from Kayleigh.

"Well, since you put it that way, sweetie, of course. Just make it quick, will ya? Here, you can write down those card numbers so I can enter them, and you ladies can help yourselves," the man said, handing his phone to Heather before expectorating a sizable amount of black liquid from his mouth.

"Oh, you're such a gentleman! If you were a bit younger, I might snatch you up," Mac teased, leaning over to give him a generous view of her cleavage.

Amused, Kayleigh couldn't help but laugh, while Heather, clearly unamused, ushered them to the back of the store.

"I'll call headquarters. You grab some food, and for God's sake, stop acting like an idiot," Heather scolded, jerking the phone from Mac's hand before leading the way to the back of the store, with the others following.

"Look, I'm not stupid. I know how to use what the Lord gave me. That's how women get ahead in the world. Women want to be feminists and not use the gifts they have. Well, I know how to use what I have to get my way. Why didn't it work for you? You've got a phone in your hand, just saying. Men are so simple-minded; you just have to flirt a little, tell them what they want to hear, and we always get our way. I'm not sure why you don't learn that, Heather. Just make the call," Mac declared, grabbing snacks and cracking herself up.

"You've lost your mind. I will never use my boobs to get a toothless hillbilly's phone. Now shut up and get food!" Heather snapped back, clearly irritated.

Kayleigh and Mackenzie grabbed two bags and filled them with drinks and snacks. Heather spent about five minutes on the phone with headquarters before joining them.

"Alright, I got in touch with headquarters. We're still about 90 miles away from our destination. They're sending a car. I don't think we should stay here too long. Let's take our snacks and start

walking along the highway. Maybe we'll come across a police officer who can give us a ride, but they are sending a car for us. I need to use the restroom; you guys settle the bill with our friendly cashier, and I'll meet you out front. Oh, and grab me some gummy bears, will you?" Heather instructed before heading to the restroom.

After restroom breaks and settling the bill, they resumed their journey. Down the long mountain road, they walked in silence, occasional questions about their ordeal breaking the quietude.

"Did they rescue Rhonda? Is she safe?" Kayleigh inquired, her curiosity piqued.

"Yes, she's fine. She's safe now," Heather confirmed, offering reassurance.

Mackenzie draped her arm around Kayleigh. "You're a survivor, Kayleigh. You're one of the strongest people I've ever met. I know you've been through hell, but you're going to be fine. You're with us now, and we won't let anything happen to you. You saved our lives."

As they continued their silent walk, Kayleigh couldn't help but marvel at the dense woods surrounding them, wondering how far they had truly come from the ominous building that had held them captive.

"Hey guys, Krissy will likely send people to search for us soon. There probably aren't many roads in and out of that place. I'm not sure if we should just be walking on the road like this. Perhaps,

when we hear a car approaching, we should run into the woods. I don't think it's safe for us to be here in the middle of the road," Kayleigh suggested, her concern evident.

"Yeah, you're right. When she arrives, sees that her henchman is dead, and the little Asian dude is missing, and we're nowhere to be found, all hell will break loose. She'll send others to look for us. Let's walk on the side of the road. We should meet our car in a couple of hours, and we all know what an FBI vehicle looks like," Heather concurred, her voice determined.

They adjusted their path, walking along the edge of the road toward the woods. Being on the lookout for the typical black SUV, they knew they would be able to hear a car approaching from miles away, allowing them to assess the situation before it reached them.

Silence enveloped them once again, broken only by the sounds of chirping birds, rustling leaves, and occasional gusts of wind through the woods. As the sun rose, the temperature climbed, and with the exertion of walking, it began to feel warm. Kayleigh's insulated wind suit made her sweat profusely at that point.

Hours passed, during which they engaged in sporadic conversation. Kayleigh, feeling a mix of relief and anxiety, found solace in being out in the open, away from the confines of a room with four walls and a door.

Mackenzie was the first to hear it—the sound of a car approaching. They swiftly retreated from the road, taking cover in *the woods. Fortunately, the car was navigating a curve, granting them a clear view from a distance. It appeared to be some sort of security vehicle, not exactly a police car, but possibly belonging to a security guard. Assessing the situation, they decided Heather should step out first and attempt to stop the vehicle, ensuring it was safe before they revealed themselves.*

Heather cautiously emerged onto the road, waving her arms to halt the approaching car. As it slowed to a stop, Mackenzie and Kayleigh watched from the woods. Mackenzie reached into her back pocket and pulled out a large hunting knife.

"Where in the world did you find that?" Kayleigh asked, surprised.

"I found it in that truck," Mackenzie replied, eliciting a giggle from Kayleigh.

As they observed intently, Heather approached the car with great caution, only to stop abruptly, her mouth hanging open in shock. Recognizing her tension, Mackenzie prepared to jump out of the woods. Kayleigh grabbed her arm, urging caution.

"Wait a minute, hold on. We don't know what's up there; just wait," Kayleigh cautioned, concerned for their safety.

After a few moments, Heather turned back and motioned for them to approach the car. They approached warily, and Kayleigh couldn't believe her eyes. It was the little Asian man, his face contorted with concern. He looked pale, sickly.

"Hurry, get in. We don't have much time. They'll be looking for you. We've got to go NOW!" he urged urgently.

The three women scrambled into the car. Making a U-turn, he sped down the mountain road. Once inside the vehicle, they realized it was a hospital security car.

"Dude, did you break out of the hospital and steal this security car?" Mackenzie questioned, her curiosity piqued.

"I had to. She already sent someone to kill me. I had to get out and reach you. I'm fine," he replied, his eyes focused on the road ahead.

For the first time, Kayleigh had a good look at him. He was small, with a thick Asian accent that made it hard to understand him at times. Despite the winding mountain curves, he navigated the car with an alarming speed, driving unlike any ordinary person would.

"Okay, who are you? Why did you help us? Where are you from? How are you involved in all this? You need to start talking, because right now, I'm not sure if we're safe in this car with you," Kayleigh demanded, surprised to hear her own voice carrying the weight of authority again.

"I understand you're all confused. Please, allow me to introduce myself. I am Lam. I work for the State Security Ministry in China. I was brought here by the CIA to assist with this case. As you know, the Body Auction operation has spread across multiple countries,

and China was involved. The Chinese government learned that several young women were sold into the auction, shipped to the states, and resold here," Lam explained, his eyes flicking between the road and the rearview mirror.

"It's been a major embarrassment for our country, bringing dishonor upon us. I managed to infiltrate the inner circle of the auction and worked undercover. The plan was to hold another auction in Nashville, as you might have figured out. When Krissy discovered Layla's intended location, the entire operation was relocated to Nashville. She can't let it go. She must have Layla at any cost. When your FBI discovered that my partner, Jody, and I were following her, they sent these two agents, Heather and Mackenzie. Krissy ordered us to kill both of you. But fortunately, you were both quite attractive, so I used that to persuade her to include you in the auction. That bought me more time to devise a plan to rescue you. The FBI knows something's amiss. They know wealthy individuals have been pouring into Nashville over the past few weeks, so they are aware," Lam explained, steering the car with unwavering determination.

Infuriated, Heather chimed in, her face etched with anger. "Why weren't we informed? We were agents sent there to protect Layla. Why weren't we told about the auction? I'm furious."

"Only a handful of people within the FBI were aware of the upcoming auction. They had to be extremely cautious about *sharing the information, suspecting a mole within the bureau. Somehow, information keeps leaking out. So, only a select few have access to any details about the auction. Agents from multiple countries have infiltrated the group, which has been invaluable. I'm here to assist you, to help Layla, but most importantly, I'm here to put an end to this evil organization," Lam clarified, his voice resolute.*

"I can't believe this. We should have known. It would have been immensely helpful if we had been informed about what was happening. Why do they think there's a mole in the FBI? That's preposterous. They've invested so much time and resources in finding Kayleigh. Please, for the love of God, slow down!" Heather pleaded, her tone filled with desperation.

Gradually easing off the gas pedal, Lam took a deep breath as the color drained from Heather's face. She went from a pale shade of pinkish-green to ghostly white.

"I'm so sorry; I didn't realize the complexities of your government, your CIA, or FBI. I can't provide you with that information. There seems to be animosity between your agencies, a situation we don't have in China. Our citizens are highly vigilant, and we have the State Security Ministry. The way our government functions is vastly different from yours. I'm not privy to your government's intelligence. I only know what I've been briefed on. They didn't initially bring me to the United States for this case.

I was wrapping up a personal family tragedy investigation when they asked me to stay and assist before returning home," Lam explained, his voice calm despite the gravity of the situation.

Mackenzie, being herself, reached over and touched his arm. "Well, we're really glad you're here, dude. You saved our lives. We owe you."

"I can tell you what you owe me. A pair of Nikes. Those were my favorites!" Lam quipped, and the car filled with laughter. Kayleigh looked at the shoes, feeling immense gratitude for those seemingly ordinary sneakers.

"Do you know where Layla is now?" Kayleigh asked, her voice steady despite her underlying anxiety.

"No, I don't. But that's where we're headed–to find her," Lam replied, his eyes focused on the road.

"I called headquarters, and they're sending a car for us," Heather added, seeking reassurance.

Lam's expression shifted, his face contorting with concern. He slowed the car, practically turning to face Heather. "Wait, who did you call? And did you mention that you have Kayleigh with you?"

Heather's face drained of color once again. "Yes, of course I did. I didn't know I wasn't supposed to. I mean, the agency has been searching for her for so long. I thought everyone would be thrilled that we found her. Oh my God, what have I done?"

Without a word, the gas pedal was to the floor. Kayleigh

wasn't sure it was the curves or the new information, but Heather vomited all of her snacks into the small bag. Her hands shaking. For the first time, she saw fear radiate from Heather.

Kayleigh wasn't scared though, she was ready. She was ready for it to be over. And what was worse, she actually wanted to kill someone; she needed to kill someone--she needed to kill Krissy. She had to be the one.

Chapter 25

Alisondra's house struck me with its perfection, just as I had anticipated. Every corner gleamed in pristine white, meticulously decorated to an immaculate standard. We indulged in a meal of margaritas and light conversation, granting me a temporary escape from the looming hospital situation, which remained unspoken.

In her expansive walk-in closet, meticulously color-coordinated, I discovered an unexpected array of revealing outfits. "Good grief, you dress like a hooker!" I exclaimed, and we shared hearty laughter at her bold fashion choices. "Well," she retorted with a smirk, "my motto is, if you got it, show it to the world!"

My eyes widened as I pulled out a pair of stunning Lucchese boots–light beige with delicate crystals adorning the sides. They seemed to be worth a fortune. "Oh my, I love these. Are you sure?" I questioned, to which she replied, "Of course! Now, let's find a shirt. Do you have a jean mini skirt?"

"No, I didn't bring my whole closet for a travel gig," I explained. Alisondra surprised me again by producing a bag containing a perfect jean mini skirt. "I guessed your size. I hope it fits. Here, try this shirt with it," she said, her generosity touching my heart.

"You shouldn't have done that. I'll pay you. Thank you so much," I insisted, but she waved off my offer. "No, it's my gift. You've been a great friend, and I hate to see you leave. I wish I could convince you to relocate, but I understand you won't. Just promise you'll visit!" Tears welled up in her impeccably lined eyes as she spoke.

Overwhelmed with gratitude, I embraced her tightly. I would miss her, quirks and all. Trying on my new ensemble– the skirt, the shirt, and those exquisite boots–I gazed at my reflection in the mirror. With my new hair and makeup, I felt undeniably fabulous.

"Oh, girl! You look amazing! For your age, you are pretty hot," Alisondra complimented, making me giggle in response. "Sorry, that sounded bad. I just hope I look like you when I'm old. Oh crap, there I go again."

"Yeah, stop while you're ahead," I teased, laughter bubbling between us. "I think this is the outfit. Thank you so much. I love it. My friend Krissy will go crazy about it. You'd like her. I hope you meet someday."

"Is she a ho like me?" Alisondra inquired bemused by her own joke.

"No, no. She's very conservative, quiet, almost meek. She doesn't have a bad-girl bone in her body," I replied, defending Krissy's character.

"Nope, I wouldn't like her. Ok, well, I hate to cut this girls' night short, but I have a booty call," Alisondra chimed in, steering the conversation in a different direction.

"Oh, with Colton?" I questioned, trying to glean more information about her complicated relationship.

"Yeah, I'm just going to watch a movie and hang out," she responded casually. "Y'all seem more serious than you admit. Why the secrets?"

Before I could answer, I began putting the boots back in their box and hanging the shirt and skirt. As I stood up, my eyes drifted to the end rack in the closet, where something caught my attention–a black hoodie and black leggings.

While Alisondra continued speaking, I couldn't help but fixate on the black section of her closet. "Well, we have a long history. He's a great guy, but he got messed up in the military. I love him, though. You know he had a thing with Angel for a little while," Alisondra shared, drawing me back into her narrative.

"No, really? What happened, and when was that? Is that why you guys don't get along?" I asked, intrigued by the unexpected revelation.

"No, we've always hated each other since kindergarten. But Colton and her were in the military together, and they were close. He was close to her dad too. She was there for him when he had mental issues. I don't know the details, and that pisses me off even more. Military, confidential bull crap drives me crazy. I can get him so drunk he can't even stand up, but he won't tell me what happened. But anyway, I guess I don't have to worry about her anymore. She is going to fry!" Alisondra said, her giggle escalating into full blown laughter. It was actually kind of sick. Why did I like this woman?

"OK, well, on that note, I'll head home. I'll call you and bring your stuff back ASAP! Thanks again." After exchanging hugs, I left. My plans were to return and start packing things up.

Upon arriving, I decided to check on Mr. Reavis. It was getting late, so I went around back. Walking there, I noticed the backyard was very dark, so I hurried inside.

He was seated on a chaise in the corner, eyes closed. Was he asleep? I quietly approached the boards to see if there was anything new.

"What's up?"

"Oh gosh, did I wake you? I am sorry."

"No, just resting my eyes."

"How are things? Anything new?"

"No, not really. The Asian dude disappeared, so no idea

what's up with that. Angel refuses to talk and lawyered up, of course, with some fancy guy who knew her dad. They refuse to even make a deal. I asked her if she wanted to see a psychiatrist."

"How did that go?"

"Oh, she came unglued at that. I actually thought she was gonna slap me in the face. Said I was looking in the wrong place and other people would die because of it. What did your texts mean? What did you find out?"

"Well, I had a hair appointment, and you know women."

"Oh dear Lord..."

Laughing, I continued. "Colton's Aunt was there and had verbal diarrhea. She said that Angel's dad had cancer because of something he was exposed to on a mission. That the other guys survived and he didn't. Angel took it all very hard. Was very bitter and angry and hated the military group because of it. Felt like they turned their back on her dad after all he did for them. She rambled on about how that group was crazy and made them all insane. But hey, it makes sense. She has it out for the survivors. Like I texted, PTSD."

Pulling his cap back, he scratched his head as if contemplating what I had said. "Yeah, it sure does. But still..."

"What? What are your reservations now? We have a why, a how, and the evidence. Were her fingerprints on the bottle of insulin?"

"Yep."

"OK, well, the case is closed. Stop overthinking this. Will they set bail?"

"No bail. Because she is a flight risk, her military background, and the nature of the crimes. She will be moved to the women's prison in a few days."

"Well, OK, I'm heading up to start cleaning my stuff up. I will be gone tomorrow, but I will see you before I head home. Get some rest!"

"You too, goodnight."

Ascending the stairs, I felt a peculiar heaviness in my chest, a sense of melancholy settling in. It was almost over, and I knew I would miss these people dearly. Upon entering my apartment, I abandoned my plans to pack and instead sat like a lump, my thoughts swirling with an undeniable state of uneasiness.

Unable to shake off the nagging feeling, I hastily changed into comfortable clothes and rushed outside in my bare feet and pajamas. Mr. Reavis remained seated in the same spot, but he leaped up in surprise when I flung the door open.

I hurried to the table where I had worked the previous days, frantically sifting through photos. Finally, I found it–the photo that had caught my eye a few days ago. Holding it up alongside another photo, my eyes widened with realization.

"What in the Sam Hill are you doing?" Mr. Reavis questioned, perplexed by my sudden urgency.

"Look at this, look at this photo of Colton's battalion, then look at Marvin... they look just alike," I exclaimed, desperation tainting my voice.

"So, what's your point? That's not a shock. That's his son," he replied, his words punctuated with a touch of sadness.

"His *son*? How did I not know that Marvin had a son? How was I never told that?" I gasped, shocked by this newfound revelation.

"Well, probably because it had nothing to do with the case. He was in that same unit, but he was killed in the line of duty. They went out on a mission and he never came back. It broke the old man's heart. I think that's why he does the little flags. But no one ever really talks about it. Colton and him were like brothers. They've always been best friends since they were little kids. His name was Bailey. You couldn't ask for a better kid who grew into a great man. It devastated the whole town," Mr. Reavis explained, his voice tinged with sorrow.

"Wow, that's a lot, a lot that I didn't know," I murmured, my mind reeling from the revelation.

"Like I said, it was not relevant to the case," he reiterated, emphasizing the irrelevance of the information in our investigation.

"Was Angel there when he died? Did he die from injuries or literally on a mission?" I pressed, seeking closure on this newfound piece of the puzzle.

"I really don't know the details. As you know, getting any details is almost impossible," Mr. Reavis replied, his frustration evident.

"Okay, well, I guess you're right. It had nothing to do with the case. I just feel like I should have known it. Well anyway, goodnight," I said, my voice trailing off as I retreated back to my apartment.

"Goodnight, *again*," he responded, his tone carrying a hint of irritation.

Alone in my apartment, I couldn't bring myself to pack. Instead, I sat there, staring at my box of belongings, lost in my thoughts.

Chapter 26

The drive from my little town to the restaurant spanned over two hours. I hadn't anticipated the journey being quite so long, but it was tolerable. On the way, I encountered some road work, necessitating a detour. With nothing else to occupy my time, I opted to take the detour in stride. My mood didn't lend itself to packing, so I spent the morning meticulously preparing myself. I was on my way to meet Krissy at Luke's 32 Bridge, a fantastic bar and hangout spot to gear up for the concert. I felt a surge of excitement, not just because I would be seeing Krissy, but also because I would finally get to experience Luke Combs live. I remembered how he had just started out when he used to perform at Appalachian State. Aubrey and her friends used to watch him at a tiny bar when he was still relatively unknown. Despite his newfound fame, he still appeared humble.

I endeavored to clear my mind of the events of the past few days. After revisiting the details the prior night, I found myself once again questioning Angel's involvement. However, after a restful night's sleep, I had reached the same conclusion: it *had* to be her. I needed to put my doubts to rest.

A lingering sense of Mr. Reavis's discontent with me nagged at my conscience. As I attempted to bid him farewell before leaving, he was engrossed in a phone conversation and brushed me off with a swat, so dismissively that I was irritated as I started to drive away. But as I was about to pull out, I noticed him in my rearview mirror, gesturing frantically. He seemed to be running towards me, trying to convey a goodbye. His gesture was sweet and endearing; I waved back with a smile and sped off.

Navigating the bustling streets of Nashville proved to be a challenge, with the traffic crawling at an exasperating pace. Eventually, I managed to find public parking and took a moment to freshen up my makeup. I sent out texts to Tripp and Aubrey, informing them of my arrival and apologizing for the delay, promising to call them the next day. I also messaged Krissy, asking if she had arrived yet and letting her know that I was on my way to the bar.

Walking in boots was a cumbersome task; they pinched my feet, hindering my pace. Despite the discomfort, I felt a surge of confidence–I looked good, and that was all that mattered. Since Krissy hadn't replied yet, I took the opportunity to snap some pictures, including a few selfies.

Standing in front of the bar's entrance, I adjusted my hair and captured a few more photos. Once satisfied with a shot, I sent it to Tripp and Aubrey. Suddenly, I felt a strong grip around my waist, nearly causing me to scream. Turning around, I saw Krissy and squealed instead.

"Oh, my gosh! It is so good to see you," I exclaimed, relief washing over me as I hugged her tightly.

Our embrace lingered for a moment longer than usual, a testament to the depth of my genuine affection for my friend. Krissy looked stunning as always, her beauty manifesting in a different way than Alisondra's. Despite being fully clothed, she exuded sensuality. She wore a blue jean mini dress–not too short, but just short enough to highlight her curves. Her outfit, completed with pink lips, matching nails, and rhinestone-studded cowboy boots, made her resemble a country music star. I had felt confident about my appearance until I saw her.

"You look gorgeous!" Krissy complimented, her eyes shining with genuine admiration.

"So do you. I've missed you so much. I'm so glad we're here. This is going to be a great night," I replied, smiling as we held hands and entered the bar together.

We spent the next couple of hours engrossed in conversation, catching up on each other's lives. Krissy had been working long hours, and there was still no news about

Kayleigh. I updated her on my case, although the loud music made it challenging for her to hear me clearly.

Finally, we made our way to the concert venue. It was an unforgettable experience. Luke Combs's performance was mesmerizing, with hundreds of people dancing and singing along. Surrounded by the joyous energy of the crowd, I couldn't help but feel ecstatic. When Krissy went to get us drinks, she missed my favorite song. Undeterred, I stood there, singing along at the top of my lungs.

After the song ended, I felt parched from all the singing. I eagerly gulped down the fruity drink Krissy handed me. "What is this? It's delicious!" I exclaimed, savoring the sweet taste.

"It's a Shirley Temple, virgin, of course," Krissy replied, her understanding and support evident in her choice of drink.

That was one of the things I loved most about Krissy–her acceptance of my choice not to drink. Unlike some of my other friends, she had never pressured me or made fun of me for abstaining from alcohol.

As the night wore on, we continued dancing, fueled by the delectable fruity drinks. Sweat poured off me, and I began to feel lightheaded. The room, hot and crowded, seemed to spin around me. At first, I attributed it to exhaustion from dancing, but the dizziness grew more pronounced. I clung to Krissy's arm for support, my words slurring as I tried to speak.

"I don't know. I feel really dizzy. Are you sure that drink was a virgin?" I managed to say, my speech barely coherent at this point.

Minutes passed, and my legs grew increasingly unsteady. Krissy was talking to a tall, hairy man beside her, desperation etched on her face. "Excuse me, sir, can you help me get my friend outside? She's not feeling well, and I don't have the strength to hold her up."

The man's hairy arms encircled my waist as he practically carried me out of the concert venue. I felt wretched, my condition worsening in the cool night air. Despite the chill, my eyes refused to stay open.

"I'm so sorry. I don't know what's wrong with me," I mumbled, my words barely intelligible by this point.

Krissy's expression was intense, it looked like a mix of concern and something unfamiliar, maybe fear? I saw her speaking to the man, but the roaring in my ears drowned out their words. Fear and regret filled me–I had ruined our night, and I couldn't understand what was happening to me.

I had never felt that way before, except once... back when... Darkness engulfed me, shrouding me in its embrace.

Layla

The car sped around the sharp curves, a sense of intensity, anticipation, and anxiety permeating the vehicle like the lingering smoke from a stale cigar. The atmosphere was thick with tension, pressing down on them. Despite Kayleigh's attempt to alleviate the unease by rolling down the window, the oppressive atmosphere persisted. She was the first to break the heavy silence.

"Okay, guys, everything is fine. What are you so worried about, Lam? I mean, I am with you guys. Are you concerned about those corrupt agents you mentioned?" Kayleigh asked, trying to infuse some reassurance into the situation.

"I don't know who I can trust anymore. I've only dealt with a couple of agents, and my handler was very specific about keeping everything confidential. There are so many people involved, from politicians and FBI agents to local police departments. I just want to get you safe and find Layla," Lam replied, his voice laden with concern and uncertainty.

"She's right. We'll stick together, and everything will be okay. We need some phones and a weapon. Why don't we just get a phone and call Layla? Wouldn't that be the smartest move?

She's intelligent, and if we tell her what's going on, she can protect herself," Mac interjected, attempting to inject a glimmer of optimism into the conversation.

"I noticed a small store about an hour from here. We can stop there and get a couple of burner phones. Getting a gun, well, that will be more challenging," Lam suggested, focusing on finding a practical solution.

For the next hour, silence enveloped the car as they continued their journey. Heather finally broke her silence when the store came into view.

"Y'all get the phones. I need to rinse my mouth out and use the restroom. I'll be quick," Heather announced, her sense of urgency apparent.

"Are you okay, babe? Do you want me to come with you?" Mac offered, concern etched across her face.

"No, Mac, I'm fine. I'll be right back," Heather reassured her, stepping out of the car.

Stretching her legs felt refreshing as they waited for Lam to return from the store.

"Hey, is Heather okay?" Kayleigh inquired, noticing Mac's worried expression.

Mac smiled, attempting to dispel the tension. "Yeah, she's fine. She just gets intense before things happen. She'll be alright."

Lam emerged from the store, accompanied by Heather, who

carried a burner phone. "Okay, Mac, you call Layla. It's getting late. I hope you can get her to answer. Be vague, just tell her to get to the police station and stay put. Don't reveal too much. We're on our way," Lam instructed, handing Mac the phone.

Mac nodded, her determination evident as she dialed Layla's number repeatedly. No answer.

"She's not picking up. I'll call Mr. Reavis," Mac announced, frustration creeping into her voice as she reached for her phone.

They all stood watching, their hope resting on Mac's conversation with Mr. Reavis. A smile broke across her face, indicating that he had answered the call.

"Hey, Mr. Reavis? It's Mackenzie, with the FBI. I was one of the agents on the detail for Layla Matthews. Yes, sir, we are fine, now anyway. Yeah, we were grabbed... that's a long story..."

Heather grew impatient, signaling for Mackenzie to hurry up. Layla's safety was at stake, and they needed to move.

"Sir... yes, sir... if I may interrupt, sir, I need to tell you something important. I know you are always in contact with Layla. You need to get her and take her somewhere safe and secure. I mean very secure. They are coming for her soon, probably today... Hello? Mr. Reavis? Are you there?" Mackenzie's face showed confusion and frustration.

"What happened? What was that about?" Lam asked, clearly irritated.

"Well, first of all, he wouldn't shut up, asking a hundred questions about what happened to us and where we had been and how worried they were, blah blah blah. Then when I was finally able to speak, he said, 'Oh crap, hold on.' Then I heard him running and yelling Layla's name. Then he was gone."

The phone rang.

"Mr. Reavis? Yes... Oh, I see. Ok, great, we are on our way to you. Please keep this confidential; we have been informed we have a mole. Yes, sir. See you soon!" Mac hung up and turned to the others before continuing, "Well, she was driving away when I called; Mr.Reavis tried to run after her, but she didn't stop. He has a tracker on her car, and he will follow her and get her. We are to meet at his house. He has tried to call her also, but she isn't picking up. He did say the signal is sketchy in the mountains."

"Ok, let's go, we still have a while to get there," Kayleigh interjected, urgent to ensure Layla's safety. Refreshed and more optimistic than they had been mere moments prior, they were back on the road.

The bumpy cadence of the old road was soothing. The phone rang again and Mac picked up. Putting it on speaker, she spoke up,"Hey, Mr. Reavis, go ahead, I have you on speaker so my partners can hear. Is Layla with you and safe?"

"I am afraid not. Someone has removed the tracker from her car, and she's not answering her phone. She was going to Nashville

for a concert. She is with her best friend from back home. Christy maybe? Kristina? Anyway, she should be okay if she's not alone, right?" His voice betrayed his uncertainty.

"What?" Lam's booming response startled Mac, and she almost dropped the phone.

"Who is that?" Mr. Reavis's confusion amplified.

"Long story." Heather said as she took the phone. "Ok, Mr. Reavis, listen, you need to do just as I tell you, fast. Call the Nashville FBI and have them dispatched to the concert venue. They need to find her, now. They need to be discreet. The lady she is with, Krissy, is extremely dangerous and almost certainly armed. Krissy will likely have her team around her also, blending in, and they will also be armed. This is a very volatile situation. Time is of the essence; they cannot, under any circumstances, let Layla leave with her."

"Ok, I have so many questions, but clearly, there's no time for that. I will call now. I feel terrible; I had no idea she was in danger. I never would have let her leave" His tone mimicked that of a worried father.

"It's not your fault; there's no way you could have known. Make the call, now." Heather offered little comfort for the old man and hung up the phone abruptly. There was bloated silence in the car for a second before she spoke again, "We need to prepare for the worst."

"What do you mean?" Mac questioned, her eyebrows knitting together.

"Lam, pull the car over. We need to regroup before we go any further, pull into the woods where we won't be seen." Doing as he was instructed, Lam pulled the car off the road and maneuvered as far into the trees as he safely could.

"Alright, spill it. What do you know?" Mac's demeanor shifted.

"Well, we know that they probably have Layla by now. Krissy has the upper hand. Losing us was inconvenient, but her main focus tonight is that auction and getting rid of Layla. She will proceed as planned; we can be sure of that. She has no idea how much we know. She's got millions on the line. That will be her priority. We need to know where she'll keep the victims. Think. Because, that is where we need to go; we won't save her sitting in an old man's basement. Where will the auction be held? Do you have any ideas?"

Lam's eyes brightened, rejuvenated. "Yes, yes you are absolutely correct. Let's go find her. And I have an idea where all this will be, yes. I was never informed specifically, but I overheard talk of a luxury camp hidden outside the city; large luxury cabins used by wealthy people so they can have a 'taste of nature'. Yes, I remember mention of a restaurant and a clubhouse and conference hall. There were maps and staff lists in the office a few weeks ago, I didn't make the connection right away. That must be right. Krissy has replaced the staff with her own people. If I had to guess, the auction will take place tomorrow."

"That's it! That's got to be it! That's where they will be, and if there is indeed a mole, they will expect us back at Mr. Reavis's, which is precisely why we aren't going there!" Mac was almost screaming with excitement.

"I don't mean to be Debbie Downer, but how do you plan on finding this place?" Kayleigh, not sure of the plan. "I mean we have no GPS, no decent phone, and most of all, no weapons."

"You are right, but I can call my FBI contact, the one I trust and ask him to trace my location with the burner. He should be able to locate the camp on an aerial map based on the general location I can give him from my memory, and then meet us there. He will keep secure. I know he will." Lam reached for the phone before he finished his sentence.

"Ok, go for it... that's the best option we have at this point." Heathers voice with a tinge of anxiety. "Just hurry."

"Do you think Krissy would kill Layla before the auction? Layla has cost her so much. She's a liability." Kayleigh voiced her concerns aloud. They all looked at one another, considering the gut churning possibility.

As they were waiting for Lam to be connected to his contact, two black SUVs flew past... FBI vehicles.

"There go our guys, are you sure we can't trust them? I mean, *that would solve our problems right now." Mackenzie with urgency, looking as if she was going to jump from the car, still finding it hard to believe there would be a mole in her beloved Bureau.*

"No, no we cannot, especially with Kayleigh with us. It's not safe. We are not safe, I need you to trust me!" Lam almost shouted.

"She's got a point. We don't really know you do we? What if you're still working with Krissy and taking us on a wild goose chase? What if you're leading us to our own deaths? How do we know that our salvation didn't just drive by? Tell us why we should trust you over our own people?" Heather stern, eyes hard and voice firm.

"You have no reason to trust me. None at all. If you want to take your chances and follow them, tell me, and I will follow. But know, you are putting us all in danger."

The only sound was their breathing and the rustle of leaves outside the car. An impasse. A crossroad between trust and mistrust.

"Hand me that phone. Have you all forgotten that I am FBI?" They all stared at Kayleigh. "Hand me the phone. Now!" Lam blinked once and passed the phone to Kayleigh.

Dialing a number, they all sat silent, they had underestimated Kayleigh.

"Yes... I need to be connected to Aubrey Matthews, it is urgent," Kayleigh stated with authority, her resolve evident.

Chapter 27

I despise recurring dreams. Since the auction, I have often found myself trapped in the same nightmarish loop, plagued by these tormenting visions. Thanks to my therapist, I learned coping mechanisms to prevent full-blown panic attacks that used to strike me a few times a week. As I realized I was once again ensnared in the clutches of a familiar nightmare, I kept my eyes shut, practicing deep breathing to calm my racing heart. "Layla, you are safe. This is just a dream," I repeat to myself like a mantra.

After several cleansing breaths, I managed to open my eyes. This morning's dream had been unusually vivid; the coldness on my bare back had felt chillingly real. Despite my disoriented state, I forced myself to focus. I was in a large room, but the walls were not sterile; they were constructed of massive logs. Logs? Confusion flooded my mind. Where was I? This wasn't a dream.

"Hello? Hello?" My voice was feeble and hoarse.

My heart pounded in my chest, the sound resonating in my ears. I realized my arms were bound tightly at my sides. Panic seeped in as I assessed my situation. After struggling to clear my thoughts, I finally managed to observe my surroundings. The room was expansive, its walls made of rough-hewn logs. I was baffled, wondering about the location.

This was *not* a dream.

My mind struggled to piece the memory together. Krissy and I had been at the concert, dancing. I felt dizzy, and Krissy had grown concerned. Oh, my God, my Lord, Krissy! *Help Lord*! My heart cried out in prayer. My heart ached for my friend. How had they found me? But Krissy, dear Krissy, she wouldn't have the strength to endure this ordeal.

Hot tears streamed down my face. The warmth was oddly comforting. I screamed out, louder this time. "Hello, who's here? I know you can hear me. Summon the courage to face me! Let her go. You want me, not her!"

Someone had drugged me at the concert; that meant they had her too. But where were we? The FBI had been monitoring the situation. Aubrey had warned me about something happening in Nashville. Why hadn't I heeded the warning? I had been too engrossed in my role as an pretend agent. How stupid. Who? Why?

I struggled to free myself from my restraints, but they held firm. This place was peculiar. As my mind cleared, I noticed the surrounding oddity. It was a vast room with log walls, devoid of furniture. The earthy scent of wood filled the air. Preserved animals adorned the walls, once magnificent creatures now lifeless ornaments. A photograph of a mountain range hung on one wall, contrasting sharply with the grand rock fireplace on the opposite side. Silence reigned, the house eerily quiet. Hours seemed to pass, and I must have drifted to sleep. Suddenly, the sound of voices jolted me awake.

"Hello, hello... someone answer me, please."

No one responded.

Finally, two tall men entered the room. "Well, look who's awake. Did you enjoy your nap?" The very tall man, dressed in a suit, approached and caressed my cheek. His breath reeked of vodka and cheap aftershave.

"Don't touch me, you creep! Where am I? Where is my friend? What have you done to her? I swear, if you've harmed her, you're dead. The FBI will be here soon!" I exclaimed, my defiance undeterred.

Laughing, he continued stroking my cheek. In a swift movement, he slapped me so hard my ears rang. "Don't worry about your friend. You need to worry about yourself," the other man interjected, his accent barely discernible, possibly Peruvian.

"We're bringing you some company; don't worry, you won't be lonely for long," he added, before they both burst into laughter and exited the room.

Soon, the large doors on the opposite side creaked open, revealing people approaching from outside. I continued to shout, but my cries fell on deaf ears or were deliberately ignored. Finally, the two men wheeled in tables like mine, some with women and, to my surprise, a few young men. I felt embarrassed seeing them naked and vulnerable.

"You've *got* to be kidding me. *Another* auction? How is this even possible? The FBI shut this down. What in the world is happening?" Did I just say that out loud? Yes, I did, though my words were weak. My voice echoed my disbelief.

Oddly, I felt the subtle sensation of indifference wash over me. This would mark my third time in such a nightmarish scenario. My psyche shifted into a place of understanding and familiarity. I had become a seasoned expert. Body after body rolled in, devoid of movement. The men seemed unfazed by my outrage and attempts to struggle, occasionally patting my head or winking at me. Their humming and carefree demeanor juxtaposed the gravity of the situation. They were seemingly content, happily living their lives as part of this grotesque world.

Finally, the deliveries ceased, and the door closed, enveloping the room in silence. My neck ached from my desperate attempts to survey my surroundings. To my right, there were five women, a stark contrast to the previous auctions. These women didn't fit the stringent criteria of youth, fitness, and beauty. One of them, a blond woman with unkempt hair and acne, lay snoring on the table, her figure far from the previous standards. The next woman was Latina, young, and stunning–a perfect contrast to the others. As I glanced around, I counted approximately fifteen tables, each with varying shapes and sizes. There were five men, seemingly plucked from the previous auctions, young and muscular, one white man and the rest Latino or black. Their youth, their young bodies exposed in this vulnerable state, made me flush with embarrassment.

Panic attempted to consume me, but I suppressed it with the assurance that the FBI must be aware of this ongoing horror. I attempted to awaken my fellow captives. I could see that some of their restraints appeared fairly loose, and they might have a chance to escape.

"Hey, wake up! Wake up!" I implored, trying to shake my body and kick, but there was no response. Whatever sedative that had been administered had left them nearly lifeless. The room remained eerily quiet except for the snoring woman, who,in truth, sounded like a grizzly bear. I couldn't help myself, my NP brain kicking in. She needed a sleep study. I resolved to suggest a sleep study if we survived the ordeal.

Time stretched on, and I succumbed to sleep.

I was roused once more, this time by Krissy, who hovered over me, whispering urgently.

"Layla, Layla, wake up! We have to go!" she pleaded, attempting to free me from my restraints.

"Oh my God, Krissy, are you okay? I'm so sorry you got dragged into this. We'll be alright. The FBI is on their way. Untie me!" I urged her, my desperation mounting.

"I know, I'm trying. We have to hurry and get out. Oh my gosh, Layla, what's happening?" Krissy's voice trembled with fear.

Just as the door opened, I heard Krissy gasp. I screamed, "Please don't hurt her! Please, don't hurt her!"

Tears streamed like rivers down my face as I fought against my restraints and pleaded for my friend. As Krissy bent over, attempting to help me, she screamed as someone grabbed her from behind.

Chapter 28

I squeezed my eyes shut, unable to bear the horrifying scene that would unfold before me: Krissy, sedated, and placed naked on a cold metal bed. Her screams pierced the air, they were distorted. They sounded like a shrill laughter. What? My mind couldn't reconcile the sound. Yes, laughter. Slowly, I opened my eyes, compelled by the echo of sound in the room. I strained to see Krissy's blonde head, standing about six or seven feet away, her back turned, and her body convulsing with laughter. A pair of small, dainty hands wrapped around her waist, adorned with rings and pink-painted nails, reminiscent of Krissy's. I fixated on those hands, unable to process the reality before me.

The small hands moved from Krissy's waist to her bottom, caressing and rubbing, accompanied by more giggles. As the forms turned, Krissy's blonde head stooped into an intimate kiss with the mysterious person attached to those delicate hands. It was a surreal sight, a stark contrast to the woman I had known. Krissy, usually elegant, now wore a short, tight black dress, her cleavage spilling out of the low-cut top, uncharacteristic spiked heels accentuating her transformation.

"Not her. That's not her," I thought. But it *was* her. The Krissy before me was unrecognizable, her eyes devoid of warmth, replaced by a cold, malicious glint. We locked eyes, tears blurring my vision, while Krissy's remained dry. A smile spread across her face showing teeth that now seemed more like fangs to me. The hand-person, now revealed, stood beside her, arm in arm, their gaze fixated on me.

Krissy's voice, once familiar, was now chillingly different. "So, have you put things together yet, babe?" she sneered. "For goodness' sake, wipe that stupid look off your face. You make me sick." Beside her, that dainty pair of hands impatiently urged for my demise, her lips pouting as she flirted with Krissy.

"Now, now, love muffin, we need to wait," Krissy continued, her tone dripping with menace. "What I get out of her, I am keeping for myself. I want a new car, I deserve it. So, I have a special buyer for her. He is coming all the way from Dubai to get her." Malevolent laughter escaped her lips, filling the room with an eerie ambiance.

I mustered the strength to speak, my voice cracking with fear and disbelief, "How could you kill all of those innocent women? What kind of psychotic person could ever think of something like this?"

Krissy, reveling in her victory, leaned down and grabbed me

by the face. "Speak! Speak, you typically never know when to shut the hell up. I am sure you have plenty to say, don't hold back now. I have endured your stupid jokes, stories, and bubbly sister crap for over a year now. I am sick of hearing your stupid country accent. What do you want to know, Layla? Ask me anything."

My throat felt like sandpaper, but I managed to utter one word, "Why?"

"Perfect, just the question I hoped you would ask," Krissy replied with a sinister grin. She left the room briefly, returning with a chair which she placed beside the cold metal table. She sat down, her eyes level with mine, while Whitley settled beside her.

"This may take a while," Krissy chuckled darkly. "Where do I begin... Well, let's start at the beginning. Let me introduce you to the love of my life. This is Whitley." Laughter filled the room. "Your face, Layla, you are killing me. I know, isn't this great? Surprise! She's not dead! She was never dead. She was a test run, so to speak. Some of the things I told you were true. She has always been my best friend. I love her just like I told you. But you see, we fell in love. Her parents were too conservative to let us be together, so we had to hide our love. We went to PA school and quickly realized it would be too hard work for not enough money. It was a happy accident that we found out what the physicians were trying to organize, and with our input, as a group, we developed the system for the Body Auction.

Whitley was a test case. She wanted to disappear, so she 'died,' and it worked. Her family had her funeral, everything worked like a charm. That's when we knew we could do it. But then *you* happened, you messed up everything. I was sent in to fix the situation, and you were so easy. So gullible, so sickeningly innocent, from the moment I walked in, you thought you were training me. My tears melted you. You are such a pushover, so easily manipulated, so trusting, we became best friends so quickly. You brought me right into everything, and the ignorant FBI just opened their doors. It's hilarious if you really think about it. Did you know that the FBI thinks they have a mole?" She laughed a boisterous belly laugh, unlike anything I'd heard escape her lips before

"It's *you* Layla, you are the mole. You tell me everything, every mission, where you are going, where Aubrey is, what's happening with the case, you *are* the mole, you idiot. So much for following protocol; you never keep your mouth shut." She was laughing so hard, mocking my pain, that her eyes became wet. Whitley stood next to her, stroking her arm and hand, laughing a low rolling laugh every time Krissy guffawed. She continued. "Wait, I'm not done... hold on for the best part.

You see, we became besties, and that is when my love bug here came up with the best plan. We let you and the FBI kill off Ricardo and 'dissolve the auction?' Or rather, let you *think* you did. So, I helped you, as much as I could. I would drop little details and help the FBI here and there just enough for you to catch the 'bad guys,' but not us. We wanted those male chauvinists out of the picture. They always thought they deserved better cuts and more of the pie. Typical. We plotted their downfall, and you helped us do that, so thank you, Layla."

"Yeah, thanks Layla," giggled Whitley, her voice dripping with irony.

"Now we are in total control, and I run this business much better than any man ever could. I have added to the menu, I mean, people have different tastes. I have also added men. Why was it always women? Equal opportunity and such... and these young, cute men actually bring a nice price." With that, Krissy walked over to one of the tables where the youngest man lay. She caressed his muscular arm and stared at his genitals in a sinister, obscene way, cocking her head to the side and adding, "I don't see the appeal."

Evil laughter filled the room. She then grabbed Whitley by the waist and kissed her again. It seemed this horrifying business was an aphrodisiac for both of them.

"Why not just leave me alone? I wasn't even looking at the

Body Auction any longer. I was moving on. Why kill me? Did you have no love for me? None at all? Has our entire friendship been a lie?" My voice found unexpected strength amidst my despair.

Krissy pushed Whitley off her and approached the table. Silence hung heavy in the air. I could smell her perfume, Coco Chanel Mademoiselle, her favorite. She gently brushed some hair away from my eyes and tenderly wiped a tear away.

"Layla, oh my sweet Layla," she whispered, her voice almost melancholic.

"You were my dear friend. I love my friends. I am naive, I agree, but I am a true friend. I would do anything for you, Krissy. Please don't do this, please."

Krissy leaned down, her lips close to my ear. "You must die, my darling, for you have something I want, something I need. I will miss you. You are certainly fun, and I will probably shed at least one tiny little tear for you. At your memorial, well, I will get a Grammy for that, but no, my dear, I have no plans on saving you."

"It's Oscar you twit. You'll get an Oscar..." My broken heart fueling my anger, I seethed a retort.

I'd hit a nerve, "Whatever," she spat. "Shut up."

"You will never get away with this. They will be here any moment," I challenged, desperation fueling my defiance.

"Oh, your precious FBI you mean?" She mocked me, "Well, I hate to tell you, but they won't. Remember that little detour, when you had to wait in traffic? We disabled all of your tracking and your phone. They have no way of finding you. No one knows where you are. Everyone thinks you're living it up downtown. By the time they realize you're missing, you will be long gone."

A final glimmer of hope flickered within me, and I mustered the strength to make one last request. "Can I ask you one thing? You at least owe me that before you kill me."

"Why not, we are *sisters* after all." Krissy responded mockingly.

"Kayleigh... What happened to her? Please tell me," I implored, my voice cracking with the last shred of hope that she might still be alive.

Help

"Hello... Hello, Aubrey?"

"Who is this? How did you get this number?" Aubrey's voice quivered with uncertainty.

"Aubrey, it's me... Kayleigh." A loud gasp echoed over the phone.

Aubrey's response was barely audible, almost a whisper. "What did you say? Who did you say this was?"

"Honey, I know this is a shock, and I know you need answers, but there is no time. Pull yourself together. Your mom is in danger."

Silence hung in the air, pregnant with worry.

"Aubrey!" Kayleigh's voice shifted abruptly from sweet and nurturing to stern, demanding attention.

"I am here. What is going on? What do you mean? I have you on speaker. I am at the field office in Atlanta. Go ahead." Aubrey's voice, although stronger, trembled with a mix of fear and determination.

"Okay, I need you to trace this call and see where I am located right now. This is a burner phone. I am in the mountains of Tennessee, not far from Nashville."

"Nashville, of course," Aubrey muttered, piecing things together in her mind.

"I have two other agents with me who were missing as well," Kayleigh continued, moving the phone closer to the others, "Heather, ID Alpha 33678, and Mackenzie, ID Beta 88876. Have someone else look for a type of lodge or resort out in the middle of the woods outside the city. It will have multiple cabins and a conference hall. It's a ritzy vacation spot. I need to know how to get there from where I am. We need backup to that location ASAP. That's where your mom is."

The urgency in Kayleigh's voice prompted immediate action. Voices in the background shouted orders over the phone speaker.

A man's voice broke through the chaos. "Kayleigh, we almost have this call traced. Keep the line open; it's difficult because of the poor signal, not many towers to ping off."

"Got it. We think agents are on the way to get us now. The two other agents had called earlier for help. Do you have agents in this area? If so, they just passed us, but we are not sure who to trust."

"Hold on, let me check... As you know, you are not calling the field office handling your case, but I am connecting with the Washington Bureau now. We will continue this call," the man replied.

Lam shouted out, "NO! Don't do that, please!"

"Hello? Who is this? State your name and ID, please," a stern voice demanded.

"I am an agent working with your FBI; I am with the State Security Ministry from China. We have reason to believe your agency is compromised. Please use caution and do not make this an open call. If the people we are after think we are on the way there, they will kill all parties involved and flee," Lam explained urgently.

"Aubrey, do you have the location? We are wasting time," Kayleigh pressed.

"I am here, yes, we have your location and also the area you are looking for..." Aubrey's voice cracked with emotion.

"What is it, Aubrey? What's wrong?"

"You are still at least 80 miles away. What if you don't make it? You have to let us alert the other office. We need people there now, not two hours from now," Aubrey pleaded desperately.

"Text me the information; we headed there now. We will drive as fast as we can. Somewhere along the way, we will get weapons. Aubrey, you have to trust me. It's too risky, and we cannot let her get away."

"Her? Her who?" Aubrey's voice was filled with confusion.

"It's a long story. Just send the info, send backup. Only people you trust. Keep this intel within a small group. I mean it, guys."

"Okay, sending now. Be safe, and Kayleigh," Aubrey hesitated, her voice laced with fear, "please save my mom..."

"I plan on it."

Just as the connection seemed about to end, the same man's voice intervened in the nick of time.

"Wait, we looked into who was sent to pick you up, and they seem trustworthy. Can we reroute them to your location? It's just four agents, but they have weapons and GPS."

"Can we trust them?" Kayleigh questioned.

"They seem solid. I'll contact them. Hold tight. They will be back to you."

"Okay, thanks, we are out."

"Good luck, guys, be safe!"

Click...

Silence settled in the car. Lam, visibly angry, couldn't contain himself. He cursed under his breath. "You did exactly what I told you not to do. Why do you trust these people? You have probably just single-handedly killed Layla and compromised the whole mission. I see why your country's FBI has not been able to fix this situation; you are all incompetent."

*"Look, you arrogant prick, that was Aubrey, Layla's daughter. If there is anyone on earth you can trust, it's her. And those agents heading back here, well, whether they're good or not, an entire separate branch of the FBI knows who they are, so they won't do anything to implicate themselves. Aubrey will bring a whole different team as soon as she can, so shut up about things that are above your pay grade. Remember, we don't know **you** either,"*

Kayleigh's sharp tone sliced through the tension, silencing Lam instantly. Heather and Mackenzie sat in wide-eyed astonishment, witnessing the force of Kayleigh's conviction.

After a few moments of loaded silence, Heather spoke, "Well, alrighty then, it seems you have awakened the beast. We always heard you were some kind of badass. Glad you decided to join the party!" Heather chuckled.

"Heck yeah! There she is, there's my girl! Let's get this party started!" Mackenzie cheered, and just at that moment, the black SUVs pulled up.

They all jumped out of the car and into the SUVs, anxiety lurking beneath the surface. Could these agents be trusted? For now, they had to act on faith. During the two-hour drive, they shared every piece of intel they could. Heather and Mackenzie took the lead, while Lam simmered with fury and frustration. The burner phone in Kayleigh's pocket chimed; it was a text from Aubrey:

Is it really you? I can't believe it, we have been looking for you.

Please save mom, please save yourself.

Tears welled up in Kayleigh's eyes as she responded:

Yep, it's me. I'm back, and I intend to. See ya soon.

Chapter 29

"Kayleigh, well, that's not what I expected you to ask, but okay. Well, she's dead. Sorry, I left her back in that basement, in Dubai. Remember when you were there? Well, so was she. You practically killed her. I mean, are you guys idiots? Of course, they took her there, so she stayed locked away in a dark room, starving to death."

The air was gone from the room. I couldn't breathe; I was having a panic attack, hyperventilating. This couldn't be true. My mind went wild, thinking of my friend dying that way— alone, hungry, scared. My heart broke into a thousand pieces.

"What, no comments?" Krissy's voice was filled with twisted amusement.

"Okay, pull yourself together. I have wonderful guests arriving, and they will be here soon. Now, I am torn... I want you awake, to see and feel everything that's going to happen. You see, I run my system differently. But, you look terrible, your face all red and bloated like that. Ew. Nor can I have you running your fat country mouth, scaring the buyers. So, what should I do, my little sexy thang?" Krissy looked at her lover for advice.

"Can we just tape her big mouth shut? I mean, they will understand since she is the only one awake. All the other merchandise is still out cold."

"Good idea, but tape is so ugly... let me think. Wait? What if we give her just enough paralytic to prevent her from talking, but not enough to put her out. It's a delicate balance, but she'll be awake and she'll still feel and hear everything. I could even take her restraints off."

"Great idea. I'll go get the supplies!"

I glared at Krissy, my anger boiling over. "I am going to kill you. One way or the other, you will die."

"Oh, I thought you *loved* me. I thought you would *do anything* for me. You couldn't kill a fly, you stupid little troll. Now shut your mouth. I have to go get ready. I have to look my best. Have fun tonight!" With that, she flipped her hair, smiled wryly and turned and left the room.

Shortly after, Whitley arrived, carrying medical paraphernalia. She was humming while she placed an IV in my arm and started a drip. Here we go again, paralyzed and unable to move. I couldn't speak, or cry out. I could only pray that they gave me too much, enough that I would stop breathing. That would be best. Who did she say wanted me? Someone from Dubai? So, it must be someone from the original auction seeking revenge. Please just let me die.

I had no idea of the time, no idea if anyone had missed me. What if she was right, and no one ever found me? This might be it... In my state of forced stillness, I drifted off to sleep. The large room was quiet, peaceful. The hint of wood and pine filled the air. I was at peace, but it was a fragile, fleeting peace amidst the nightmare that surrounded me.

Chapter 30

I was roused from my slumber by the sound of chatter and laughter echoing through the room. Music filled the air, signaling that the party had commenced. A fog of lethargy hung over me, a consequence of the sedatives in my bag. My body felt heavy, unresponsive, but oddly tranquil. Although I longed to draw a deep breath, my lungs burned in protest, refusing to comply. An itch teased my left thigh, but I was powerless to scratch it. My eyelids remained shut, my movements restrained.

Amidst the music, her voice slithered into my ear, a sinister whisper cutting through the haze, "Hey, girl, are you in there? I think my dear has overdosed you, but don't fret. I'll ease it down a bit. You deserve to witness the grand finale." With a subtle adjustment of the drip, relief slowly trickled in, allowing me to breathe more freely. My vision slowly cleared, and I could finally open my eyes. As I began to struggle against the weight of my eyelids, I heard Krissy speak again "Good, good. Take in the view. You'll recognize some familiar faces. Rest assured, I'll be your constant companion," she declared, her voice laced with laughter.

As my focus sharpened, I observed a diverse crowd milling around the room, each person cradling a drink. The ambiance resembled the initial auction, yet with a more casual atmosphere. Gone were the roses and waiters bearing trays of champagne and finger foods. Buffet tables were laden with food, and attendees served themselves. The shoppers sported an array of outfits, from ostentatious western wear to elegant ensembles. One man, of Asian descent, wore cowboy boots and a broad-brimmed hat, an incongruous sight that would have amused me under different circumstances. Women and men of varied ethnicities, sizes, and shapes filled the room, emphasizing the diversity of this grotesque gathering.

I marveled at the number of people scrutinizing the young men on display. Plaques atop the tables provided detailed information, akin to shopping in a store.

{Male}

{Age: 19 years old}

{Weight: 130 pounds}

{Health: No concerns}

{Option: ORG/ WHOLE}

{Starting Price: $1 million}

My curiosity piqued, I wondered about the meaning of

"ORG/ WHOLE." Could she truly reduce a person to a mere commodity, complete with a price tag? Krissy, sensing my thoughts, appeared at my side, her presence a bittersweet reminder of our closeness.

"Oh, are you perusing the information sheets? I prefer transparency with my products. Interested in seeing your details? Alright, let me fetch it," she chirped, her excitement palpable.

While I watched, she circled my display table, her attire a shimmering black jumpsuit, blonde curls cascading perfectly around her face. The delicate pink nails and lips had given way to fiery red, accentuating her aura of power and beauty that, in different circumstances, might have inspired pride in her fellow women.

"Let's see your card... It reads:
　　{Female}
　　　　{Age: 35}
　　　　{Weight: 135 pounds}
　　　　{Health: No concerns}
　　　　{Option: ORG only}
　　　　{Starting Price: $500,000 (per organ)}

"Now, allow me to explain. I omitted your age as a courtesy," she chuckled, "and 'ORG only' indicates that you're not for sale as a whole. You're designated for organ donation, each part priced at $500,000. I'm aiming for the best value, especially for your kidney–asking half a million for it! It's because we're besties, you know. I want the finest price for you; you deserve it!" She planted a kiss on my cheek, her gesture mirroring the betrayal of Judas towards Jesus.

I could only glare at her, incredulity flooding my senses. Why was she doing this? Her attention wavered as a crimson-faced man approached, inquiring about the obese woman lying next to me. Their conversation turned my stomach, its grotesque nature nauseating me further.

"Yes, sir, how may I assist you?" Krissy's tone adopted a salesperson's professionalism.

"Can you provide information about this beauty here? She's precisely what I've been seeking. I attended previous events but found the offerings lacking. I prefer a more voluptuous female." The man's thick southern accent marked him as unmistakably American. His flushed face spoke of habitual indulgence, he had fat little fingers that looked like sausage, adorned with a distinctive pinky ring, a stubby cigar protruding from his dry lips.

"Certainly, sir. I took your preferences to heart and curated samples accordingly. She's a stunning specimen, isn't she? At 25, she weighs 190 pounds, stands at 5'4", and boasts excellent health. No prior pregnancies, but our physicians confirm her fertility. She's available in both options, whole or for organ procurement. Perfect for your desires. What specifically did you have in mind for her?"

"I want her for my pleasure. I have a secluded hunting lodge where I unwind. I have a wife, kids, run an oil company in Texas–I just need a new plaything. You know how it is. I go to church, I'm a deacon you know, and a family man. But everyone has their secrets, right? I'll take her. Consider her SOLD! What's the price tag?"

I couldn't fathom the horror unfolding before me. Bargaining over a human life as if it was a mere commodity was beyond my comprehension.

"Her starting price is $750, but if you prefer, I can exclude her from the live auction and offer her to you at $850,000," Krissy stated.

"Quite steep. How about $775k, considering she's not the typical preference around here?" the man countered.

They haggled over this young woman's fate, a grotesque spectacle that made my stomach churn.

"Alright, $800. That's my final offer," the man declared, extending his sausage-like fingers for a handshake. Krissy agreed, motioning for the men to prepare the helpless girl for transport.

"We'll prepare her for your trip. She'll remain sedated for another eight hours, after which you can handle her as you please. Pleasure doing business with you. I hope you'll return," Krissy said, a veneer of professional cheerfulness covering the macabre transaction.

"I certainly will, and I'll recommend you to my friends with similar tastes. I appreciate the changes you've made. I'll be flying out as soon as she's loaded," the satisfied client responded.

"It's been my pleasure," Krissy said, bidding him farewell.

Leaning close, her breath minty fresh, she whispered in my ear, "That's how it's done, my friend. That's how it's done." Her pride was evident, but I couldn't bear to look at her. With what little movement I could muster, I turned my head away.

"Feeling sad, are you? Well, your guy just arrived, so you won't be here much longer," she chuckled before walking away.

Surveying the surrounding scene, I found myself in an absurd situation. Under different circumstances, this gathering could have been enjoyable–the room was elegant, the food tantalizing, the music soothing. People mingled, laughing, and chatting. Who would have guessed that these seemingly normal members of society hid such monstrous tendencies? It made me reevaluate everyone I had ever known, reminding me that darkness could lurk beneath the facade of civility.

Then, he appeared–a dark-skinned man, his demeanor serious, devoid of joy, arriving with a singular purpose: to dismantle me, piece by piece.

The Rescue

The winding mountain roads stretched endlessly as Kayleigh shook off her daze, immersing herself in her laptop, searching for crucial information. She delved into Krissy and Whitley's backgrounds, acknowledging the brilliance of their plan. The FBI and Layla had placed unwavering trust in her. Determined to ensure everyone's safety, Kayleigh dismissed any inclination to adhere to rules. This time, vengeance was her sole agenda—she intended to leave with Layla and consign the rest to Hell.

In the car, Heather and Mackenzie toiled in silence, Lam's visible distress palpable. Attempting to diffuse the tension, Mac implored Lam, "Look, I want you to know how much we appreciate you helping us. We trusted you, now we ask the same from you. We can never repay you for what you have done for our country and saving our lives. So stop sitting there being mad and start helping. We need to all get a plan together and know what we are walking into." Taking a deep breath, running his small hands over his face, he succumbed to her pleas.

Taking charge, Lam initiated the discussion. "What do we know so far? The venue is vast, but the event will be in the conference lodge. Pull up the map... we have eight agents for now until backup arrives. Kayleigh, text your contact and check their ETA." His petulance transformed into determination as he sprang into action.

"They just landed at Nashville airport. We'll be there in approximately 30 minutes, while they'll take an hour," Kayleigh reported, her fingers flying across her phone.

"We have a full weapons closet in the back. One of you ladies, crawl back there and start distributing them. Let's gear up," the previously silent agent, who had been focused on driving, finally spoke up.

"I'll crawl back," Mac, always the flirt, maneuvered through the seats, teasingly presenting her perky butt for their new companions. Kayleigh chuckled, but Heather's swift smack on Mac's behind echoed through the car, leaving a handprint behind. The atmosphere lightened momentarily, except for the stoic driver, seemingly devoid of emotion, a mere machine.

"I'll connect the other agents so we're all on the same page," Lam declared. The SUVs synchronized through the earpieces, forging a unified front.

"Lam, how much security will be there? How many guards?" Heather interjected; her voice now assertive.

"For this event, approximately fifteen. But her security choices weren't stellar. Jody and I were hired, which should tell you something. We'll park a mile away in the woods, approach on foot, neutralize the guards, and secure the perimeter."

"Agreed. Who's the best shot?" Heather inquired, her determination shining through.

"Andrew, the driver in the other SUV, is a sniper. I can handle that position too," the robot responded.

"Perfect. You two take out as many guards as possible. Mac, Heather, and I will head to the building. You'll provide cover. Once it's secure, get inside," Kayleigh said, simultaneously distributing ear radios and weapons. Guns and clips circulated through the vehicle, heightening the anticipation. The SUV hurtled forward, adrenalline mounting.

Suddenly, a hand, that same hand that had been a beacon of hope in her cell, emerged from the back of the SUV, gently grasping Kayleigh's arm. A touch filled with love and concern.

"Are you okay? Can you handle this? It's a lot to bear, considering what you've been through. No one would blame you if you wanted to sit this one out. We can't afford anyone freezing up; it's too risky," Mac voiced her worry.

"I've got this. I have to do this, or I'll never heal. But fair warning, I'm tossing protocol out the window. I won't be taking prisoners. That mindset got us into this mess. So don't try to stop me," Kayleigh's voice was fierce, her resolve unyielding.

"Hey, I've got your back. After all, we're emotionally distraught *from the kidnapping, so we can't be held accountable for our decisions due to trauma, right?" With a wink and a smile, that hand was gone and was instead loading a firearm. The irony made Kayleigh smile.*

"Okay, we're nearing the perimeter. We go dark and move on foot. Are you all ready?" The voice from the other SUV broke the tension.

"Ready. Switching to ear mic now. Let's go silent," Kayleigh declared.

With those words, the headlights vanished, and the black SUVs melded into the dark woods. Not a word was spoken, only hushed whispers guiding them through the shadows. Eight people moved stealthily, a remarkable feat of silence.

Kayleigh's gratitude extended to her Nikes, ensuring her silent footsteps. She exchanged a glance with Lam, but he remained impassive. The distant lights quickened her heartbeat–the lodge, an idyllic sight amidst the dense forest, beckoning them.

The circular drive boasted a fortune in high-end vehicles– Mercedes SUVs, Teslas, and even a red Ferrari. The presence of such influential figures only underscored the gravity of the situation.

As predicted, six guards patrolled the perimeter, indicating more inside. When all agents were in position, a single shot initiated their assault. The guards fell swiftly, and the team surged towards the nearest entrance, catching the unsuspecting attendees off guard.

Approaching a side door, Mac, Heather, Kayleigh, and Lam silently opened it. The guard turned but found himself incapacitated as Lam's blade slashed his throat. The women, although shocked, maintained their composure.

Cautiously moving around the kitchen entrance, they discovered staff uniforms. With a shared nod, they donned the disguises and concealed their weapons. Déjà vu gripped Kayleigh as she spotted lifeless bodies sprawled on tables. Men, women... she needed to find Layla. For a moment, nobody noticed them. However, when Whitley spotted Lam, their cover was blown.

"Well, well, well, who do we have here?" Whitley, a Snow White doppelgänger, had her arm wrapped around Lam's neck, his face already a strained purple, and a small .22 caliber pistol pressed against his temple. Her eyes met Heather's and Mackenzie's, both of whom knew that with a close-range head shot, a .22 bullet is just as deadly as any other. "I could blow a hole in his pretty little head right now, but I'd prefer not to disrupt business. Why don't you ladies follow me to the library?"

Silent nods passed between them as they complied, ushered into a vast library. Whitley hadn't noticed Kayleigh's presence.

"Where's Kayleigh? I know she's with you," she demanded, tightening her grip on Lam.

"She isn't here. She couldn't make the trip; she was too weak.

I led them here," Lam attempted to reason, struggling against her grasp. In a swift move, he broke free, but Whitley managed to fire a shot, leaving Lam crumpled on the floor. Mackenzie lunged at Whitley, but another shot rang out. Mac fell onto Whitley, a bullet grazing her, as she wrestled her to the ground. With a swift twist, Mac snapped Whitley's neck, rendering her silent forever.

"Are you okay? Did she hit you?" Heather, unfazed by the gruesome sight, inquired.

"Yeah, she nicked me, but I'm fine," Mac replied, checking on Lam. Thankfully the shot missed his head, but had entered his upper abdomen. "He's alive but not good. He was already weakened from the stab wound, but this was close range, it might do him in. We need to get him help." They applied pressure to his wound, moving him to the sofa in the library. "We have to find Kayleigh."

Surprisingly, amidst the music and chatter, nobody noticed the commotion. Business continued as usual. Layla, lying on a metal table, noticed what seemed like a ghost–Kayleigh's eyes locked with hers. Tears streamed down Layla's face, mirrored by Kayleigh. Kayleigh fought to regain control; Mac's warning echoed in her mind–no one could afford to freeze.

Suddenly, doors slammed shut, signaling the arrival of the other agents. They had neutralized the guards and stormed in, prompting screams from the wealthy psychopaths. Attempting to escape, they were met with a hail of bullets. Kayleigh and Heather stood side by side, picking off anyone attempting to flee.

"Wait, what are you doing?" the agent in the black suit protested, incredulous. "You can't just shoot them; they're supposed to be arrested, tried. This isn't protocol. They're unarmed!"

No one paid him any attention, and eventually, the fleeing ceased. "Line up against the wall, you pieces of crap!" Heather's voice dripped with disdain, commanding the attendees.

On cue, the side door creaked open. Krissy, attempting to mask her shock, addressed the agents, feigning indifference.

"Well, it's a party now, isn't it? Let my buyers go; they haven't committed any crime. You've already killed innocent people. I doubt the FBI will approve of your guerrilla tactics."

Kayleigh marched over, her fist connecting with Krissy's face, the impact resonating with a loud crack. Blood gushed from her once-perfect nose, now askew. Her eyes pouring tears as rapidly as her nose poured blood, Krissy lay on the floor, clutching her face.

"Shut up! You shut your mouth!" Kayleigh screamed, her voice raw. As Heather moved forward to disconnect Layla's IV, Kayleigh's voice rung out again. "Stand up and face me."

Krissy, bleeding and broken, her tiny button nose misshapen, whimpered. "I'm going to kill you right now. But I want you to understand—after this moment, I'll never think of you again. You didn't win; you're a pathetic excuse for a human being and an even worse excuse for a woman." Kayleigh's grip on the gun tightened, her voice unwavering.

"Kayleigh, no, don't kill her. We need her," Mackenzie pleaded. Other agents advanced slowly toward her.

"No, Mac, I warned you. She must die today. Now! This is redemption. She has to pay for her sins–for what she did to me, to Layla, and all those innocent people!" Kayleigh's conviction blazed in her eyes.

In a desperate attempt to stop her, an agent lunged for Kayleigh's gun, but it was too late. The deafening shot reverberated through the room, silencing Krissy instantly. Her lifeless body crumpled to the floor.

Kayleigh turned to Layla, who laughed amidst her weeping, her weakness clear. Though too weak to move, she managed a shaky smile, finding internal strength in their shared victory.

Chapter 31

Krissy had introduced the man to me and had left the room to get some paperwork when the commotion started. Yells, screaming, a gunshot—then I saw her. I saw Kayleigh. I couldn't believe it. As my IV was pulled from my arm, I wanted so much to jump up, but my body wouldn't allow it. But as I lay there, I saw my life come back together.

I watched the man who had just bargained for my organs run to escape only to be shot in the back, falling to his death. I watched one dear friend, or who I thought was a friend, shot to death by another. I was so relieved, so happy it was over. Kayleigh was right; redemption was necessary.

The other agents gained control, and the shooting stopped. It seemed like only a few moments had passed. The room was filled with FBI personnel. The next thing I knew, my sweet Aubrey was running to my table. As she ran, she took off her FBI jacket and threw it over my cold, naked body. In the commotion, I had completely forgotten that I was naked; and at that point, I didn't even care.

"Mom! You're OK!" She was crying so hard she could barely

breath.

"Kayleigh is here," were my first words, my body slowly waking up.

"I know, I know. Here, let's sit you up."

Looking around, Aubrey took in the scene.

"Oh, Mom, Oh no, it's Krissy, she's dead. They had her too?" Her expression was one of deep grief.

"Oh honey, there's so much I need to tell you. Go check on Kayleigh; I'm fine."

Aubrey ran to Kayleigh and threw her arms around her body, engulfing her in a hug that seemed to last forever. Mackenzie came over and helped me steady myself. "Are you okay? It shouldn't take long before these drugs wear off, and you'll be okay. Everything's gonna be fine."

"Thank you so much. Thank you for what you did. I'm so glad you're alright." My voice was still breathy.

"Girl, I am fine! I am just glad to see this nightmare come to an end." She flashed that huge smile.

What happened next was a flurry of activity. The woods were quartered off, US Marshals, FBI, law enforcement from local agencies all poured onto the scene. This time, no one escaped. The idea of hosting the event deep in the Tennessee mountain woods turned out to be a mistake; those who had managed to slink away were quickly captured. Those who had attempted to flee from the viewing room lay dead on the floor. The two primary players were dead.

Unfortunately, we did lose a great man. Kayleigh, Mac and Heather were visibly broken. Lam had been a great man; he had saved their lives, and mine.

One thing that kept playing over and over in my memory was the word Kayleigh had used. "Redemption." She said she needed redemption. When I was finally able to walk, Kayleigh, Mackenzie, Heather, Aubrey, and I walked out, arm-in-arm with strained faces, dirty, exhausted and emotionally drained, but victorious; we left that house of horrors and didn't look back.

Kayleigh and I spoke very little. We *wanted* to talk, we needed to say so many things, but it was not the time nor place. We all wanted to cry, to break down, to be vulnerable and weak. There would be time for that. In that moment, we all had to be strong. So many women had been tortured, sold, literally hollowed out alive, their organs stolen from them as easily as someone might pluck a flower from a pot, so at that moment, we needed to be the strongest we could possibly be, for us, for them--the ones we lost.

Redemption.

I did not mourn Krissy because I never knew her. She wasn't real. She was a persona, a character. I would miss the made-up person I had known, but not the person she truly was. No one would miss Whitley because she had already been declared dead. I wasn't sure how the FBI would handle that. Would they tell her family? Who knew?

We left a huge mess back in that lodge. But you know what? Men like to take control, take charge, clean things up. So, we let them, and none of us batted and eye.

That one word rang in my mind constantly: *redemption*.

Chapter 32

I had to go pack up and say goodbye to everyone, especially Mr. Reavis. Finally getting my phone back, it seemed to ring incessantly. Tripp was worried sick, and everyone just wanted me back home, but there were loose ends I had to tie up–one particular loose end I couldn't ignore.

While lying on that metal bed, I had ample time to contemplate what had transpired, to reflect on the events that had unfolded. The words about redemption echoed in my mind, sparking a new line of thought regarding my case.

As I pulled into the driveway, Mr. Reavis was waiting for me.

"Oh my goodness, thank God you're okay! I'm sorry. I didn't know. I tried to stop you..." he began, his voice laden with concern.

"Stop it!" I embraced him tightly, reassuring him, "You couldn't have known. It's not your fault. I'm fine. But we need to talk. I have to speak with Angel. I know it might blow my cover, but I have to."

He looked shocked, pulling away from my embrace. "What? What are you talking about? Why? They're transferring her today. That case is closed, Layla. Let it go."

"Just trust me. I need to talk to her. I'm leaving now. Call ahead and let them know to let me in." I jumped back into my car, speeding away before he could protest further.

Driving through my quaint little town, I cherished every detail. I had grown immensely as a person here, learned from my mistakes, and though I had a long way to go, I was determined to make things right.

Upon my arrival, I was swiftly escorted to a holding room. I sat at the metal table, patiently awaiting my friend.

When she walked in, I could barely recognize her. No makeup adorned her face, and she wore the typical orange jumpsuit. Her hair was tangled and unkempt, her body language exuding defeat. Before me stood a woman who had been broken, someone who had given up all hope–a feeling I knew all too well.

"What are you doing here, Layla? What do you want?" she asked, avoiding eye contact.

"Look at me, Angel. I'm not who you think I am. I'm an FBI consultant. They sent me here to gather intel for the unexplained deaths investigation." Startled, she looked up, her eyes darting between my face and my badge.

"You did this? You had me arrested for something I didn't do, Layla?" she asked, her voice filled with disbelief.

"Angel, I didn't do this. The evidence led them to you, but I believe you're innocent. I think they've got the wrong person, but I need your help. If you want me to help you, you have to help me. Do you understand?" I implored.

"How can I *help* you, Layla? They've basically already convicted me. I've told them everything I know."

"Yes, but Angel, you have to understand that the evidence points to you. You administered insulin to every patient, and it was found on your cart. There's video footage. You need to understand our perspective, too. That's why I need you to be honest with me."

"Honest about what, Layla? I've already told you everything I know."

"No, you haven't. I know about your involvement in the military battalion, your sworn secrecy about missions. There are some things that I believe could help your case, but you need to tell me." Her head shook slightly.

"Okay, Angel. So, you're saying you're willing to spend your life in prison for murders you didn't commit? Because you're protecting a military group, even though you haven't served in years? Is that really worth it, Angel? Tell me it isn't true," I pressed.

"Why would it help, Layla? Do you actually think someone from that group is responsible for this?" she asked, her face buried in her hands, struggling with inner turmoil.

"I don't know, but I believe you and I can figure it out. Let me share my thoughts with you. I recently heard a word that has been haunting me–redemption. I've analyzed every aspect of it in my mind. That's why I need you to tell me about that mission. I need you to tell me about Bailey. Tell me everything. Don't shake your head no. I understand it's top secret, but your freedom depends on it. All the recording devices are turned off. It's just you and me.Your secret will be safe. What you tell me will stay here. I promise you; I won't reveal anything about the mission," I swore to her.

"Do you really think this has something to do with the murders?" she asked, her face tear-streaked.

"Yes, Angel, I do. Tell me everything you know. Tell me about that mission," I urged.

The agony was evident both on her face and in her voice as she began to speak. "We were doing Recon in Afghanistan, targeting insurgents. We came under heavy fire, and Bailey got badly injured. He stepped on an IED while we were evacuating, and it blew both his legs off. Colton picked him up and carried him to the chopper. We had to go dark–no lights inside the aircraft due to enemy fire. The military is cheap. We were using outdated night goggles, and Bailey was screaming, yelling for Colton to help him, crying, dying, both his legs missing. He kept pleading for our help, saying his legs were burning, but his legs weren't there. He was conscious the entire time. He felt every last second of pain, and we weren't *allowed* to help him. We couldn't even see to administer morphine," she said, her voice trembling. Tears flowed freely now, and she took a deep breath to steady herself.

"It's okay, take your time," I reassured her.

"We did everything we could in the pitch dark, with the limited resources we had and could feel our way through using. Colton begged to turn the lights on and get help, but our pilots refused. It would have jeopardized the entire mission, our lives, *all* of our lives. In the end, Bailey bled out in the dark, begging for help that wouldn't come. He died because of *protocol*, and Colton never recovered. He never forgave the Corps. It shattered him mentally, and truthfully, it me, too. We were sworn to secrecy and threatened by leadership. If the public knew the Marine Corps would intentionally allow a young man to die, it would be a PR nightmare. So, like any dark blot on the image, they classified the mission and covered it up. The military's secrets, their protocols, have cost so many lives. Protocol killed Bailey, protocol killed my dad, too," she revealed, her voice laden with pain.

"He had been on a top-secret mission with the same unit years earlier. He inhaled some kind of known chemical weapon, and the government knew what he was walking into. Rumor has it they knew because the chemical itself had been created by the U.S. government and then someone sold it to a terrorist operative.

They knew he'd been exposed, and they had an antidote that would have neutralized the poison before it became systemic, but they refused to give it him. Releasing the antidote would have exposed the fact that they had prior knowledge of the chemical weapon in the first place. So they let my dad suffer and die, eaten alive from the inside. I couldn't bear it anymore. I had to leave the military. I couldn't work for an organization that would let their own suffer like that.

If I could, I'd rip this tattoo off my arm, erase every connection. Colton is still haunted, grappling with severe PTSD because he watched his childhood friend die in his arms, screaming. I visit him in psych hospitals when he's there. He's always heavily medicated, and I understand him, but Alisondra hates me for it. She can't comprehend what we went through that day. She can't fathom why he can't just move on like she demands. She can't understand the horrors we witnessed, the agony we endured. I could face criminal charges for telling you , Layla, but I swear to you, I did *not* kill anyone, outside of wartime I mean. That's the truth," Angel confessed, her voice breaking.

"I believe you, Angel. What you've told me makes perfect sense and I think I know who's behind all this, and I think I understand why," I said, conviction in my voice.

"But why would someone do this? Why kill innocent elderly people who surrendered their young lives to military service? I just don't understand," Angel questioned, her confusion palpable.

"Just hold tight. I'll get you out of here. You will *not* be transferred today, I promise you. I promise you, and soon this nightmare will be over. I know you're innocent, and to answer your question of why, why someone would do it, it's simple. The answer is simple; redemption.

Chapter 33

Trust me when I say I was more than ready to be home. The longing to return to Tripp and Aubrey had consumed me, but Kayleigh's situation demanded her attention with extensive debriefing sessions and psychiatric evaluations conducted by the FBI. Though we had exchanged texts, a proper conversation with her would have to wait. I still had unfinished business here. I had messaged Alisondra earlier, letting her know that I was stopping by the hospital to go through some records and clean out my locker. She had wanted to meet me for lunch.

As I strolled down the dim, lengthy corridors of the hospital's basement, I eventually reached the supply room, where I found Marvin, the kind man I had met weeks earlier.

"Well, hello, Miss Layla. How are you?" he greeted me warmly.

"Oh, I'm good, Marvin. Do you have a moment to talk?" I inquired.

"Sure, what can I do for you?" he replied.

"I want to discuss the recent deaths in the hospital," I started, the air growing tense. "I want you to know that I'm aware of your son, Bailey. I am truly sorry for what happened to him."

His entire demeanor shifted. The sweet old man I once knew transformed into a vengeful, angry figure right before my eyes. His frail, slumped posture straightened with pride, and his eyes, once weak and tired, turned dark and intense.

"Don't mention his name. Don't you dare mention his name. You don't know a thing about my Bailey. Why are you bringing this up? What do you want?" He spat, his anger palpable. His voice grew deeper as he continued.

"I'll tell you what I know, Marvin. He died a terrible death serving this country. I know he was a great man. I also know that Colton came home and shared the details of that mission with you," I said, met with cold, angry eyes and an eerie silence.

"And I know about redemption... Let me tell you something else I know. Every time a veteran with that tattoo on their arm comes into this hospital, you ensure they never leave. It's your way of seeking retribution for what happened to your son. You've been in every room, and yet, you're 'just the housekeeper'... No one would *ever* suspect you," I stated firmly.

There was silence. He didn't blink, and his gaze never

wavered from mine.

"You can never prove any of that. It's all speculation. You have no evidence," he retorted defiantly. "Even if it were true, they deserve everything they got because of that group, because of those fanatics. My baby boy didn't just die; he suffered, begging for his life. And Colton, my son, even if his skin is a different color than mine, he is still my son. He is my family. He's been driven to the edge because he pleaded for my son's life, but they discarded him like trash. They cast him aside because he couldn't handle what they put him through mentally and they destroyed him in the process. So hypothetically, if it *were* me, yes, they all deserved everything they got. But you're wrong because it wasn't me. This is all speculation."

"You're right. We'll have to review some footage, take more fingerprints. But I know it was you, Marvin. I know it was you, and I know you had help. Thank you for your time." With that, I left, convinced I was right.

Exiting the hospital, I called Mr. Reavis. He would be issuing the search warrant immediately, and Marvin would be arrested. But there was one more person I needed to see. I went over to the hospital and was greeted by the beautiful, smiling blonde, Alisondra.

"Hey, how was the concert? Was it the best ever? I missed

you," she greeted me.

"Well, I had quite a wild weekend, to say the least, but yeah, the concert was great. I have your clothes and your boots in my car. If you'll walk out with me, I'll give them to you. I've really enjoyed working with you; you've been fantastic," I replied.

"Oh, girl, it's no problem. Let's go get some lunch," she suggested cheerfully.

Knowing full well I couldn't return Alisondra's clothes and boots because I didn't have them anymore, I had to come up with an excuse as we walked to the diner next to the hospital.

"Isn't it a beautiful day? Let's just walk over to dinner. I'm in the mood for a hot dog. How about you?" I said, trying to divert the conversation.

"Oh, Layla, you really should eat better, and then you'd be skinny like me. But okay, sure," she replied in her typical fashion.

We placed our orders, engaging in small talk about the concert before I broached the topic I really needed to discuss.

"Alisondra, I know you love Colton. I know you both have a history, and I know his life was shattered when Bailey didn't come home," I said gently.

"What? Why are you bringing all this up? Why are we talking about this? I don't want to talk about this. This is none of your business, Layla; you're crossing the line," she protested.

"Alisondra, I know you want to marry Colton. I know you want children, but he can't. He can't get married because he's emotionally unstable, and I know you can't have children due to the psychotropic drugs he's on. I know he's refused to marry you. Do you want to know what else I know?" I continued.

"This conversation is over, Layla. Screw you. This is none of your business. You come in here, work for a few months, and think you know everything. You know nothing! You don't know me. You don't know about our lives here. Just leave. Get out of town, and don't ever come back!" she exploded in anger, venom pouring from her words.

I kept my composure, continuing to sip my iced tea and munch on another cheese fry.

"I know that you and Marvin are seeking redemption," I said calmly.

"We what? What are you talking about? Have you lost your mind?" she retorted.

"I know that you and Marvin had a plan. I know that when military personnel were admitted, he would place a little pot in the room with the flag upside down to signal you that they needed to die. You and Marvin had an agreement to eliminate anyone from that group who had harmed the two men you love, Colton and Bailey. I know it was you. I knew it was you when I was in your closet and saw your black suit hanging there because I saw you on the video walking to one of the rooms. You placed the insulin back on the cart when you bumped into Angel. I know you framed Angel. You despise Angel just as much because she sympathizes with Colton, and she truly understands him. I know you're seeking redemption and revenge for what happened to Colton and Bailey," I said, confronting her directly.

"I hate you. I hate them," she cried, tears streaming down her face. "They ruined my life. We were supposed to get married, have children, and live in a house with a white picket fence. Now he can't even have sex, he can't sleep, and when he needs comfort, who does he turn to? Angel. They all deserve what they're getting!"

As I relayed her confession through my earpiece, the chief entered the diner. He didn't speak, but made eye contact with Alisondra and she knew. She knew what was coming. Alisondra never uttered another word; the only thing she said was, "I want my lawyer."

I held my breath until he led her away. I didn't even realize I had been until my lungs started to burn and I let out a long slow exhale. Could it be over? Could it really be over?

Relief oozed into my blood like Maple syrup. Every muscle in my body relaxed as I realized that, yes, it *was* finally over.

Church

A month passed, and life had deviated far from the ordinary. Texas, with its majestic cattle and sprawling ranches, stood serene and magnificent, a world away from the hustle and bustle of the city.

Ah, the charm of a Southern Baptist church! The heavenly melodies of the choir singing praises echoed through the air. Occasionally, worshippers would raise their hands high in devotion, their fervor palpable. Seated in the pew, I basked in the divine atmosphere, feeling a profound connection, rooted in my upbringing as a preacher's daughter.

Positioned just behind the first row, where the deacons sat, I observed the deacons' wives in their exquisite suits, some donning hats adorned with feathers. Amidst the sacred ambiance, my anticipation peaked for the sermon. The topic of the day resonated deeply with me—John 3:16, my father's cherished verse from the Bible.

Yet, the pinnacle of the service arrived when a plump hand, its fingers resembling sausages, adorned by a single pinky ring, ascended in praise. Patiently, I awaited the opportune moment, *mirroring the movement of praise with my own hand, I lifted my hand. My involvement in this momentous event was a result of persistent pleas to Mr. Reavis and several other agents. They seemed both reluctant and excited to grant my request. The thrill of the occasion surged within me. It felt like victory. I couldn't get over the audacity of this man, to raise his hand in praise, despite the sin and evil in which is sausage fingers dabbled. I went unnoticed by the congregation, just another visiting worshipper, until I clicked the ring of a shiny handcuff around the deacon's wrist. Triumph flooded my heart, and a smile of accomplishment played on my lips.*

A thin, dark-haired woman rose from her seat, her voice piercing the air. "Just who do you think you are? What are you doing? Get that thing off my husband. What's the meaning of this?"

Murmurs erupted. Interrupting his sermon, the pastor demanded an explanation, but before another word was spoken, an undercover agent seated nearby stepped forward, reading Sausage Fingers his rights. Simultaneously, multiple FBI agents entered the sanctuary, dispelling any notion of a joke or prank. My smile widened as they completed the handcuffing of the red-faced Deacon. I glanced at his pinky ring, a symbol of his fall from grace, and vowed to remember that moment.

Silently, they led him out of the church. Unbeknownst to him, agents had already located his hunting lodge and rescued his "plaything" that very morning. I still planned to suggest a sleep study at some point, though her recovery would likely take much more than rest. However, I also yearned for his confession, for him to acknowledge the depth of his depravity. His façade of arrogance crumbled as I stepped toward him, staring into his eyes with silent knowing. My hushed knowledge of his heinous crimes left him visibly uncomfortable. His false bravado dissipated swiftly as they escorted him past the church pews.

Not a word escaped his lips as he was placed in the back of the black SUV, his demeanor similar to that of a distraught child. In the back of the FBI vehicle, he cried like a girl. I couldn't help myself. And no one stopped me. I grabbed him by his fat round face and said, "You're going to rot in jail, you piece of crap," I sneered, my voice laced with contempt. "And you know what? When I was praising the Lord in there, that's what I was thanking Him for–the fact that I found you and that you will rot in prison for the rest of your life and everyone in your life will know exactly what you really are."

Redemption

The anticipation bubbled inside me as I hurried home, my footsteps echoing with purpose. Upon my arrival, I found Tripp in the shower. His voice echoed through the bathroom, "I'll be right out, baby! I'm so glad you're home!"

"Okay, honey, take your time. I'll change and start dinner," I replied, my heart swelling with contentment. The familiar surroundings of my house and the prospect of preparing a meal for my husband filled me with joy. Kayleigh was safe, the harrowing auction was finally over, and the man with sausage-like hands was behind bars. A sense of relief washed over me, and I couldn't help but smile.

Being home and preparing dinner for my husband in our house made my heart smile. Kayleigh safe, the auction finally over, and the sausage hand man in prison.

I was happy.

As I hummed while preparing dinner, I couldn't help but chuckle at the chaotic state of our home. I knew I'd be cleaning up the mess for the next week, but I embraced the task with a sense of fulfillment.

While bundling up some trash, my eyes fell upon a small gift bag nestled at the bottom of the bin. Did Tripp buy me a gift? I hesitated for a moment, debating whether I should peek inside. "I shouldn't. It will ruin his surprise if I peek," I thought, "but, oh, I can't help it!" I squealed as my curiosity got the best of me, I couldn't resist.

To my shock, I discovered a receipt for Coco Chanel Mademoiselle inside the bag.

The breath caught in my chest and a wave of sudden emotions crashed over me like a storm. Confusion and disbelief mingled with anger, and my mind raced to make sense of what I was seeing. I read the line again, and again. The realization hit me like a punch to the gut.

Krissy's perfume.

Not mine.

The implications hit me hard, shattering the happiness I had felt just moments prior. In that instant, my world turned upside down, and a cold determination settled in the pit of my stomach.

Just as I absorbed the weight of the revelation, I heard the shower turn off, and I sprang into action. I loaded my gun with a shaking hand, my fingers moving with both hesitation and purpose, and the bitter taste of betrayal fueling my resolve.

Redemption.

With trembling fingers, I composed a brief text message to

Kayleigh, Mac, and Heather, urgency bleeding into my words:

> *I need you at my house NOW.*
>
> *No radios, this stays between us.*

Acknowledgements

First and foremost, I want to express my gratitude to my Lord and Savior, Jesus Christ. Without Him, I am nothing.

I extend my heartfelt thanks to my family, including my husband, Todd, and daughter, Amber, who consistently encourage me, regardless of the nature of my unconventional ideas.

Special appreciation goes to my brother, Bryan, for offering invaluable advice and daily love.

To my "BFF," Paula Farmer, you are the best cheerleader and support a person could ever pray for; you are a priceless jewel.

Kristin Himes, Whitney Moose, Alicia Albanez, and Angel Blackburn, thank you for your unwavering friendship. I acknowledge that I can be a handful sometimes, and I am especially grateful for your willingness to be characters in my book.

A tremendous thank you is owed to my wonderful publisher, Vertu Publishing, and Tylie Eaves. I cannot express my gratitude enough for your patience with me.

I want to express my perpetual gratitude to the staff of

Iredell Health Systems. You are my biggest fans, a continued source of inspiration, and dear friends. Your encouragement, laughter, and entertainment have fueled my ability to write.